I0740119

SIC TRANSIT TERRA 2

THE OTHERNESS FACTOR

ARLENE F. MARKS

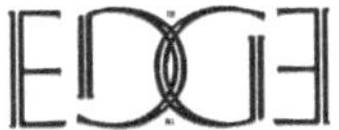

EDGE SCIENCE FICTION AND FANTASY PUBLISHING
An Imprint of HADES PUBLICATIONS, INC.
CALGARY

The Otherness Factor
Sic Transit Terra Book 2

EDGE SCIENCE FICTION AND FANTASY PUBLISHING
An Imprint of HADES PUBLICATIONS, INC.
P.O. Box 1714, Calgary, Alberta, T2P 2L7, Canada

The EDGE Team:
Producer: Brian Hades
Acquisitions Editor: Ella Beaumont
Edited by: Emily Stanford
Cover Design: Brian Hades
Cover Art: Lyn Perkins
Book Design: Mark Steele
Publicist: Janice Shoults

ISBN: 978-1-77053-140-6

EDGE Science Fiction and Fantasy Publishing and Hades Publications, Inc. acknowledges the ongoing support of the Alberta Foundation for the Arts and the Canada Council for the Arts for our publishing programme.

Library and Archives Canada Cataloguing in Publication
CIP Data on file with the National Library of Canada
ISBN: 978-1-77053-140-6
(e-Book ISBN: 978-1-77053-135-2)

FIRST EDITION
(20180317)
Printed in USA
www.edgewebsite.com

Publisher's Note:

Thank you for purchasing this book. It began as an idea, was shaped by the creativity of its talented author, and was subsequently molded into the book you have before you by a team of editors and designers.

Like all EDGE books, this book is the result of the creative talents of a dedicated team of individuals who all believe that books (whether in print or pixels) have the magical ability to take you on an adventure to new and wondrous places powered by the author's imagination.

As EDGE's publisher, I hope that you enjoy this book. It is a part of our ongoing quest to discover talented authors and to make their creative writing available to you.

We also hope that you will share your discovery and enjoyment of this novel on social media through Facebook, Twitter, Goodreads, Pinterest, etc., and by posting your opinions and/or reviews on Amazon and other review sites and blogs. By doing so, others will be able to share your discovery and passion for this book.

Brian Hades, publisher

The Sic Transit Terra Universe Series:

Novellas:

Lydia's Royal Ace

Candles

Novels:

The Genius Asylum (Book 1)

The Otherness Factor (Book 2)

Relativity Bomb (Book 3)

The Genome Rally (Book 4)

The Cockroach Crusade (Book 5)

The Identity Shift (Book 6)

Acknowledgements

The birthing of this book has been a long process, made much easier by the support and advice I've received from my family, friends, and esteemed writing colleagues over the years. Your names are legion, and I'm grateful to each and every one of you.

Special thanks are due to my husband David for keeping me grounded while the Sic Transit Terra Universe was under construction and never once complaining about the mess.

PART I

Abner Dedrick

Abner Dyson Dedrick (b. 2363 – d. 2397 C.E.) was the proverbial 'black sheep' of the Forrand-Dedrick family and the most notorious of the Angel of Death plague dogs. Abner was the only one of the nearly 100 escapees from the Thryggian medical facility to be criminally charged by the Thryggians for the damage done to their laboratories during the mass escape. It is still unclear what Abner's role was in facilitating the test subjects' breakout, or whether he played any role at all. Available records indicate that he and another patient (known only as Rose) left Thrygg together and went into hiding on then-uninhabited Planet MF-307, where they both succumbed to an emerging strain of the plague thirteen Earth years later.

> — *Sic Transit Terra, An Unauthorized Planetary History*
> (2673 C.E.)

Earth High Council

MEMO

EARTH DATE: 5 September 2384

FROM: Edlund Warner, Secretary, Earth High Council

TO: Supreme Adjudicator (Americas) Dennis Forrand

Further to the extradition demand received by this office from the Thryggian Planetary Council one week ago, we met this morning with the liaison from the Galactic Great Council to view the evidence against your nephew, Abner Dedrick.

I'm sorry, Dennis, but it's pretty damning. The theft and vandalism can be worked around, but I'm afraid the murder charges are going to stick. Abner was never exactly a model citizen, and the High Council doesn't want to jeopardize Earth's chances of being invited to join the Great Council by sheltering an interplanetary criminal from justice, so it appears we don't have much choice in this matter. He's on the run right now, so we can delay the inevitable. Sooner or later, however, he'll be found, and when that happens we'll have to turn the kid over to the Thryggians.

I know this isn't what you wanted to hear, and I'm truly sorry. We'll do all we can to distance the rest of your family from the repercussions of this unfortunate incident, including ensuring that Ensign Gael Dedrick is posted to a deep space exploration vessel, effective immediately.

Warmest regards,
Ed

1

Okay, first things first. To whoever finds this voice log: the ship and everything aboard her belongs to me. If the Thryggians claim otherwise, just check with Earth Data Management. You'll learn that sprint cruiser alpha delta five nine one one seven is the property of Abner Dyson Dedrick, citizen of Earth, Americas. That's me.

By the way, be advised that I'm carrying a passenger at this time, rescued from the aforementioned Thryggians. The girl is Human, I think — well, humanoid, anyway — and looks to be about sixteen years old. I'll add her name later on, when she stops sniveling in the corner and tells me what it is.

You're safe now, dammit! A little gratitude might be in order here.

I'm recording this because I want the Thryggians to get what they deserve, whether I'm alive to see it or not. The bastards disappeared two of my friends, Ian McCormack and Paul Travanti. They tried to murder the girl as well, and they probably would have killed *me* if I hadn't escaped when I did. And there was something else going on there, I don't know exactly what, but it sure as hell ought to be investigated.

For the record, and again regardless of what the Thryggians might claim, let me state that the girl is innocent of any crime. All she did was point me in the direction of that lab. I was the one who—

(Pause)

I'd better explain.

It all began on my twenty-first birthday, when Ian and Paul and I were celebrating at Dante's Hotspot in Atlantica. Everybody knows Dante's — red strobes sweeping the room, naked girls with little horns on their foreheads hanging off the balcony, waving pitchforks...? The three of us were well-toxed when Paul brought up the idea of flying to Thrygg to get me a special birthday present. He'd heard that the Thryggians had discovered a way to extend the Human lifespan almost indefinitely. It seemed like a grand thing to do on one's birthday, like wishing for more wishes from the genie in the bottle. Even toxed, we were aware of the Council's ban on travel to Thrygg, so we filed a bogus flight plan to get departure clearance. Ian knew how to set the navcomputer to avoid being detected by the critical beacons en route. The three of us partied all the way there.

I want to be absolutely clear on this point: we were toxed, but we weren't alzhammered, so there's nothing wrong with my memory. There were three of us on this field trip. We flew to Thrygg together, we entered the medical facility together, and we sobered up together. The next day, Ian and Paul watched me being taken into the treatment room for the longevity procedure. I waved to them as the door slid shut between us. When I woke up from the treatment, they were gone. The sprint craft was still at its tie-down beside the landing apron, but my friends had vanished, and nobody I spoke to could recall even seeing them.

That was just the beginning of the nightmare.

The Thryggian doctors insisted on keeping me for observation following my treatment. Ten days. It seemed reasonable enough. Only, ten days stretched to fourteen, and then twenty. Each time I was assured that I could go home the following day, a new symptom would pop up, or I would have a reaction to something, and my departure would have to be pushed back again. Eventually, I figured out that I was being held prisoner. I barged into the office of Doctor Arristo and demanded to know why.

Arristo took one look at me and flattened himself against the wall farthest from the door. His fear was understandable. I'm a full two meters tall and mass over a hundred kilos, and at that moment I would have welcomed an excuse to hurt him.

In case you've never actually seen a Thryggian, imagine a being about a meter and a third tall, with grayish skin and the head of a snapping turtle. Now give this creature the body proportions of a Human infant — oversized head, short arms and legs, prominent belly — and the neck and shoulders of a wrestler. Make him smell faintly like fresh-baked bread. Round the skull and cover the cranial surface with a dense network of blood vessels that blue the skin and make it throb perceptibly, more so whenever he's excited.

Arristo's scalp was beating out a quick samba rhythm. "But— But you are not a prisoner here, Mister Dedrick," he chirped. "Are you locked inside your room? Are you shackled? If you are feeling anxious, perhaps a mild sedative, yes?" This last sounded like a plea.

"No! Am I free to go?"

"If you feel you must. Leaving prematurely, you would have to sign a waiver, of course, protecting us from any legal action if your treatment should prove fatal."

He'd come down from the wall. I took a menacing step toward him and sent him scurrying to the other side of his desk, beyond my arm's reach. "Why should it prove fatal?" I demanded.

"It is an experimental procedure, with possible dangerous side effects. You knew that when you arrived. You signed the form, agreeing to participate in the experiment and to let us monitor your condition until it stabilized."

I didn't remember signing any form, and told him so.

"Oh," he replied brightly, "of course you do not remember. You were — what is that quaint phrase?—'toxed to the rafters'."

That was Paul's expression. Or maybe not. But I'd never heard anyone else describe a beer-and-Manica ride that way. My gut began twisting itself into a knot. Arristo had met at least one of my 'hallucinated' friends and was now manipulating like crazy to keep me from leaving the planet. Suppressing the urge to kill the turtle-faced bastard, I stomped out of his office.

I went directly to my little green cell of a room and glared at the light screen on the wall. It was showing yet another documentary about the wildlife native to Thrygg. The damn thing had no control switches. Except during sleep periods when the sound was muted, it was constantly on and constantly loud, and all those fangs and claws and screams of dying prey had been driving me bonzo since the day I arrived. Well, I might not be able to eliminate the Thryggian irritant from my life, but I sure as hell could do something about that screen.

I remembered seeing a flat-screen video once about a prisoner who used a thin metal slat from his bedspring to confound the electronic lock on his cell. There wasn't a spring under my mattress, but there was a sturdy metal tray under my midday meal. I jammed the corner of the tray under the frame around the light screen and pried it loose all the way around. Then I began experimentally pushing the tray into the narrow space between the screen and the wall. On my fifth try, I hit something and felt it give way. I rammed it again, hard, and heard a crack followed by a sharp hissing and the ozone smell of a spark. Sound and picture died together, along with much of the light in the room. There was still some sunlight overflowing from the hallway, and it let me see what I was doing as I carefully removed the tray — its beveled edge was only slightly scorched — and pushed the frame back into place.

It's always daytime on the inhabited side of Thrygg, so all the hallways and public areas are skylit, while sleeping chambers, storage closets and so on are enclosed and therefore dark. There are no windows in the walls of Thryggian buildings. If you need light in an enclosed space, you either give it a door that opens into sunlight or install some kind of artificial illumination — like the light screen that I had just killed.

Belatedly, I realized what I had done. The patient zone of the facility was regularly patrolled by pairs of uniformed Thryggian guards wearing sidearms. They never blocked the hall or even questioned anyone trying to pass them, but they were there, and they were watchful. Each door in the facility had a slot cut into it maybe seven centimeters high and nearly the width of the door, set at Thryggian eye-level.

As they passed each room, the guards could scan its interior at a glance. The darkened screen would make it difficult for them to do that; so, the next patrol would lose no time reporting it to maintenance. Arristo wasn't stupid. Knowing how I felt about being kept in his facility, he would have me put under close surveillance in case I tried to sabotage something else. He might even decide that the best way to control me was to drug me senseless and lock me in my room. Before that happened, I had to find Ian and Paul — assuming they were still alive — and come up with a plan to get us all the hell out of there.

I needed to take a walk. There were a couple of patient cubicles four corridors over that I hadn't yet checked out, and the exercise would clear my mind. I stuck my face out the door to make sure there were no guards around, then headed double-time for the perimeter hallway of the facility. By now I knew the fastest route to just about anywhere in the building.

After the treatment, as soon as I could stand upright, I'd begun taking long strolls around the inside of the complex. It was laid out perfectly for the purpose, like a large wagon wheel. The central reception area was circular, illuminated by a huge skylight. This hub had corridors radiating off it like the spokes of the wheel, ending at a circular hallway that defined the circumference of the building. Corridors through the patient and treatment zones opened into the outer ring as well as the hub. But there were other hallways, evidently passing through restricted areas, that showed only a locked door to anyone walking around the perimeter.

At first it was the walk that was important. When Thryggians guarding the inner-ring entrances to the laboratory zone politely but firmly refused me entry, I made a mental note and then filed it away. Sometimes a guard challenged me, and I explained, truthfully, that I had to exercise every day to maintain the calcium level in my bones. The first few times, Arristo insisted that I be accompanied by an orderly in case I passed out from the exertion. When it became clear that I wasn't the fainting type, my attendants drifted off, all having better things to do. That left me unguarded, free to begin visiting and questioning the other patients. Somebody had to have seen Ian and Paul, even if only for a moment.

That day, I was on the clock and on a mission. I stopped five rooms down the corridor to show another Human — I'd met him earlier; I think his name was Grant — how to kill the screen using his food tray, and I asked him to spread the word to the other patients.

Diversionary tactics. Confuse the enemy, buy some time.

Grant wasn't the only zombie I'd found, by the way, staring dull-eyed and under the influence at the images floating across that damned screen. There had to be a hundred patients in the facility, apparently not one with the strength or the will to fight his way out of the toxic stupor. So, no surprise, none of them had seen Ian and Paul, or had any idea what might have happened to them.

Over time, we'd talked about other things too, comparing our reasons for being there and treatments undergone, as patients in a hospital are wont to do. And this is where it gets even more suspicious. Every last one I spoke to, all thirty or so of us Humans and many of the aliens, had come to Thrygg for the longevity procedure — but no two of us had received exactly the same treatment. I was the only one who'd been surgically opened. Grant had been given a series of injections. Others had been smeared with ointments, had inhaled mists, had ingested capsules of various colors. We were part of an experiment, all right.

I realized that it had probably never been the Thryggians' intention to prolong anyone's lifespan. I also doubted, aloud, whether they ever intended to let us leave the complex.

When they heard this, the other patients all chorused their agreement. Then they decided that I should be their leader. It was pathetic — the sheep choosing a shepherd. I hadn't done anything that they couldn't have done for themselves, and I hadn't reached any conclusions that they couldn't have — no, *shouldn't* have reached on their own. If they were offplanet, then they had been certified Eligible, and that implied a certain level of intelligence, dammit! I told them I wasn't there to save them. All I wanted to do was find my friends and get clear of Thrygg. But they wouldn't hear of it. They bleated at me to call meetings, draw up plans for a mass escape. They simply wouldn't let up. So, my first escape was from them. How dare they make me responsible for their freedom when I could feel the clock ticking away the seconds on my own?!

Oh, crap, she's unconscious again. Just as long as she isn't bleeding. Okay, good.

The girl knows more about the Thryggians than she wants to talk about yet. As soon as she does, I'll add her voice to this log.

Now, where was I? Oh, right…

The day after I killed the screen, it still hadn't been repaired. Good old Grant. Screens were probably gasping their last all over the place, while turtle-faces ran diagnostic after useless diagnostic on their transmission 'ware. Anyway, I was sitting in the lounge, thinking dark thoughts and, quite appropriately, staring at a plant that must have come from the dark side of the planet, since it was called a nightbloom. It was deep purple and had no leaves, of course, but about a dozen tendrils ran from the sides of its thick, woody stalk down to the loamy soil in its container. The name implied a blossom of some kind, and I had taken to visiting the lounge a couple of times a day to see whether a flower had appeared.

That day was the first time I saw the girl. Well, to be accurate, she saw me first. I was just sitting there, trying to figure out a way to get into the restricted zone without alerting any guards, when suddenly I felt these eyes on me. I glanced up and there she was, in a pale green tunic and leggings, bent the way I'd been bent for the first week or so after surgery, and pressing a hand to her side. Backlit in the doorway, she was beautiful, in a fragile, otherworldly way that made my breath catch in my throat. A cloud of blond hair, delicate, perfectly proportioned features—she was like a doll. In another time and place, I would have tried to play with her. I still may, if she can manage to stay conscious long enough.

To be honest, I thought about it even then, but her eyes stopped me. They were pale blue and huge with suffering, and they were trained accusingly on my face. It was no wonder I'd felt them on me before. Looking into them now sent a shiver across my back. And then she dropped her hand from her side, and I saw the red spot on her tunic that meant she was bleeding through a bandage and had no business being on her feet.

"You should be in bed," I told her.

She clamped her lips together and shook her head. "I needed to find you," she said. Her voice was low-pitched and taut with pain. Each word was a struggle to pronounce.

Now I was intrigued.

"The masters have plans for you. For me." Gritting her teeth, she managed a smile. "And I for them."

Revenge. I understood immediately. We had a lot in common, this girl and I. But it bothered me to hear her refer to the turtle-faces as 'masters', as if she were some kind of slave.

I watched her hobble slowly to the only other chair in the room and sink down onto it with a gasp. When she could speak again, she continued in that same strained voice, "They cut you, took tissues. Me too. Our lives are joined."

"They did more than that," I told her. "They made my friends disappear. May have killed them."

She shook her head even more decisively than before. "They are not your friends."

She was in a lot of pain, for which she clearly had not been medicated. I could feel anger swelling inside me. Even a slave deserved more compassion than that.

And what the hell did she mean, saying that Ian and Paul weren't my friends?

Wincing, the girl heaved herself out of the chair. The red spot had grown larger. When I reached out to steady her, her fingers wrapped around my wrist like narrow steel bands. She took a step toward the door and I followed, dragged along by the astonishing power of her grip.

She didn't say another word after that. Speaking took too much of her strength, and she was obviously determined to lead me somewhere important. Marveling at whatever force was driving her to keep putting one foot ahead of the other, I let her pull me down the corridor to the outer ring, and then along that curving hallway for a while.

At one of the locked doors in the perimeter corridor, she stopped, and I thought, *Okay, this is it, she's finally going to pass out.* I braced myself to catch her when she fell, nearly tumbling over myself when she didn't. Instead, she reached out and pressed her right palm against one of the tiles in the doorframe. It backlit and chirped something at her in Thryggian. And, to my utter amazement, she chirped back, evidently giving it the correct password, because the door unlocked with a brief rumbling sound and slid aside for her.

Whatever her relationship was with the turtle-faces, she'd been at the facility long enough to learn the Thryggian language, and the password to unlock a restricted zone door. I made a mental note to take her with me, if and when I ever got out of that place.

Obviously, since I'm recording this log and she's aboard ship, I have, and I did.

The entrance was unguarded from the inside, and the sentries at the hub end of the corridor weren't watching for intruders behind them. She signaled me to be silent as we made our way to one of the laboratory doors and went through the same palm-print-and-password exercise to open it. Abruptly then, the girl's condition caught up with her. Her fingers slid off my wrist. Leaning weakly against the wall, she pointed inside the lab and repeated in a fading voice, "Your tissues. Experiments."

I couldn't believe what I was seeing in there. First of all, it wasn't skylit. Where wall met ceiling, a band of artificial illumination ran like a ribbon around the entire perimeter of the room. In this soft bluish-white light I could see metal tables supporting a series of complicated glass constructs. Each network of clear tubing ended halfway up a transparent, fluid-filled container. I counted more than a dozen of them, each holding — each holding—

(Heavy breath.)

They were artificial wombs.

The 'tissues' the turtle-faces had stolen from me had to be sperm cells.

Days later, my chest feels tight just thinking about it. At the time, however, rage began pouring into me as if someone had opened a spigot. That's the only way I can describe it.

I've had a lot of experience with anger — one of the side-effects of being the youngest member of a dynasty, I suppose. Many people envied me, and told me so. 'Born with a silver spoon in my mouth.' Well, let me tell you, saliva tarnishes silver, and the taste of that spoon gets pretty foul after a while. Are you listening, Uncle Dennis?

From the day I was born, people have been telling me what I was going to be and how I was going to get there. No one has ever asked me what I want, and no one has ever heard me when I talk about it, least of all dear Uncle Dennis, whose only concern of the moment seems to be preserving his reputation. He hates having his name dragged through the tabs, and of course, that's something else I've had plenty of experience with. The point is, all my life I've been living off handouts: from my mother, from Uncle Dennis, from people wanting to kiss up to The Great Man. I never got a thing that way that meant a damn to me, but nothing that mattered seemed to be coming from anywhere else — so I settled. Don't be shocked. I'm an Eligible. It was the lesser of two evils. (The shrink that he blackmailed me into seeing put a catchy name to what was screwing me up, but even she had to acknowledge that as long as I was trapped in The Great Man's gravity well, there could be no lasting cure.)

Anyway, in all the universe, the only thing I really felt I owned and controlled was my physical body. I decided what went into it, and I decided where to put what came out of it. And, in particular, I was the one who decided how and when and with whom to share my sperm.

Every second that I stood there staring at the obscene crèche they'd set up, my outrage grew. Fury just flooded into me. It filled me almost to bursting, then exploded into a red-hot mist inside my skull, obliterating every other feeling. No more thoughts of fooling Arristo, finding my friends, plotting an escape. No more thoughts, period. All I wanted to do was barrel into that lab and smash every bit of glass in the room. As I was bunching my muscles to do it, I was hit from behind, hard enough to knock me off balance but not hard enough to bring me down. I whirled and found myself facing half a dozen Thryggian guards, all waving weapons and chirping at me like a nestful of homicidal chicks.

Clearly, someone had called in a security alert. The two guards at the inner end of the corridor probably hadn't been unaware of us at all — they'd simply been waiting for reinforcements.

Time was up.

I waded into them. What else could I do? I began grabbing their weapons and throwing them away. Two of them discharged sizzling blue bolts of energy, one over my shoulder as I curled my fingers around the business end of the thing and yanked, the other over the heads of the Thryggians as it smashed end-on against the wall. The guards surged around me, reaching in vain for my neck and shoulders before locking their stubby arms around my waist, my thighs, trying to bring me down with their combined weight. Fortunately, my arms were free, and they had big beefy fists at the ends of them. I bruised my knuckles against turtle-faces over and over. As each guard chirped defeat and released his grip, another one grappled himself onto me. More guards came running. At one point there were an even dozen of them, most on me and the rest surrounding me, watching for an opportunity to join the fray. I realized they were spelling one another. Unable to bring me down, they had decided to wear me down. And they'd kept me out in the corridor, where I couldn't do any real damage to their 'experiments' — their test tube babies, created from my stolen sperm.

I felt a fresh wave of fury break over me, and then something truly bizarre happened, something that had never happened to me before. My mind became detached from my body, and my body kept on going, as if on automatic pilot. I could see and hear through it, but I was powerless to influence what it was doing. And what it was doing was finishing the fight.

My hands were breaking Thryggian arms and legs and cracking Thryggian skulls. They were hurling bodies up, down, and sideways, effortlessly but with lethal force. The Thryggians left smears of blue-green blood when they landed. Other guards came running. My hands reached one of them as he was pulling a communication device off his belt and snapped his neck before he could chirp anything into it. The air was thick with the smoke and smell of spent energy bolts. Scant minutes later, the hallway was littered with motionless Thryggian guards leaking alarming amounts of blood.

Unopposed, my body strode into the laboratory and resumed breaking things. It didn't leave a single piece of glass intact. It found the contents of every 'womb' and ground the life out of it with a booted heel. It overturned every piece of furniture in the room. I heard more glass shatter as a series of cabinets hit the floor.

Behind that sound I heard another, a commotion of raised voices and things breaking elsewhere in the complex. Of course! The other patients had been talking mass escape. Perhaps they had counted the number of guards running toward the laboratory zone and decided to take advantage of the diversion. And perhaps I could now take advantage of this further diversion and, in the confusion, find an exit, race over to the landing apron, and lift off in my ship…?

My body must have heard me. I winced mentally when it reached for the girl, by now lying unconscious on the hallway floor. But all it did was sling her over its shoulder and stride away in the direction of the reception area.

All hell was breaking loose, all over the patient treatment zone. Without the guards to protect them and quell the riot, the turtle-face doctors were taking quite a beating. It looked good on them. My body waved to the Thryggian clerk cowering behind the reception desk in the central hub. Then it — *we* — walked out the front door of the facility, unchallenged.

There was nobody guarding the tie-down area, either. By the time we reached the sprint craft, my mind was back in my body again; and it was a damn good thing, because the Thryggians had disabled my ship.

They'd probably done it as a precaution, in case I called their bluff and tried to leave. "Oh, Mister Dedrick, your ship is broken, such a shame. You can stay here while our mechanics repair it." And so on, and so on.

Fortunately, Human technology has built-in redundancy. It took me about five minutes to initialize the bypass circuits and fire up the thrusters. By then there were other escaped patients out there, starting their own ships without any difficulty at all. Interesting. Arristo had apparently expected me to make a break for it but not anyone else. Not even after the screens had started dying.

I guess there is something to be said for the element of surprise.

We've now been in space for three days. The girl has been awake and aware for just over half that time, but not all at once. Those turtle-faces really did a job on her, so I'm going to have to give her a chance to heal before interrogating her about her 'masters'. I'm still trying to figure out what they did with Ian and Paul, as well as what the hell they did to me.

I know they did something. There's no way I should have won a battle against a dozen Thryggian guards. Even weirder, my chest and back are splashed with fresh energy burns, all hurting like hell right now. Just one of those bolts should have seized up internal organs and knocked me out, but I hardly remember taking them. There's much more to this than stolen sperm cells. I don't know yet what it is, but I'm willing to bet that the girl can enlighten me on it.

For the record, please be advised that while I made a bloody mess of the entire corridor, I only demolished one laboratory. It contained no sentient life, just a lot of tissue samples, illegally obtained. They were my property, and I had the right to destroy them, and I did.

And that's what really happened on Thrygg, no matter what the Thryggians may claim. They'll probably accuse me of mass murder; and I've no doubt there are Humans on Earth who would agree with them, even though the turtle-faces did throw the first punch. Uncle Dennis has clout, but this may be bigger than even he can smooth over. So, I'm going to look for a small planet or moon that can support life, where we can go to ground until the heat dies down and it's safe to return home.

I'm hoping to deliver the preceding information in person, preferably as testimony at the Thryggians' trial, but in case something happens to both me and the girl and you find the sprint ship abandoned, please take this voice log to Supreme Adjudicator Dennis Forrand. He'll figure out something official to do with it. He always does.

2

I wasn't going to continue recording, but after viewing the latest Gate transmissions I figured I'd better take a page out of Uncle Dennis's book and cover my ass.

It's been 23 days since our escape from the medical facility. According to the tabs, the Thryggians are jumping up and down over the damage I did to their laboratory, claiming that I willfully destroyed over a dozen experiments at critical stages and set back scientific research on their planet for several generations. Naturally, they're screaming for my head, since a crime against science is a capital offence on Thrygg. And the Gate Broadcasting Authority approved the story for galactic transmission, so it must be top-of-the-page news all over Earth space.

Of course. Forget about all those Humans who were tricked into breaking the travel ban and then subjected to secret experiments by unethical alien scientists. We're selling downloads here, folks. 'Nephew of Supreme Adjudicator Flees Extraterrestrial Justice' — now, that's a headline. A real scandal-spawner, that one. It'll keep the muckrakers busy for months, not to mention Uncle Dennis's spin-flunkies.

Total morons, the lot of them.

I've been trying to figure out which of the patients I met at the facility on Thrygg was the journalist. That's the only way a story like this could have made it to the news media so fast from a planet that nobody was allowed to visit. And if a journalist was embedded on Thrygg, and the only news story to emerge from what happened there was about me disgracing my family and tarnishing The Great Man's rep, that raises other, even more disturbing questions. The girl told me earlier that Paul and Ian weren't my friends. It's beginning to look as though she was right. When we get back to Earth, I'm going to—

(Pause.)

I think we'll just lie low here for a while. I've landed the sprint cruiser on the fifth planet of a system that doesn't appear in my navigational data bank. It's a little farther than I meant to go, but still within Gate monitoring distance.

The exo-environmental scan reads friendly to Human life — breathable air, carbon-based flora and fauna — although, since it's supposed to be our hiding place, I could wish the planet looked a little less inviting from space.

The girl is outside right now, naming things. She named herself, too, a couple of days ago. She wants to be called Rose. From what she's told me, I gather that she was kept prisoner inside that facility for a long time. She jumped ship as soon as I popped the hatch, and she's been running around, devouring this world with her eyes ever since.

I don't begrudge Rose the happiness she's found here. Clearly, she's enjoying her new-found freedom. But this place is so hospitable that it makes me nervous. What if there's already a colony ship on its way here from Earth?

Rose may not like living in the sprint cruiser, but we're hiding out here, not settling down. I'll be closely monitoring all Gate activity. From the time a ship passes through, we'll have less than fifteen minutes to remove all traces of our stay here and lift off.

Planetfall Day 15

Still no ship movement through the Gate, although the data transmissions have been interesting. The Thryggians have taken their extradition demand directly to the Earth High Council. Their timing is impeccable — the matter has been tabled until the Council's next judiciary session, in about five Earth months. By then, hopefully, the story will be old news, not worth the energy required for a Gate transmission.

Meanwhile, I'm starting to have feelings for Rose, and they scare the hell out of me. Now that she's healed up, she's begun flirting with me. In fairness, I'm pretty sure she's not doing it purposely. After all, she's spent most of her life surrounded by Thryggian scientists. How is she supposed to know what happens to a Human male in the presence of an attractive female? Normally, sex wouldn't be a problem. After all, we're both young, both Human, and it's consensual, right? Except that every time little Willie raises his head I can feel that spigot inside me open up another notch. Just the thought of losing control again and hurting Rose the way I hurt the Thryggian guards makes me feel sick inside.

Long story short, I've been taking a lot of cold swims in the river.

<u>Planetfall Day 21</u>

Well, it finally happened. Now Rose is avoiding me completely, keeping as much of this planet between us as she can. She hasn't even returned to the ship to sleep. Not that I blame her. I've been using the exo-scanner to track her, so that I can pick her up quickly if a ship comes through the Gate.

I don't think we're going to be friends any time soon. That's a shame, because I could use a friend right now. I honestly never wanted to hurt her. And she isn't helping matters by hiding from me like this.

Never mind — we have a more serious problem to worry about. Something is killing the small rodent-like animals that inhabit the woods and fields around the ship. I've found hundreds of little carcasses on the ground, all seething with a foul-smelling blue fungus. The stench is pervasive. It even penetrated the filters of the envirosuit I wore to gather tissue samples for analysis.

I never fully appreciated the medical and scientific datanalysis packages on the ship's computers until now, although I wish they would work a little faster. I have to find out what is killing all these animals and be sure that Rose and I won't be affected.

<u>Planetfall Day 22</u>

I can't believe she's still hiding from me. It isn't because she's unaware of what's happening here. You can't take two steps in the forest anymore without encountering dead, stinking birrels and skwunnies. And it's really starting to burn me that she would prefer their company to mine.

<u>Planetfall Day 23</u>

The test results are in, and they aren't good. The computers have identified deadly toxins in every sample I collected, including all the shrubs and grasses, the fruits we've been eating, the water, the soil, and Rose's and my blood. (You wouldn't believe what I had to do to get a sample of her blood for testing.) I would love to be able to say that these lethal substances are probably native to the planet, that *it* has contaminated *us*; but the timing of this 'plague' clearly indicates that it was recently introduced into the ecology, most likely through the water supply. At least, that's what the computer tells me. I'm willing to bet that the toxins were released by some alien organism that came with us from Thrygg.

So why aren't we sick or dead? Good question.

And why are the animals dying while the plant life seems to be thriving? Another good question. And there's probably a Thryggian scientist somewhere out there who can provide the answers.

I'll have to do some further testing, culling samples from my own body first, then Rose's. I've brought her back to the ship, where she'll live from now on. She isn't happy about this, but I think she understands how necessary it is if I'm going to keep us safe.

<u>Planetfall Day 30</u>

A thousand dead on Venturi 5. Agricultural plagues on at least ten worlds. Disease that seeks out and kills the young, or the old, or the female, or the dark- or light-skinned. Reports have been coming through the Gate nonstop for the past week. Each new outbreak opens the spigot another notch, making me want to feel something shatter under my fists.

The Disease Control Department is calling it Angel of Death, and they suspect that all its manifestations are mutations of a single virulent organism. They're putting every inhabited planet in Earth space under quarantine until they've tracked Angel of Death to its source and figured out how it was carried. Then they can begin to work on developing a cure. To this end, the Thryggian scientific community has kindly volunteered its facilities and expertise.

Those lying bastards!

I've seen the organism, a microscopic virus shaped like a corkscrew, in samples of my blood. I've measured the toxins it puts into my semen, saliva, urine and perspiration. I know where Angel of Death originated and how it was carried, and so does every other patient who left Thrygg that day. No wonder the Thryggians let their 'patients' escape instead of simply discharging them.

When the plague the turtle-faces have unleashed is eventually traced back to them, they'll have a ready-made excuse, and a convenient scapegoat — me. After all, I was the one who started the commotion that pulled all the guards out of the patient treatment zone, making the mass escape possible.

There's no question anymore of my — of *our* leaving this place, not until I can figure out a way to destroy the virus, or at least purge it from my system. Rose's samples are now registering as alien on the computer, which probably means she was vaccinated against the plague and its toxins back on Thrygg. I have no doubt that the strain of Angel of Death in my blood is what killed all the animals here. I also believe that it has poisoned this planet, and that anyone else who tries to settle here will end up just like the birrels and skwunnies.

(Pause.)

Just thinking about what those damned Thryggians have done to me makes me want to—!

(Pause with heavy breathing.)

Still, you've got to admit that the idea has a certain — I don't know. A certain savage irony, perhaps. I mean, I went to Thrygg in the first place because I was bored with my life.

So the Thryggians took it away. Now all I've got are a planet and a woman, both damaged.

Thanks to those turtle-faces, Rose has scars inside as well as out. I've promised to try not to hurt her, but she has to help me stay calm.

After all, the two of us are all we've got, right? And she *is* living on my planet.

A whole planet, just for me. Dedrick's Planet. It has a nice ring to it, don't you think?

<u>Planetfall Day 47</u>

I've felled some trees to build a shed and made some tools to store inside it. I've also dipped into the extra clothing in my cabin to give Rose something to wear besides her green hospital outfit. If we're careful and keep them clean and mended, these garments should last us for years. And, since we're evidently going to be here for a long while, I figured it would be a good idea to begin growing our food.

Rose has been helping, as much as she can. Life in that Thryggian lab didn't exactly prepare her to be farm labor, but she loves being outdoors and she's trying her best. I guess that's something.

I'm preparing a couple of fields for cultivation and have been using the ship's computer to analyze the food value of some of the native plants. So far I've found two roots rich in vitamins and a berry bush that puts out a second crop: pods containing flat white seeds that read high in calcium and iron. We'll have corn, too — I found some popping corn left over from a party — and wild fruits and berries to round out our diet.

Of course, all these foodstuffs will be loaded with toxins absorbed from the soil, but that's okay. I'm not growing them for outsiders.

Meanwhile, Angel of Death continues to spread in spite of Disease Control's quarantines, and the Thryggians are still pretending to be the good guys. So, we're just going to sit tight here, keep a low profile, and concentrate on staying alive on Dedrick's Planet.

Year 1, Day 121

She's pregnant. She's pregnant with my child and she wasn't going to tell me. She claims she had no idea what was happening to her body, but I know better. She was probably planning to convert the third room of the house that we're building into a nursery one day while my back was turned.

I suppose she thought giving birth would be easy, like going to the washroom, that she could just step into the woods for a moment, drop the kid, and hurry back before I'd missed her. Well, she's in for a shock. It mystifies me that she was even able to conceive this baby. And if the Thryggians left her as screwed up inside as I suspect, her chances of surviving its birth may be slim. If she doesn't survive, I'm left alone here with a child I never wanted. If they both die, I'm left alone here, period. I think I'll take door number three, thanks — Rose lives, baby dies.

I've begun coming out to the ship once a week to check on Gate traffic and run tests on myself. There's no indication so far that the Angel of Death virus has any kind of lifespan. I'm just as infected now as I was when we landed here. Still, I have to believe that a cure will eventually be found and I'll be able to go back home to Earth to live a normal life.

Well, as normal a life as it's possible to have when you've been altered by the Thryggians. Once Rose realized that not helping me stay calm could put her life in danger, the flow from the spigot reduced to a trickle. Working the fields and building the house seems to be taking care of the rest of my anger for now. I feel almost like an ordinary man, able to see Rose as an ordinary woman. No, that's a lie. Rose will never be an ordinary woman. The Thryggians saw to that.

Year 1, Day 265

According to the ship's chronometer, today is April Fool's Day back on Earth, a perfect date to announce that I am now the father of a baby girl. Rose is calling her Lania. Well, why not? She's named every other damned thing on this planet.

The delivery was terrifying. Things broke loose inside Rose from the force of the contractions. There was blood everywhere, and her screams were deafening. She passed out a couple of times. Hell, *I* nearly passed out. I was sure she was going to die in childbirth, but she surprised me. I guess she's much tougher than she looks. Anyway, she's walking funny right now and sitting in the stream a lot. *I* may never recover from this, but I'm pretty sure she's going to be just fine.

She's calling Lania our miracle baby, and I suspect she may be right. Lania appears to be a perfectly normal Human infant, with all the right parts in all the right places. And she gurgles and coos and suckles and wets her diapers, just like a regular kid. What makes her special is that her body is apparently oblivious to Angel of Death. I've done all the tests two or three times. It's as though her body chemistry is specifically adapted to filter out and neutralize the toxins produced by at least this one strain of the plague.

Now that I know they're both healthy, I'm glad Rose fought me off when I tried to abort her pregnancy earlier. There's plenty of work here for three people. I have a feeling this kid will be able to start pulling her weight at an early age.

Fortunately, she doesn't cry. She stares, though, with huge eyes that remind me of Rose's except they're dark brown instead of light blue. Mainly, she stares at me. I wish she would stop doing that. It really gets on my nerves.

Rose has begun nattering on about our duty to provide the best for our daughter. She says I shouldn't deprive the child of a normal lifestyle. When I asked her how the hell she would know what a normal lifestyle is, she told me some of the stories she'd heard from the patients at the Thryggian facility while she was growing up. I then pointed out that normal lifestyles are for normal people, which, thanks to the Thryggians, we are anything but.

Rose has also been dropping careful hints about the sprint cruiser. I've informed her that the ship is mine and it doesn't lift off without me. Which means that until I can leave this planet and return to civilization, nobody else can either. End of discussion.

<u>Year 12, Day 275</u>

Well, it's taken them long enough.

After five years of fruitless detective work, the Disease Control people finally quit trying to track down the plague and instead dedicated all their resources to fighting it. Two years later, they came up with a broad spectrum vaccine that they claimed should protect against virtually all known strains of the virus; and three more years of clinical testing proved that they were right.

The bad news is that once a vaccination program was well under way and some of the planetary quarantines could be lifted, the Council reactivated the colonization timetable. The first of four ships came through the Gate nearly a week ago. There are now well over a hundred trespassers on Dedrick's Planet, not including livestock.

Their leader fits into both categories, being a real jackass. He paid us a visit yesterday — just strolled up to the front door, bold as brass, and started a conversation with Rose and the brat while they were working in the kitchen. I cut it off before he could find out too much. I told him we were the Joneses, but from the look on his face, I could tell he didn't believe me. He said he was surprised to discover settlers on 'their' planet but reassured me that the colonists would be glad to have us as neighbors. His face fell when I informed him that good fences make good neighbors, and that I would be billing the settlement for any damage done to my fields by their sheep and cattle.

I could warn the colonists about the birrels and skwunnies and scare them off right now, or keep my mouth shut and see whether this wonderful vaccine of theirs really works. If it doesn't, we'll be rid of them soon enough. But if it does…?

(Pause.)

Interesting thought. Meanwhile, regardless of what she pretends to my face, I know that Rose is curious as hell about these newcomers. I've forbidden her and the brat to talk to them, but just about every day Rose has been finding an excuse to wander over toward the river. From a certain spot, there's a clear view of the colony's landing pad, and she likes to stand and watch the people swarm around the ships, like flies on bloated gray carcasses.

Watching is all right, I suppose, as long as she doesn't make contact with anyone. Since her near-fatal … accident earlier this year, I've tried to ease up on her, but Rose doesn't seem to appreciate that. Lately it seems as though she's bent on provoking me.

I've even seen some temper from her. She comes at me whenever she thinks I'm hurting the brat. She's overreacting, of course. Our 'miracle child' bounces back like a rubber ball from any sort of injury. It's unbelievable how rapidly she heals. Anyway, Rose fought like the devil to have this kid, so I guess it's natural that she would fight like the devil to protect it.

My chest feels tight most of the time now. But I'm not going to blow up. I am determined to keep control of my temper for as long as there's a colony on this planet.

<u>Year 12, Day 283</u>

A cluster of domed structures has gone up about three klicks away, probably serving as temporary shelter while the colony is being built. It looks as though there are about 30 families living there. One of the women wandered over this morning to chat with Rose, but I headed her off. Good thing I did. She was nosy as hell. How did we get here, she wanted to know. Where was our ship? Where were we from? How old was our daughter? Would we put her in their school?

When I flatly refused, she hastened to assure me that every member of the colony had been certified toxin-free and then vaccinated by Disease Control before being allowed to join, so there was no need for us to worry about the plague. Naturally, I agreed with her on that point.

Her next offer I did accept. Since we were Human, like the colonists, they could share their surplus materials with us. If we needed anything to improve our homestead or our quality of life, all we had to do was show up at one of the supply domes 'with a wagon and a smile'. I cut the conversation short after that, remembering to thank her before sending her on her way.

Then I walked over to the ship to test my blood (still no change), and to check out the engines. I'm glad I thought to camouflage the sprint cruiser before any other vessels could arrive. Fuel levels are steady and all system indicators show immediate readiness for liftoff, in case we need to leave in a hurry.

That need could arise fairly soon if the wonder vaccine doesn't work. Once a colony reports an outbreak of the plague, the Disease Control Department is quick to become involved. These colonists were all vaccinated, so the DCD investigators would realize that 'the Joneses' must have been the carriers, and they'd waste no time coming to pick us up. That's provided the Thryggians didn't hear about it and get here first.

Since I'd rather this all transpired later rather than sooner, I have decided to keep my own counsel for now and let these trespassers make themselves at home.

<u>Year 13, Day 20</u>

I knew we wouldn't have to wait very long. The plague has started its sweep through the colony, beginning with the livestock. You can tell when a homestead has been stricken, by the huge plume of black smoke hanging in the air over what used to be the barn. Once it takes hold, Angel of Death is swift and merciless. The skies are dark right now above much of the settlement. In a short while there'll be more smoke, a column of it rising from the burning ruin of each family's house.

Meanwhile, a Disease Control Department ship landed near the supply domes yesterday to investigate the outbreak, and DCD officers in envirosuits have been taking water and soil samples for analysis from each homestead. The planet is apparently under strictest quarantine. Sensors have been placed in orbit to detect anyone trying to escape before the plague has run its course; and patrol ships are posted nearby with orders to turn back or destroy any unauthorized traffic entering or leaving the system. Containment is a cruel policy, but it works.

I have a plan to fool the DCD and foil the quarantine, but I can't implement it until the patrol ships have been recalled.

That won't happen until all the colonists are dead. So, we wait.

As long as some of them remain able-bodied, they should be able to tidy up their own messes. Towards the end, however, that won't be the case. Much as I would love to just leave the final few bodies to rot, the plague has an overpowering stench to it, and we're downwind of the settlement. So, as it comes down to the last several families, incinerating and burying the remains will become *our* chore – mine and the brat's. I'm actually looking forward to spending some quality time with the kid, far away from Rose and her damned maternal instinct.

Once I know the patrol ships are gone, we'll take off, just Lania and I. I don't really want to leave Rose behind, but she's made it clear that she will never accept the kind of relationship I want to have with her daughter.

As for the brat, her attachment to her mother is touching, but Lania's just a kid. She'll get over it. She can't hate me forever. Not when we're both fugitives and I'm the only one she can trust to keep her out of the hands of the Thryggians.

PART II

Lania Dedrick

Lania Dedrick (b. appr. 2385 C.E. – d. unknown) was part of the 'lost generation' of the Forrand-Dedrick family. Beyond the fact that she was born on MF-307, the daughter of Abner Dedrick and his companion Rose, very little is known about her as any official records mentioning her were apparently wiped from Earth's database. Data-tampering charges were briefly brought against Lania's cousin, Watch Commander Gael Dedrick, but were later dropped for lack of evidence.

— *Sic Transit Terra, An Unauthorized Planetary History* (2673 C.E.)

Obituary

January 30, 2398

Abner Dyson Dedrick

Taken by Angel of Death in his 35th year, on Planet MF-307. Co-deceased by his partner Rose. Son of the late Carl and Emma (née Forrand) Dedrick. Nephew of the late Dennis Forrand and the late Thomas and Regina (née Forrand) Dedrick. Survived by his first cousin, Watch Commander Gael Arthur Dedrick, currently assigned to the Fleet star cruiser *Marco Polo*.

3

They found them all inside the house. The four children lay in their beds, where they'd undoubtedly been sent by their mother as soon as the sickness took hold of them; and the two adults sprawled on the kitchen floor, their bodies and faces contorted with the final agonies of the disease. The corpses were blue, their skin already pocked and seething.

Lania could well understand why the last few settler families might be unable to bring themselves to dispose of their own dead. The first time Abner had brought her out to a plague-stricken homestead, she had reeled in speechless horror, sure that the human flesh seeming to writhe and twist beneath that bright blue skin was being consumed alive. The faces were most terrifying of all. Jaws worked, cheeks bulged and hollowed, as if the victims were struggling to speak. She had backed away and would have turned and fled if not for the certainty and severity of Abner's punishment.

By now, Lania had seen too many plague-dead bodies to be disturbed by their appearance. Now it was the smell that made her stomach lurch, the sickly-sweet pall that hung like a heavy curtain in every room of the house, strong enough to mask even the penetrating stench of decomposition.

"Go stack the wood in the yard," said Abner, his lip curling with disgust as he flexed his hands inside his heavy gloves. "I'll bring them outside."

Lania raced out the door, gulping lungfuls of blessedly fresh air. The wagonload of wood that they had brought stood just beyond the front yard. She pulled her work gloves back on, scrambled up onto the wagon bed, and began pitching short logs down to the ground, visualizing as they landed the quickest way to construct the shape she would need.

Lania was only twelve, but she was getting plenty of practice at creating funeral pyres — this was the seventh family they'd had to see to in less than twenty days. She was grateful that they didn't have to burn the livestock as well. The settlers themselves had done that.

Abner had knotted the children's bed sheets around their bodies and dragged them all out into the yard. He turned and stared critically for a moment at what Lania was building.

"Spread it out, brat!" he commanded sharply. "I don't want to have to stack them too high."

He brought the adults out wrapped in sheets also.

Once the pyre was wide enough to suit him, Abner tossed the linen-shrouded bodies onto it like so many extra pieces of wood. Then he lit the kindling.

Flames danced all around the wooden pyre, poking at the larger logs like orange and yellow fingers. After several minutes the center collapsed, spilling its burden down into the heart of the fire; and with a sudden roar, the flaming fingers leaped upwards and closed like a blazing fist around the entire structure. Sparks and ashes floated skyward in a great cloud of black soot, and the air was drenched for a hundred meters around with the hot, smoky-sweet stench of the disease.

The first time they'd had to perform this chore, Lania had retreated hurriedly from the smell. But the overpowering odor had still managed to permeate her clothing and her hair, remaining in her nostrils for days after she thought she'd scrubbed it off.

She risked a covert glance at Abner and saw him nodding with satisfaction. Lania could easily guess what was going through his mind: twenty-seven families down, only three left to go. These colonists had never been anything but a nuisance to him. A blight. An infestation. If there hadn't been any Angel of Death on this world, he would probably have forced Lania to help him exterminate them some other way.

"Come on, brat, let's do the inside," snapped Abner.

This was the part she really hated. Lania sighed inwardly. She pulled her gloves a little tighter and stepped through the front door as her father returned to the wagon for his ax.

There was hardly any smell left inside the house, she noticed. Or perhaps her nose had simply been numbed by the stink rising from the pyre outside. Inside the gloves, her palms were sticky with perspiration. Just knowing that they were there to obliterate every trace of the family that had lived in this house was enough to make her stomach churn.

She'd wanted desperately to get to know these people.

Ever since Lania could remember, Rose had been telling her stories by the flickering light of their kitchen hearth — made-up stories about heroes and princesses, singing trees and talking animals — and it had never mattered whether Abner was close enough to hear. With the arrival of the colonists, that had changed.

The first story, whispered quietly while Abner was outside chopping firewood, had been about a family, a mother and father and a little girl. But it wasn't about their family. The father and mother spoke kindly to each other. The father never beat the little girl. The mother never screamed or sobbed at night after the father had joined her in their bedroom. There was laughter and sharing and happiness in this very normal family, and Rose assured her that there were families just like it living in the settlement across the river, where Abner had expressly forbidden them both to go.

Cautiously over the next few days, Rose continued telling her daughter the story of normal family life, stunning her with descriptions of birthday parties and picnics, things that sounded too good to be true even as they resonated in Lania's mind like long-buried memories struggling to resurface. The details gripped her imagination and would not let go. Day and night, they shimmered just out of reach, tantalizing and tragic, like a desert mirage.

"Move it, brat!"

The bonfires. Lania hurried through the living room of the settler home and into the first bedroom. It was a child's room. The furniture was all white and red and yellow. Small stuffed animals perched on the wall-shelves, miniatures of the creatures that the colonists had brought with them, but with brightly-colored fur or patchwork skin. Depicted on the window shade, a pudgy baby animal with a horn growing out of its forehead leaped, grinning, over a rainbow. Lania stepped over to the wardrobe and looked inside. Pink underwear and ruffled blouses. A little girl had lived here. And died here.

From the living room came the insistent thudding of an ax, punctuated by the dry crunch of wood tearing as Abner broke up the furniture. Lania sighed, remembering the richly polished cabinetry she'd stared at briefly earlier. When Abner was done, it would all be firewood. And when the fire was done, there would be only ashes.

And when the fire in the front yard was done— Abruptly, Lania realized that she was fingering the lace collar of an embroidered pale yellow tunic. Steeling herself against the tears already stinging her eyelids, she grabbed a double handful of the little girl's clothing and dumped it in the middle of the bed. *Quickly*, she told herself, *quickly, like pulling funnel tree sap off your skin. It will hurt for an instant and then you can forget about it.*

With frantic haste, she built the bonfire on top of the mattress, emptying the wardrobe and all the drawers, snatching the stuffed animals off the shelves and toys out of the toy box, even throwing the toy box and the shelving onto the pile when she realized they would burn.

Then it was on to the next bedroom, and the next, rushing to finish the grisly job before the fortress around her thoughts collapsed.

Lania tried not to think about the things she stacked on top of the bonfires. She didn't want to know what these people had owned or which item belonged to which member of the family. She didn't want to visualize them dining together, or imagine what they had discussed in the evening, when their day's work was ended. She didn't want to have to remember anything about them at all. She especially didn't want to dream about them, about lives cut short, about what might have been. There was no room for wondering and regret in a life fully occupied with survival. It was enough for her just to have the moment, to drag from it whatever she could against the day when she and her mother would finally be free.

At last it was done. Abner took the tater-alc out of the wagon and sprinkled some over every bonfire they'd built in every room. He left a tater-alc trail from room to room, finally emptying the cannister in the front hall. Then he lit a stick of wood and threw it inside. He and Lania made for the wagon and watched as flames raced to fill the house, exploding with a fierce roar in every room, shattering windows and melting the roof with their intense heat.

It pressed against her face like a wall, that heat. It kindled tiny, searing flames in her eyes, so that she saw fire everywhere she looked.

"What's this?" demanded Abner scornfully, grasping her chin and pulling her around to face him. "Are you crying?"

Lania shook her head. "It's the smoke," she blurted, wiping away the tears with the back of her hand.

"Well, don't let me catch you crying for *them*," he warned her as he pulled the shovels off the wagon bed and thrust one into her hands. "They had no business coming here in the first place. This is my planet, Dedrick's Planet, and don't *you* forget it either." And Abner turned and bit his shovel into the soft ground at the edge of the yard.

Flexing her fingers thoughtfully around the handle of her shovel, Lania stared for a moment at the back of Abner's head. There were still three families left in the settlement, three families they would have to cremate, and she knew she lacked the strength to position an adult body properly on a funeral pyre. Reluctantly, she let the blade drop to the ground.

Lania cast a furtive glance over her shoulder at the pyre she had built that day. The fire was almost out. Once the embers cooled, she and Abner would bury the Human remains. That part wasn't too difficult. A charred body didn't look very Human at all. With a final shuddering sigh, Lania turned her back on the blazing homestead — but not on Abner — and began helping to dig a grave.

It was nearly dark when they pulled the wagon the last few meters up the path to the Dedrick homestead, a squat, crudely-built house beside a large quonset tool shed with padlocked double wooden doors. Lania remembered helping to build that tool shed, using supplies taken from the settlement domes shortly before the livestock had begun dying off. She also remembered what Abner had done to her the day he'd caught her inside the shed, curiously inspecting what he'd put on the shelves. As usual, Rose had interfered with the beating, preventing him from killing her. However, by the time Lania had recovered, he'd installed the lock, blocking any further exploration.

"Go lose that stink, brat," growled Abner. "I'll put away the tools."

Just then the front door swung open, and Lania saw her mother silhouetted in the shifting light from the kitchen. Rose shivered and wrinkled her nose as Lania scurried past her, around the house to the big water barrel beside the back door.

Lania drew a bucket of water, set it carefully down on the ground, and stripped off her overalls and shirt. The soap was gritty and didn't like to lather, but with rapid, practised movements she scrubbed her hair and skin with it until she burned all over. Then she rinsed off by pouring the bucket of water over her head.

And not a moment too soon. Heavy footsteps were coming around the side of the house. Naked and dripping, Lania darted through the back door just as Abner turned the corner.

She stood quietly in her room, her spine rigid as she listened for the warning creak of the door. Water dripped off the ends of her short, dark brown hair and streamed down her back and her chest, until she was standing in a puddle on the rough wooden floor. When finally she heard the muted splash of the bucket being dipped into the rain barrel, she breathed a sigh of relief.

Lania took her clean shirt and overalls off their hook and lightly toweled her skin with them before putting them on. As she prepared to leave her bedroom, she glanced around at the bare, rough-hewn walls, the plain wooden bedstead with its grass-filled mattress and stained cotton sheets, and the sagging, faded curtains that couldn't quite cover the almost-square pane of her window. For one treacherous instant, her mind flashed the image of red hearts on a puffy white bedspread, a floppy doll with rouged cheeks and yellow pigtails, and a grinning baby animal soaring over a pastel rainbow.

Lania's heart clenched briefly and finally in mourning.

—— «» ——

"We need to leave this planet," said Rose quietly.

Abner barely even glanced up from his dinner. They'd had this conversation before.

Lania sat, chewing slowly, and watched her mother's features harden into an expression of stubborn resolve.

"I mean it this time," said Rose, the quietness of her voice together with the look on her face offering a reckless challenge to his authority. Lania's chewing stopped altogether as she became aware of Abner's flinty eyes, trained like a weapon on her mother's face. There would be an 'attitude adjustment' that evening, for sure.

"Remember what that woman from the settlement said? The colonists were vaccinated against the plague. Abner, if they can do that, surely they can find a cure for the strain you're carrying. You can go home again. Even if the ship won't fly anymore, there are still the supply shuttles. After the quarantine is lifted, one of them could take us to Earth. And, Abner...? Maybe there's a doctor on Earth who can repair me inside."

The look of revulsion that swept across Abner's face at that moment made Lania shiver. "You're fine just the way you are," he snapped. "Besides, as soon as an Earth doctor saw those scars, he'd demand to know how you got them. And once you'd told him, he would be forced to hand you over to your legal owners, the Thryggians."

Thryggians.

Abner threatened her mother so often with that word, wielding it like a club to force her to stay, to submit. *Be good and do what I tell you, or I'll send you back to your alien masters.* Rose never talked about what the Thryggians had done to her, but Lania had seen the pale lacework of scars on her mother's body and understood instinctively that they hadn't been put there by Abner.

"Why? The Thryggians don't want me. They were prepared to destroy me because they had no further use for me. Why should they care about me now?"

"Because they don't know about *her*," he replied, jerking his head in Lania's direction. "What was that you told me back on Thrygg — our lives are joined? You knew *how* they were joined, too, didn't you? Well, I turned that genetics lab into a pile of ground glass, so now the Thryggians will have to start over, with fresh samples of your DNA and mine. And if they ever learn that we went ahead and produced the next generation of the experiment ourselves—"

There was no need for him to complete the thought. Her eyes shining with sudden tears, Rose declared, "I'm not going back to Thrygg! And neither is Lania!"

"Of course, you're not, baby," he agreed, smiling benignly now. "None of us are. We're staying right here, safe and sound on Dedrick's Planet." And his charcoal eyes caught the fire of the wood-burning hearth behind her, forcing her back against her chair in silent but unmistakable warning.

As the color left Rose's cheeks, all the fight seemed to drain out of her as well.

Abner nodded slowly to himself and went on eating. Rose's throat was working as though to keep something down. She picked up her fork and began dividing the now-cold vegetables on her plate into smaller and smaller portions. And Lania resumed putting food into her mouth, chewing and swallowing without tasting any of it as her mind struggled to digest all the startling revelations of the past few minutes.

Rose had mentioned a ship. Maybe Abner was keeping it behind the locked doors of the tool shed; or perhaps he had concealed it somewhere else on the planet. Wherever it was, Lania decided, she had to find it.

If it had brought Abner here, it could take her and her mother away.

—— «» ——

Abner Dedrick was tall and straight and strong, with muscles that bunched and shifted like cords just beneath his skin when he moved. Today his long legs had attained a ground-devouring rhythm that didn't slacken as he entered the forest. Abner strode along the path, shouldering his way through the low-hanging branches of the funnel trees, brushing aside the dangling, ropy tendrils of birrelweed that wove them all together.

He walked with purpose, never looking to the left or right, nor over his shoulder; for Rose was still recovering from her latest 'attitude adjustment', and Lania had been given an entire field to cultivate and threatened with punishment if the work wasn't finished when he returned. And who else was there with the time or inclination to worry about Abner's comings and goings? Not the colonists — there were only two families left at this point, and they had much more important things to be concerned about.

So, Abner walked with his shoulders back and his head held high, making no effort to conceal his progress. Lania was grateful for that, for it made him very easy to track from a distance.

With the onset of the plague, Lania had begun keeping a record of the days, and it had dawned on her as she studied her calendar that once every seven days, without fail, she worked alone for half a day, and Abner was nowhere to be found. Where did he go? Today she would find out.

She watched him stride purposefully past their farthest fields and directly into the woods. Then, with only the slightest hesitation, Lania entered the forest as well, choosing her footsteps carefully on a light-dappled, leaf-strewn path that roughly paralleled her father's.

Abner emerged from the woods and set out at once across a span of bright green, gently rolling hills. Lania forced herself to wait until he had topped the crest of the first hill before she left the cover of the forest and followed him. Three hills later, he plunged back into another thick growth of trees that encircled a large grassy hillock.

Lania counted slowly to ten. Then she scurried down the long slope, her legs swishing noisily through the knee-high bayonet reeds and flatgrass. Not until she was out of sight behind the thick bole of a rubberleaf tree at the near edge of the thicket did she dare to draw her next free breath.

From her hiding place, Lania strained to hear sounds of Abner. Nothing. Cautiously, she raised her head and peered around, half-expecting to find him standing ten meters away, glaring wrathfully at her. But he wasn't anywhere in sight.

As quietly as possible, Lania made her way through the wood, stopping every few seconds to listen and look all around. Then, once she had crossed to the inside of the wooded circle and knelt in the protective shadow of a huge, bifurcated funnel tree, she finally found Abner. He stood with his back to her, digging his fingers into the grass on the side of the hillock.

Lania froze. All that separated them was a clearing perhaps five meters wide. Remaining motionless, afraid even to take a deep breath, she watched as he made a hole large enough for his hand and thrust it in up to the wrist.

A sharp click and a low rumbling sound issued from somewhere inside the hillock. Abner pulled his hand free and set to tearing another hole one meter over from the first. This time the grass tore more easily, parting almost like a curtain. Once he had an opening nearly as tall as he was, Abner bent slightly, stuck his leg into it, and stepped through.

Lania gasped softly. She stared at the teardrop-shaped hole that had swallowed Abner up. This was no ordinary hillock. Hillocks didn't growl when they were touched, and they weren't hollow. This was something cloaked with grass to make it look like a hillock. Perhaps the ship that her mother had mentioned?

Abruptly Lania's common sense took over, and she realized that now, while he was still inside, was the perfect time for her to start back home. Now that she knew how to get here, she could find a way to return and investigate further. And she would, she promised herself, most definitely investigate further.

Lania backed away carefully, until she was halfway through the thicket and the hillock was out of sight. Then she turned and ran as fast as she could, out of the thicket, over the three hills, not daring to look behind her, not caring whether the bayonet reeds swished and crackled around her frantically pumping legs. She was in the near forest now, her arms flailing to keep the birrelweed out of her face as she raced back to the field she was supposed to be cultivating. Hardly pausing to snatch a breath, Lania rolled beneath the horizontal rail of the fence and grabbed up her hoe.

She'd made it! But she could never convince anyone she'd been routinely working a field for the past hour. Lania's face was hot, she was gulping air, and her arms and legs were shaking almost out of control. She would have to focus her energies, concentrate on slowing her body down. She closed her eyes, reached inward with her mind—

"You! Brat!"

Lania's eyes snapped open and she whirled around just in time to catch the flat of Abner's hand across her cheek. The force of the blow knocked her off balance. But Abner caught her by the shoulders before she could fall, his fingers biting into her flesh as he shook her furiously back and forth.

"So you spied on me, eh?" he roared, his eyes glittering with menace.

Lania felt the color drain from her face. She'd been so sure he hadn't seen her! "No! I — I just—"

Abner's lip curled in a cruel sneer. "What did you see? Tell me!"

The pain in her shoulders was paralyzing, but Lania gritted her teeth and forced the words out. "Nothing! I didn't see a thing!"

"Liar!" And he drew one arm back and gathered his huge hand into a fist.

Lania saw the blow coming. She knew she couldn't duck it, even if Abner weren't holding her fast with his other hand. Willing herself to relax, she closed her eyes, reached the fingers of her mind deep within, and found and held her focus. And drew herself inward, inward, until she was safe from the fear and the pain, and her body was nothing but a shell of meat and gristle that immediately went limp.

From her refuge, Lania was distantly aware of her body hitting the ground, of blows raining down on her, of her mother's approaching voice screaming, "Stop it! You'll kill her!" And then even that awareness grew unbearable, and she drifted off to a place much further inside her mind, a place of absolute peace and tranquility, where her body ceased to exist at all.

4

Slowly, Lania opened her eyes. It was morning. A sickly yellow light was pushing its way through her window. She was lying on her bed, staring up at bare wooden ceiling beams through a haze of agony and confusion.

Bit by bit, fragments of memory began piecing themselves together, and Lania groaned and then gasped at the pain that enveloped her right side. Some ribs were broken. She could feel them shift with each shallow breath she took. And she could taste blood on her teeth.

Carefully, she located her right arm, then her left, then her legs, experimentally flexing her fingers, her wrists, her elbows, her knees, assessing the damage. When she tried to raise her left arm, the knives dancing inside her shoulder nearly sent her spinning back into unconsciousness.

No matter, she told herself, *soon it won't matter*.

With a sigh, Lania closed her eyes. She reached inward with the fingers of her mind and found and held her focus. Slowly she gathered all the energies of her being and poured them onto her pain in a cool, healing stream.

Rose... Rose had leaped out of bed, interrupting her own healing process, to come to Lania's aid. Somehow Rose had known Abner was attacking her daughter, even though they were out of sight of the house. And Abner had known Lania was close by, even though he hadn't seen or heard her. Dimly, she wondered how that was possible. Perhaps it was a talent he had never learned to control, that just happened sometimes. And perhaps he had other abilities as well that no one knew about yet, abilities that would emerge haphazardly, like seeing through solid objects or touching people's minds. There was something deeply troubling about that, but she was on the brink of twilight sleep and her thoughts kept melting into wisps that floated just out of reach....

—— «» ——

"Lania! Can you hear me?" Rose's urgent whisper brought Lania back to full consciousness. As her eyelids fluttered open, she heard her mother's quavery sigh of relief.

"Oh, little one, I'm sorry I took so long to get to you yesterday. When I saw you lying there at his feet, I thought you were dead," she went on, tears in her voice. "But look at you — I can hardly believe how fast you heal."

The light in the room was darkening gold now. Dust particles swam in front of the window.

Rose leaned closer, and Lania inhaled a faint, unmistakable scent.

"I'm sorry you had to be alone today. He dragged me out to help him bury a settler family," whispered Rose. "I couldn't do much with this arm, but he insisted I come along anyway. I think he just wanted to keep me away from you. There's only one family left now, Lania. Time is running out, and he's going to keep us injured and separated so we can't plan. I hate to do this to you, little one, I really do. But if we're ever going to be free, then it must be up to you."

Rose looked so miserable at that moment that the sight of her brought tears to Lania's eyes. She longed to put a comforting arm around her mother's shoulders, but her body felt like a leaden encumbrance. Even to move her lips in speech would take more strength than she possessed.

Rose struggled to recompose herself. "You just rest and listen to me. We can do this. I'll keep Abner away from you as much as possible. Don't worry about what he does to me. Your freedom is all that matters—"

The front door slammed, startling them both.

"Where's dinner, woman?" bellowed Abner from the kitchen.

Rose bent forward and gently kissed her daughter on the forehead. "Soon, Lania, whatever it costs," she repeated in a fierce whisper. Then she was gone.

Lania lay staring at the ceiling as tears rolled from the corners of her eyes, burning two narrow paths across her temples to the pillow.

When had Rose's life become expendable? And whatever made her think that Lania would accept such a sacrifice? If anyone should be running interference for the other, it was Lania. Rose healed so slowly. And if she kept getting in Abner's way, contradicting him, challenging him, even attacking him as she had done once before—!

He'd nearly killed Rose that time. It had taken her almost the entire growing season to recover.

Amazingly, the first thing she'd done after regaining consciousness was to smile. It was only technically a smile, just the slightest upward curve at the corners of her mouth, but it was the expression of a victor.

Now Rose was prepared to endure another such 'victory', this one possibly even costlier. Somehow, Lania would have to devise a plan that would make it unnecessary.

—— «» ——

On the fourth morning after the beating, Lania opened her eyes and took an experimental breath. There was still some pain in her chest, but no movement of broken ribs.

Gingerly, she levered herself up onto her right elbow and tried out her torn left shoulder. It was a little stiff, but serviceable.

Rose had covered her with a sheet. Lania sat up and rolled it down to her hips. All her cuts and scrapes had healed without scars, and the huge black bruise on her chest was mostly yellow. By tomorrow, it would be gone. Two days after that, this whole ordeal would be a memory, and she could slip away and investigate the hillock beyond the woods.

Once she knew she could stand, Lania bent carefully to strip the sheets off her bed. They would have to be washed. Given her current condition, this was bound to be a slow process. She would probably be late for breakfast. With luck, she might even be too late to eat with Abner before he left for the fields.

Lania bundled her bedlinens and carried them outside, to the rain barrel beside the back door. Moving carefully, she drew a bucket of water and set it down where the sun had begun to warm the beaten earth. Then she knelt down, letting the early morning light warm her bare back as well; and, using the recalcitrant homemade soap, she began to wash her sheets.

All at once, her senses were invaded by the crawling certainty that something was wrong. She stopped scrubbing and lifted her gaze, and directly in front of her saw a distant plume of dark smoke rising into the sky. Lania's heart dropped.

The last settlement family had finally succumbed. In three days, four at the most, she and Abner would be over there, burning and burying them. That was when she would have to do it. She had no other choice.

Lania spread her sheets out to dry in the sun. Then, after quickly washing herself, she went inside to get dressed for breakfast.

The kitchen was quiet. For a moment as she stepped through the doorway, she thought her father must already have left for the fields. That hope died when she saw him sitting in his chair, one ankle crossed over his knee.

Abner had a lean, bearded face that scowled even when he smiled. This morning his scowl was directed at the small kitchen window, which framed the rising smoke on the horizon as if it were a picture. Across the room, Rose stood perfectly still, hugging her shoulders and staring listlessly at the same black, billowing column.

"There go the last ones," she murmured.

Lania served herself some bean porridge from the pot on the hearth and slipped quietly into her seat.

"And good riddance to them," Abner muttered back. He glanced sharply at Lania and she nearly choked on her mouthful of porridge. "Well, brat, are you going to be strong enough to help me dispose of those trespassers once and for all?"

Her jaw working, Lania nodded.

"Good. Your mother was next to useless last time."

Lania looked over at Rose, now blindly twisting a dishrag in her hands as she gazed steadily out the window. Rose blinked hard, twice, and a tear rolled over the fresh bruise on her cheek.

Suddenly the porridge tasted burnt. As Lania struggled to swallow it, she became aware that Abner was watching her with a cruel half-smile on his face.

"It never ceases to amaze me just how fast you heal. From death's door to the picture of health in...what? A few days? Well, I guess you've got the Thryggians to thank for that."

Lania heard her mother's sharp intake of breath and understood instantly the weapon concealed in his words.

Still smiling, he rose to his feet and sauntered toward the front door. "You go ahead and build up your strength, brat," he tossed over his shoulder. "Just remember I need you to be a hundred percent at the end of the week."

"I'll be ready," Lania replied softly.

He turned in the doorway and gave her a long, thoughtful stare. Lania held her breath, remembering his mysterious sensing of her whereabouts the other day, and for one terrifying moment she was certain he must have read her mind. At last he wheeled, still grim-faced, and pushed Rose ahead of him out of the house.

—— «» ——

"The wagon's loaded! Come on!" Abner stood at the doorway, glaring at her.

Lania thrust the last spoonful of compote into her mouth and exchanged a meaningful look with her mother.

Rose's eyes shone with tears. Lania threw her arms around her and received a fierce hug in return.

"Today, Mama," she whispered. "I promise."

"Yes." Rose's voice caught on a sob as she ran a trembling hand over her daughter's hair. "Today it ends."

Abner's scowl was deeper than usual as Lania walked past him. "Go wait by the wagon," he growled. "I'll be there in a minute."

The door closed between them. Lania listened tensely for the sound of raised voices but heard none. Then Abner emerged from the house, and they set out for the last homestead with their heavy load of wood.

Lania had been planning this for days. After eight burials, she knew exactly what they would be doing and in what order.

Obediently, she constructed the funeral pyre and waited for him to drag the bodies outside. Once the fire was burning strongly, she followed him inside the building, where they assembled their bonfires in all the rooms, doused them with tater-alc, and set them ablaze. Finally, Abner handed her a shovel.

"Start digging," he told her. "That was a big family. We need a big hole."

Abner turned his back on her and rammed the blade of his shovel into the ground. Lania waited until he had shifted his weight forward. Then she gathered her strength in her arms and swung her own blade as hard as she could at the back of his head.

There was a wet thud when it connected, not the sound she'd expected at all. With a cry of surprise Abner dropped to his knees. Rivulets of dark blood began flowing swiftly down over the collar of his shirt.

She swung again. And again. Lania reached deep into her mind, drew herself inside, and stayed there as the deadly weight of the shovel continued to bludgeon his motionless body.

Much later, she opened her eyes and found herself kneeling in blood-soaked clothing beside the cooling corpse of Abner Dedrick. Her shovel lay nearby, stained and spattered.

Somehow she managed to lever his body onto the wagon. For a moment, Lania had considered simply rolling him into the grave she was about to dig. Then she decided it wouldn't be right. Abner could have warned the colonists off when they first arrived, could have kept the planet all to himself without anyone having to die. He had chosen not to. That made him a murderer. And it would be obscenely cruel to make his victims share their grave with him.

Sweating and out of breath, she picked up Abner's shovel and set about burying the last unfortunate, unnamed, perfectly normal family who had tried to live on Dedrick's Planet.

—— «» ——

The house was dark and silent as Lania pulled the wagon with its grisly load into the front yard of the Dedrick homestead.

"Mama! I could use a hand here. Mama?"

There was no answer. Lania's skin began to crawl with the certainty that something was terribly wrong. She dropped the tongue of the wagon and raced inside.

The kitchen was in deep twilight. The furnishings in the room cast long shadows on the rough wooden floor, and motionless among them lay Rose.

"Oh, Mama…" Lania whimpered, sinking to her knees. Rose was cold as stone, her head cocked at an impossible angle.

So this was the last-minute thing that Abner had had to do. Lania recalled her mother's words that morning, the ferocity of her parting hug, and realized with a shock that Rose must have known all along what he had in mind for her.

"Mama, we won," she whispered brokenly, leaning closer to place a gentle kiss on her mother's brow. "I'm free. But I wish you could be going with me."

She sat on the floor beside Rose's body, tenderly smoothing the silky blond hair back from her face, memorizing her pale, delicate features. Bitterness settled at the back of Lania's throat, refusing to be swallowed.

And then she saw it — only technically a smile, just a faint upward curve at the corners of her mother's mouth. In that instant, Lania understood: Rose had not been a victim. She'd accepted her death as the price of her daughter's freedom and had paid it willingly.

This gift would not be wasted. Lania would bury her parents and burn their home. She would find a way inside Abner's ship and learn how to make it carry her off this poisoned world, to a place where nobody had ever heard of the Thryggians or the plague. And then, fulfilling her mother's final wish, Lania Dedrick would be free to live a normal life.

PART III

Ixbeth Minegar

One of Earth's first alien allies, the Kularians played a pivotal role in helping Humankind to overcome the misconceptions and half-truths that were hindering its acceptance by the other races in this arm of the galaxy. The chief architect of this alliance was **Ixbeth Minegar**, a pure-blooded Kularian born on the planet Dimmla. The first Kularian to make personal contact with Humans, she was also the first to work alongside them. She established and was the first to occupy the Human Studies chair at the Archives on her ancestral home world of Kula'as. As well, she was the author of many textbooks on the Human species, including a memoir titled *The Otherness Factor*, which is still considered required reading for any Kularians planning to venture into space.

— *Sic Transit Terra, An Unauthorized Planetary History*
(2673 C.E.)

5

Ixbeth paused to shift the weight of two daybags, her own and her mother Dallia's, as she approached the Minegar family home. The market at Turvanen had been busy that morning. Several southern crops had been harvested, and her mother had traded enthusiastically for them, bartering herbs and doses of midwifely advice for seasonal fruits and melons. Ixbeth would much rather have carried melons to market and brought back herbs. The coarsely-woven sacks slung diagonally over her shoulders were heavy with produce. They forced her into an awkward gait. Worse, they prevented her from running.

Kularian feet with their long, high arches and tough, thick toepads were naturally designed for running. Unburdened, Ixbeth could have settled into an easy, loping stride and maintained it effortlessly for hours. Her heels would never have touched the ground. Instead, she had been forced to walk three kilopaces over bruising terrain, in the full heat of a midday sun. What should have been a ten-minute transit had turned into an hour of torment. Her heels felt like two open wounds, her fur was baking beneath her shift, and she was being slowly garrotted by the crisscrossing cloth straps of the bags. Even her tail hurt.

Ixbeth vowed never to complain again about tending Dallia's herb garden.

At last she saw the semicircular entrance to their home, and beside it her litter-brother's broad back and shaggy red mane as he sat on his weaving chair, knotting bright green fibers into the warp strands of his next project.

Tal had concluded his trading and left the market hours ago. He could not have foreseen that his assistance would be needed. It was irrational to be angry with him. Nonetheless, at the sight of him so placidly and thoroughly engrossed that not even the suffering she'd been broadcasting for the past quarter-hour could reach him, Ixbeth felt her fingerclaws extend.

Tal's mane shifted perceptibly, sense hairs rising as she approached.

Finally, he was aware of her!

Without turning around, he asked, "Mother is not with you?"

Ixbeth retracted her fingerclaws, sagged down wearily at the doorway, and let the straps of the daybags slide off her shoulders to the ground. For a moment she considered getting up and going inside. Then she felt painful warnings in her hips and knees and thought better of it. The Dimmlesi-style dwelling, carved into the side of a large hill, was a cool, shady refuge; however, simply rearranging her legs took less effort.

"Sianna came to market to find her," Ixbeth replied at last, gingerly rubbing at the base of her stubby tail through the material of her shift. "Eveni has gone into the woods to drop her litter. Mother passed me her bag, stuffed some sleepwort into her pocket, and went running to help her. I doubt she'll be home today."

"How many males followed them?"

"Four, I think. Mother can handle a pack that large at a birthing. She's done it before."

Concern. "Father?"

"Not among them. He was trading his second-last chair for a cutting tool when I left."

Relief. And yet, Tal exhaled a worried breath. "I hope Eveni's twins are born close together. We lost two healthy litters earlier this year when the males became aggressive after a several minutes' delay between births and there weren't enough females in attendance to hold them off."

"Eveni's two sibsisters were at the marketplace. They were running right behind Mother. And Sianna is young, but she'll fight to protect her own newborn sibs. This isn't a singleton birth like Eveni's last one. Mother felt two kits moving inside her."

Tal nodded grimly in response, his large hands moving expertly over the threads of his canvas. Drawn by a curiosity powerful enough to make her forget all her aches and pains, Ixbeth got to her feet and stepped closer to his weaving tree to examine his progress.

The tree had once been an assignment for a course in branch sculpting, an ancient Dimmlesi art. Tal had chosen a *breha* sapling that grew ten paces from the Minegars' front door, and by patiently tying off and weighting a single branch, had coaxed it into growing absolutely straight, parallel to the ground. Even then he must have known he wanted to be a clothweaver. Five years later, he'd looped a matrix of tightly fitted warp strands between the branch and a wooden rod suspended below it, and had made his first, less-than-perfect blanket.

Now he and Ixbeth were adults. The free-hanging rod had been affixed by their father, Krodus, to an ingeniously shaped chair that would cradle a weaver's spine and legs in comfort for hours on end. And Tal's bold, colorful blankets and uniquely designed wall-cloths were in great demand in both the Kularian and the Dimmlesi communities. Today, he had received a commission from the town prefect in Turvanen and had hurried home from the market to get started on it.

This wall hanging would adorn the nursery in the prefect's home. "Which story will you be depicting?" Ixbeth asked.

"The tale of the covetous artist—"

"—who so desired to possess the soul of his beloved that he sculpted a tree in her likeness, intending to cage her spirit there after he murdered her. I haven't heard that old legend in years."

"Do you remember how it ends?"

Of course she did. It had been her favorite Dimmlesi bedtime story. "He killed her, and for a while her spirit dwelt in the tree, weeping in sorrow. But then, lightning struck the tree and destroyed the cage. And her soul escaped and flew straight up into the heart of the source, where it was welcomed and loved for eternity. How do you plan to show her spirit rising into the sky?"

"Feathers. The prefect and his mate are collecting their cast-off feathers for me to incorporate into the weaving. And speaking of cages, Ixbeth...."

"Are we back to that?"

"You can mute it all you like, but I'm your litter twin, and I can taste your sadness at the back of my throat every time we're together. Talk to me. Maybe lightning will strike."

Ixbeth sighed. This had been tried before. Their conversations usually ended with one of those rhetorical questions: When are you going to stop rejecting your heritage? What is so terrible about being Kularian? Why must you try to rationalize and explain everything?

Tentatively, she reached out with her mind, sensing nothing from her brother but hopeful concern. Perhaps this time it would work, she thought. Perhaps he was ready to listen to her. She swallowed hard and asked, "Tal, have I just wasted the last five years of my life?"

Surprise. He considered for several heartbeats before replying, "I don't know. Have you been doing what you wanted to do?"

"I have. I've been studying the workings of the intelligent mind. I can explain the symbolism of the feathers in your wall-cloth. I can predict the outcome of the bargaining at the marketplace. I've learned a lot at the Archives on Altera. But I don't *do* anything useful."

"Are you suggesting that the acquisition of knowledge is a waste of time?"

They were veering close to one of those questions. Ixbeth changed tack.

"When we go to market, Mother has her herbs to trade, and you have your cloth, and Father has his chairs and tables, and I have nothing. I help Mother tend her garden and carry home her goods, that's all."

Tal was shaking his head again. He let his hands fall from the loom and turned toward her, radiating sympathy.

"You have a great deal of learning. That's not nothing. I know you aren't a Believer, Ixbeth, but I've been studying the *Dr'rava Kula'as* for seven years, and there is no doubt in my mind that the Great Presence has a purpose for each one of us. To help us accomplish that purpose, he has given us different strengths and skills, and yours is knowledge. In a moment that belongs to you alone, Avo'or will instruct you. In that moment you'll understand with perfect clarity what a valuable gift you bring to the universe."

Ixbeth sighed, allowing him his moment of pious wisdom, and went inside to prepare their meal.

That night she had a nightmare, the first of many. Night after night, her sleep was shattered by images of death and destruction. According to her father, they were messages from an oracle on a distant world, summoning the most devout among the Children of Kula'as to embark on an ancestral quest. To Ixbeth's mind, that made the dreams even more shocking. For if what Krodus said was true, the unthinkable had happened:

Ixbeth the non-Believer was receiving this call; and her brother, a religious scholar who had been preparing for it for years, was not.

—— «» ——

Red, everywhere. Red sky. Red rocks.

Fire! Surrounded! Missiles shrieking. Flames roaring. No escape! Heat crushing, consuming. Others trapped — panic! A taste like blood.

I am a defender! Must protect!

Red smoke. Eyes burning. Chest burning. Can't breathe. Can't think. Can't—

Protect! Terror! Sudden screams. Bodies blasted, flung, broken. Kularian, Mitradean, Nandrian, Human, all fallen, so still. Death smell rising from steaming red mud.

Helpless! I am a defender. I need to— Why can't I—?

Black against red sky, upright corpse of a tree, scorched limbs stretched in supplication.

Protect!

How?

Enemy!
Where?
Listen! None left to scream.
Taste! None left to feel.
Rage! Escape! Avenge!
I am a defender! I am—
On fire!

Ixbeth awoke an instant before the death cry could leave her throat. She was lying on her pallet, every muscle aching, fingerclaws fully extended, sense hairs rigidly upright on her head. She knew that she was safe, that it had only been a dream. And yet, the smell of her own charred flesh continued to fill her nostrils and sting her eyes, long seconds into wakefulness.

Burning and shivering, Ixbeth stumbled to her feet. She groped urgently for the light control. There was none. Panic rose. Then her mind cleared and she remembered. She was on Dimmla, not Altera. Altera had artificial illumination; but Altera was thirty million kilopaces away.

Ixbeth spun defensively and pressed her back to the cool earthen wall, all the tawny fur on her arms and across her shoulders bristling. She was trapped in the dark, a below-ground blackness that she could almost feel pressing against her skin. It made her heart hammer in her ears and her breath dissolve in her chest. Her throat tightened around remembered emotions. They tasted like tears. Then she thought of the bugs. They *had* to come to her this time!

"Light!"

Nothing.

In years past, they would have responded immediately. Ever since her return from Altera, however, they'd been acting strangely. And since the onset of the nightmares, so many days ago, they hadn't wanted to come to her at all. Maybe they'd grown lazy during her long absence. Maybe they'd forgotten her. Or maybe they just didn't like her anymore.

Stupid bugs.

"Light!"

JANN GROSTA'AN VIRTOD SIMMSAL HR'RUV...

Ixbeth cried out and pressed both hands to her temples. The words rang inside her head like enormous bells, their peals sounding and resounding with deafening intensity, and then, mercifully, subsiding.

They were made of familiar sounds, but arranged in unfamiliar ways.

Her father and litter-brother had told her there would be a prophecy at the end of her ordeal. Please, Avo'or, after thirty nights without rest, let this be it!

...GRENT FAN M'MHJORDOR, GEFSAL M'MHJORDOR...

Ixbeth gasped and spasmed as the mysterious utterance battered her senses once more.

Reaching out blindly with clawed fingers, she made her way across the room, bumping into a chair, stumbling painfully against a table top. At last her hands found the smooth flat object they'd been seeking — her portascribe. Ixbeth pulled the stylus out of its sleeve and began feverishly scribbling in the dark, her ragged breathing underscoring each thundering, incomprehensible word.

...NURR KRECHTOD L'LJEV DO'OVANI. NURRSAL STRAFFMR'RAND KULA'AS ANGS'SLIM.

Finally, blessed silence fell. Sinking to the floor, Ixbeth blew out a quavering breath and clutched the portascribe to her chest. She felt her fingerclaws retract, felt her sense hairs relax, and smiled with relief. She had done it. She had captured the prophecy. Now the nightmares would end.

Heavy footsteps halted just outside her door.

"Ixbeth?" She heard her father sigh as he entered the room. "You've frightened them again."

He was concerned, but whether for Ixbeth or for the bugs she couldn't tell.

"I frightened *them*?" she snapped. "I'm the one having the nightmares, remember?"

Krodus said nothing, but Ixbeth tasted his disappointment at her outburst and felt instantly ashamed. They hadn't been ordinary dreams — even a non-Believer had to concede that. In any case, the daughter of a Guardian of Time was supposed to have a deeper respect for Kularian tradition.

Ixbeth felt her scalp contract as sense hairs rose, detecting further movement in her doorway. A moment later she heard her mother's soft voice. "Light."

Like a bright yellow cloth being drawn slowly from a hidden pocket, the swarm of fire bugs streamed to the ceiling, their wings whispering comfort. The glow of their bodies cast a living lacework of pale, fluttering shadows on every wall.

Krodus sighed again at the sight of the bugs, and Ixbeth found herself sharing his relief.

Krodus Minegar stood an average height for a male Kularian but was uncommonly broad and muscled, with golden eyes and blunt features and a thick mane of auburn hair that hung down to his shoulders, cloaking his pointed ears like a curtain. Dallia Minegar was her mate's opposite in almost every way. Tall and graceful, she had a narrow face framed by a fiery halo of upcombed tresses that couldn't quite conceal her ears, no matter how closely they hugged her head. Like any set of litter twins, Tal and Ixbeth strongly resembled their same-sex parents. A gift from the Great Presence, Tal had once called it, that Kularian mated pairs produced replacements for themselves — male and female, power and agility, complementing each other as Avo'or had intended.

"Is this the prophecy?" asked Krodus, reaching for the portascribe.

Ixbeth watched his face as he turned the tablet this way and that, squinting and scowling in an effort to decipher her manic scrawl. He said nothing, but she could taste his impatience.

"I had to record it phonetically," she apologized. "It was a strange language—"

"It's ancient Kularian." Tal stood in her doorway, shaking out his mane and pointedly yawning. "The Oracle communicates with the chosen ones in the language of our ancestors. Would you like me to translate it for you?"

Ixbeth nearly choked on the jealousy behind her brother's careful politeness. He still hadn't forgiven her for being chosen over him. As if the choice had been hers!

Wordlessly, Krodus handed him the portascribe.

Tal scanned the tablet, frowning over his litter-sister's nearly illegible scribble. "It's the old language," he affirmed at last. "See, the first word is a marker demanding the listener's attention. Then we have the message: Two hundred worlds — no, wait — two hundred *on* a world, wandering together. *Simmsal* means physical proximity only, with no emotional connection. Maybe that means coming together after wandering at the same time, but separately. This is a cycle of concealment, so I guess that makes sense." Sudden alarm. "But it seems to suggest that there are only two hundred chosen ones this time. Ixbeth, are you certain you got it all?"

Before she could answer, Krodus cut in, "Move on to the next part."

Tal drew in a steadying breath and proceeded with the translation. "Life out of death, and ... giving back death? It doesn't specify to whom, or how, so I'll say 'dealing out death'. And a machine ... of a child ... *Do'ovani* has the possessive suffix, but the linking prefix is missing." Krodus's impatience was thickening the air. Tal quickened his pace. "All right, I have it now. It's the heart of a child. A machine with the heart of a child. Together, victory, and Kula'as rises again."

"Are you sure now?" Krodus wanted to know.

"I'm certain," declared Tal. "Two hundred on a world, wandering together; life out of death, dealing out death; and a machine with the heart of a child. Together, victory, and Kula'as rises again."

Immediately, Ixbeth's stomach began tying itself in a cold, hard knot. The Oracle spoke in riddles, in phrases that lent themselves to a thousand different interpretations. Thirty days earlier, she had worried about five years possibly wasted studying at the Archives on Dimmla's sister planet, Altera. Now she was realizing that she could spend the rest of her life on this quest, sacrifice all her hopes to it, and still leave it unfinished.

As Krodus and Dallia looked on proudly, Tal drew himself up and delivered the commission: "This prophecy has been entrusted to you by Avo'or, the Great Presence, to understand and fulfill in order to ensure the next ten generations of peace in the galaxy. You must travel the stars in search of truth and carry it back to Kula'as. I wish with all my heart that I were going in your place."

He meant it.

6

The *caranth* was especially good that morning, steamy and fragrant. It left a pungent aftertaste in Ixbeth's mouth.

"I trust that you'll finally get a good night's rest tonight," Dallia remarked brightly from across the table.

Ixbeth gave her a faint smile and a noncommittal nod. Sleep? Not a chance. The prophecy had rescued her from one nightmare, only to thrust her into another.

Born and raised on Dimmla, Ixbeth had always thought of herself as Dimmlesi. Now, she wasn't sure what she was. She was Kularian and yet not Kularian. She was Dimmlesi and yet not Dimmlesi. She was by heritage a defender of a Kularian community that needed no defence, having lived in peace with the native Dimmlesi since arriving on this planet more than three hundred years earlier. Now an oracle on an alien world had sought out her Kularian blood and commanded her to undertake a quest that she had always thought was just one of her father's fanciful stories. And the word 'chosen', which for thirty days had brought her nothing but anguish, had overnight become an honored title; however, it could not be discussed with anyone outside the community because the entire Kularian race was in a cycle of concealment, having apparently been ordered into hiding by the previous oracle.

...weaponless, helpless. No escape!

At the onset of the nightmares, Ixbeth had made herself *vanoi*, withdrawing from emotional contact with the family to spare them her pain. Until she had sorted out her feelings on this matter, she decided, it would be best to remain that way. Tal was her twin and would taste faint traces of her, but that was all. A good night's rest? That would simply have to wait.

Krodus made an impatient sound. "Dallia, please. The Oracle instructs us and we obey as best we can. There will be a *mar'ruk* this evening. I have also summoned the community to *ohe'elu*. All the necessary rituals must be observed, now that the Oracle has finally delivered its prophecy. You will be there," he added with a nod to his daughter, his voice and bushy brows equally weighted with ultimatum.

"Of course, she will," declared Dallia. "She's one of the chosen ones. She accepted the commission. She knows her duty, Krodus."

But Ixbeth could tell from the dissatisfaction behind her father's eyes that he wasn't quite convinced. "The *ohe'elu* is crucial to your success on the Quest," he told her. "Especially now. If only the days of legend weren't past!"

"The days of legend?" Ixbeth echoed.

Wearing a familiar, faraway expression, Krodus leaned back in his chair. "The writings say that there was a time when the entire galaxy knew of the Reyot Quest. The chosen ones, thousands upon thousands of fine, strong young males and females, would gather in the Capital City, in the great square. At this gathering they would choose comrades to stand by their side, and then they would set off in pairs or groups on the glorious Quest. And that would be their life's work, their only profession — to bring the prophecy to fruition and ensure peace in the galaxy for the next ten generations. Everywhere they went, they were recognized and welcomed. It was considered a great honor to assist a chosen one on the Quest, with food or shelter or transportation, freely given. Those were the days of legend."

"But now things are different," Ixbeth prompted.

Krodus heaved a sigh and crossed his massive arms over his chest. "Of course they're different," he grumbled. "For ten generations, our people have been scattered across the galaxy. The Guardian of Light on Altera has had visions of our beautiful Kula'as, now a wild planet crawling with strangers who catalogue artifacts and theorize about our 'mysteriously vanished' civilization. As for the Quest, how can there be a Reyot Quest if the Kularians who would carry it out are all gone?"

Ixbeth said nothing. She knew the Guardian of Light on Altera, a computer technician named Evin Lurrlo. He spent his nights attempting to make contact, however brief, with the Central Archives on Reyi'it. What Krodus referred to as 'visions' were bits of data, stolen in the instant before the contact was detected and cut off by the Archives' security protocol. Her father's insistence on turning technology into mysticism had lately begun to annoy her; nonetheless, Ixbeth felt weighed down by the sadness behind his words.

"No, I'm afraid there won't be any free meals or free rides for the chosen ones this time." Krodus sat forward again and sipped a mouthful of his drink. "Wherever you go in search of truth, you'll have to buy your passage, just like ordinary folk."

"And you'll have to do it as a Dimmlesi," warned Tal, who had finally joined them at the table. Frowning, he poured himself a cup of *caranth* with one hand and reached for a chunk of bread with the other. "That shouldn't be too difficult for *you*, litter-sister," he growled.

As their eyes met across the table, Ixbeth felt her spine and tail stiffen in response to the challenge behind her brother's steady gaze.

Thousands of young people, her father had said. An army of chosen ones. Of all those thousands who set out on a Reyot Quest, how many actually attained understanding of the prophecy? How many dropped out, weary and frustrated, or tempted by worldly opportunities too good to pass up? Did the Oracle choose thousands because it knew that only a few would persevere to the end?

Tal would persevere. He had the training and a double portion of tenacity. But Tal had not received the call. Ixbeth had. No matter. The Quest was a debt of honor, and Ixbeth would be carrying her family's honor with her as she searched the galaxy for truth. To preserve that honor, she had to set aside her personal doubts and feelings. She had to persevere. She had to succeed.

"Tal, stop that!"

Krodus's harsh voice seemed to break a spell. Blinking hard, Ixbeth glanced in confusion around the table. "What...?"

"Part of being a Kularian is perfecting the mental discipline," Tal was arguing.

"That means controlling your own thoughts and feelings, not those of others." Krodus stood up with a scraping of chair legs, arm muscles bulging with the effort required to keep his fingerclaws retracted. "I've told you about this before."

"But she doesn't have the discipline, or the commitment. There's a reason that only Kularians are chosen for the Quest, and Ixbeth isn't—"

Now Dallia was on her feet, the fur at her neck beginning to bristle. "Be careful what you say about your litter-sister," she warned softly. "We're all Kularians at this table."

Tal's amber eyes darkened with an anger that burned Ixbeth's throat like smoke. Abruptly he excused himself and left the room.

Ixbeth was stunned. "He can control people's minds?"

"He can project his emotions into them," Dallia explained. "It's a Kularian talent. We all have it to some degree."

"But I don't have any—"

"Why do you think the bugs went deeper into their hive whenever you had a nightmare?" Krodus pointed out. "Why do you think one of us came running to see whether you were all right? You were projecting your fear. Be at the landing place in the clearing at dusk, for *ohe'elu*. You'll understand everything much better after the ritual."

Ohe'elu. Hear the truth. The Guardian of Time was the historian and rememberer of the community, the teller of ancient stories, the custodian of forgotten information. He had an important role to play at the Great Accounting, or *mar'ruk*, every year. But Krodus hadn't called an *ohe'elu* since his ascension to Guardianship, shortly after the birth of Oreil and Va'ana, Ixbeth's oldest sibs. Life on Dimmla had been uneventful. With nothing of planet-shaking importance going on, there had been no need for the entire community to be informed at once, until now.

Now a Reyot Quest was beginning, and there were announcements to make and rituals to perform. And now Ixbeth could understand her father's impatient mood. Tal wasn't the only Minegar who had spent years anticipating the prophecy. And when the Oracle had chosen her instead of her brother to receive it, Krodus had shared Tal's disappointment as well. And who could blame him? After all, she was the only non-Believer in the family. A rebel. A failure.

What could the Oracle have been thinking?

—— «» ——

The least she could do, Ixbeth decided, was find a practical way to travel around the galaxy without exhausting her family's resources. A berth, perhaps, on an interstellar ship. Fortunately, the piloting contract with the Mitrades required that a Spacefarers' Guild Hall be maintained in the marketplace in Turvanen. Immediately after firstmeal, Ixbeth made preparations to go there.

Tal watched her pack a miniscribe and some fruit into her daybag. As she hefted it onto her shoulder, he asked, "Care for some company?"

"Dimmlesi or Kularian?" she shot back.

Tal's face fell, and Ixbeth instantly regretted her words as she tasted the hurt they had caused.

"Minegar," he reproached her gently.

Brother and sister stood for a moment, turquoise eyes locked with amber in a silent exchange of feelings. Ixbeth and Tal had always had their differences, but until now, nothing had ever really come between them, not even the thirty million kilopaces separating the orbits of Dimmla and its sister planet.

"You're still there, aren't you?" murmured Tal. "Inside your head, you're on Altera. But your body is stuck here on Dimmla. That's why you've been so sad."

He was too convinced of his rightness to be argued with. Ixbeth turned with a sigh and began running in the direction of Turvanen. Today she would follow the dirt path that the Dimmlesi called 'the road'. It was ironic. On Altera, where one could choose to go on foot, with hips, tail and legs moving in effortless rhythm, she had discovered the sheer pleasure of running on a perfectly flat surface. On Dimmla, however, where going on foot was the only option, there were no flat surfaces anywhere.

Tal caught up to her, purpose in his stride as well as in his mind. As though tasting her thoughts, he declared, "You don't belong here anymore, Ixbeth. You've always known that you needed more than our simple way of life to be happy, and now the Oracle has given you a compelling reason to leave this place. But returning to Altera is not the answer, not for you. You're a chosen one. You have to look forward, not back over your shoulder, if you're going to succeed on your quest."

Her quest. Ixbeth felt a chill deep in her marrow. *Her* quest? How could any one being take responsibility for the future of the entire galaxy? It was insane. And yet, Ixbeth had accepted the commission.

Reflecting on it now, she realized that she'd never actually had a choice in the matter, and not just because thirty sleepless nights had left her too exhausted to think straight. It was because, for the first time in her life, she had tasted her parents' pride in her. It was intoxicating. After a lifetime spent falling short of Krodus and Dallia's expectations, failing at every trade and craft they had arranged for her to try, she was a chosen one. Ixbeth would have done anything, promised anything, to avoid disappointing them again. Regardless of her own feelings, she simply couldn't *not* go on the Quest.

It was only a matter of time until they figured her out. Ixbeth was a non-Believer, but in that moment she prayed that Avo'or would put a suitable job posting on the Guild Hall recruitment board for her. The sooner she left Dimmla the better.

Ixbeth stole a glance back along the path. It was lined with every shade imaginable of green. The entire planet was a garden, rich and ripe and fragrant as one growing season came to an end and another one began. The southern fields would be replanted and sprouting vines right now, sprinkled with white and pink and yellow berry blossoms. And the bean bushes would be fruiting as well, especially the long brown *lalava* beans, a Dimmlesi favorite. Those were cool weather crops. North of Turvanen the temperatures had been rising, providing ideal conditions for grain farming and for the small, soft-skinned fruits that grew on trees. And there was *drithra*, of course, a Kularian staple that grew well year-round in any kind of soil.

True, Ixbeth had been much happier on Altera, where roads were flat, and where buildings were made of stone and had front and back doors, and banks of windows to let in the daylight, and artificial lighting to extend the day well into the night as she studied. But she had been born on Dimmla. She had spent her early years tending crops with older sibs and running through cool green forests, and through meadows boisterous with wildgrasses. On Altera, surrounded by friends and knowing she was near her family, Ixbeth had felt *lemvanu* — complete. Now she was planning to leave both her homes, possibly never to return, and it was a shock to realize that the one she would miss the most was simple, difficult Dimmla.

Belatedly, she regretted not taking the cross-country route to Turvanen. It would have been a bumpier run, but much more direct.

The road began winding through a collection of hills, each with a dwelling carved into it. Ixbeth glanced backward again, and for an unsettling moment their shaded entranceways looked like heavy-lidded eyes watching her run away. Startled, she felt herself misstep. She would have stumbled if a strong hand hadn't reached out to steady her.

Tal had been running in tandem with her, his thoughts and feelings so muted that she'd actually forgotten he was there. The mental discipline, no doubt. For the first time in days, she was glad of his presence.

Staring straight ahead, Ixbeth quickened her pace. "You're the one who should be going on this quest, Tal, not me," she said.

Radiating assurance, he matched her stride easily. "No. I've been thinking about this, and Avo'or has sent me wisdom. The Oracle knew what it was doing."

"But you've spent years studying Kularian culture and history," she protested. "Tal, you've been preparing for this most of your life."

"Yes. By looking backward. Don't you see? You're the one with the thirst to learn new things. That's why you had to go to Altera, and it's also why you were chosen by Avo'or. We've both been preparing to carry out his plan, Ixbeth. You've been preparing to undertake the Reyot Quest. And I've been preparing to help you survive it."

Surprised, Ixbeth halted in mid-step and nearly overbalanced before settling back on her heels. "Survive it?" she echoed.

Tal pulled up beside her, smiling benignly. "In the days of legend, chosen ones always traveled in groups, for mutual support and protection. But this is a cycle of concealment, and you'll be alone. I have the survival skills that you're going to need out there. I can teach them to you."

"The mental discipline?"

He nodded. "Mother and Father misunderstood my intentions this morning. I swear, Ixbeth, I wasn't trying to control you. I just wanted to give you some—"

"—commitment," she supplied curtly, recalling his words at the firstmeal table.

"—some sense of how important it is that you succeed in this quest," he corrected her, patience in his voice as they resumed running together. "The fate of our entire race hinges on it. 'And Kula'as rises again' isn't just a rallying cry — it means our survival as a people. On planets where interbreeding has been possible, Kularians have been doing it for hundreds of years now. Ten generations. And with each new generation, more of what makes them uniquely Kularian has been lost, dissolved in the genetic patterns of other races. Meanwhile, our community on Dimmla has become inbred. Each generation is producing fewer normal litters than the last.

"The population on Dimmla and Altera combined is no more than one-tenth the size of the original settlement. The same thing must be happening on other worlds. Many of the dwellings we passed back there were unoccupied. And it's only going to get worse. Ixbeth, if this quest isn't successfully completed, ending the cycle of concealment, in time there won't be any of us left. The Children of Kula'as will be nothing but a memory on hundreds of planets."

"But if there are thousands of chosen ones—"

Tal shook his head decisively. "There were, in the days of legend. Now there's no way to know. Our people on other worlds may already be so assimilated that they can't even receive the call to the Reyot Quest. Dimmla and Altera could hold the only remaining community of pure-blooded Kularians in the galaxy. If so, and even if every member of the ninth generation were called, there still wouldn't be more than three hundred chosen ones on this quest That's why you must succeed, Ixbeth, and why I must help you."

Her breath turned to dust in her throat. "Stars," she whispered hoarsely. The stakes were much higher and the task even more enormous than she'd thought. Ixbeth swallowed hard as the roaring of her blood filled her ears. A heartbeat later, her legs stopped running. They folded beneath her, depositing her on the ground between the knobby roots of a centuries-old *rachjab* tree that grew beside the path.

Awed wonder. She heard Tal's sudden intake of breath and glanced up in time to see him mouth a Dimmlesi word — *ristota*.

"Destiny?" she repeated. "Where?"

"In the branches. This is a spirit tree, Ixbeth. I've passed it a hundred times and never recognized its shape. And now it's dying. I never thought I would see this in my lifetime."

Ixbeth got to her feet and stared at the tree. He was right. Seen from the path, its naked limbs formed the shape of a word.

...upright corpse of a tree, its blackened limbs reaching skyward...

"Destiny," she breathed.

Suddenly aware that she was standing alone, Ixbeth hurried to catch up with Tal, a hundred paces down the road.

"One of the oldest techniques in the *Dr'rava Kula'as* is called bonding," he explained as they ran together. "It enables one individual's consciousness to be shared with another. There isn't enough time for me to train you properly before you leave Dimmla, but if you would permit me to bond with you, a part of me could accompany you on your quest and thus continue your instruction."

As the meaning of his words sank in, Ixbeth felt her skin prickle a warning. "I'm not sure I want you living inside my head," she told him. "It's bad enough having you in the next room."

Tal grinned. "If even one twentieth of what I've heard about other races is true, then you're going to find there are worse things to have in your mind than a teacher with the voice of your brother. The bonding process is painless. You won't even feel it happening, if that's a concern."

She shot him a wary glance. "It wasn't, until now."

Tal tossed his mane without breaking stride, and Ixbeth had a brief taste of her brother's hurt feelings. "Please, trust me," he implored her. "Nothing will be done without your consent, I promise. Will you think about it, at least?" He reached out and cupped his hand over her shoulder. "I love you, Ixbeth, and I want you to be safe."

There was genuine feeling behind his words. And there was something else. Tal wanted desperately to become involved in the Reyot Quest, even if he had to manipulate her into inviting him along. Remembering the disappointment that had sat at the back of her throat for days after the Oracle had passed him over, Ixbeth made a choice.

In an instant, brother and sister were standing at the side of the road, gazing at each other through an impassible barrier, an uncomfortable awareness of hurting to come; for she knew she would refuse to let him bond, and he sensed her decision already made.

"Well, I have to be going back," he said, awkwardness in every syllable. "Good luck in town. And don't forget about the ritual this evening."

"I won't," she assured him. For several minutes, she watched him trot back the way they had come, trailing disappointment. The bitter taste was all too familiar to her.

On a barter day, the square at the center of town was a riot of colorful tents and improvised lean-tos holding sacks of produce and tables of handmade goods, all brought in to be traded by hundreds of local Kularians and Dimmlesi. In that much commotion, Ixbeth would have been hard pressed to locate the Spacefarers' Guild Hall. Today, however, the marketplace in Turvanen was empty, making the only permanent structure in the square very easy to find. Constructed to meet the minimum specifications outlined in the contract with the Mitrades, the Guild Hall was a rough-hewn wooden building five paces square and three tall.

Ixbeth approached it today with a certain amount of trepidation. The only being she had ever seen actually enter this place was the Mitradean who piloted the shuttle between Dimmla and Altera. She had no idea how the recruitment center was supposed to work, assuming it was even operational. And what if the door was locked?

It wasn't. Ixbeth eased it silently ajar, then squeezed through the narrow opening, muscles taut, tail rigid, sense hairs erect. The Guild Hall was empty. She was alone. But she hadn't been the first to come here.

A table was pushed up against the far wall, and on it sat a machine that resembled the computers at the Archives. Its screen displayed the words 'Postings Available' in Galactic Standard.

Like all the students and docents on Altera, Ixbeth had had to learn Standard in order to read the books and access the databases at the Archives. At the time, it had seemed troublesome and a little pointless to conduct one's education in a foreign language. Now, however, she knew better. Standard was the common language of space travel. Perhaps Tal was right about the Great Presence. Perhaps the Reyot Quest wouldn't be as impossible as she'd feared.

Then Ixbeth actually looked at the recruitment board. There was one posting left: the *Marco Polo*. She read the registry information and felt her fingerclaws extend as a growl climbed up the back of her throat.

It was an Earth ship. It would be filled with Humans.

And Avo'or had left her no other options.

What a cruel, capricious deity her people worshiped!

PART IV

First Contact: Zekaris Station

Gael Arthur Dedrick (b. 2362 C.E. – d. unknown), eldest nephew of Supreme Adjudicator Dennis Forrand, entered training to join Earth's spacegoing Fleet at the age of 17 and was posted to the *Marco Polo* in 2384 C.E., shortly before the first outbreak of Angel of Death. Available records indicate he was a dedicated and exemplary officer, rising rapidly to the rank of Watch Commander. His first contact with the Kularian, Ixbeth Minegar, is documented as leading directly to Earth's eventual alliance with the Kularian people.... Subsequent to the charges of data tampering being quashed in 2401 C.E., Dedrick was offered a captaincy but chose instead to retire from the Fleet and become a licensed independent ship owner. His arrow-class vessel, the *Liberty*, disappeared while en route to Earth's meeting with the Galactic Great Council in 2417, leaving his fate and those of his two registered passengers unknown.

— *Sic Transit Terra, An Unauthorized Planetary History*
(2673 C.E.)

Fleet Control Headquarters, Earth

MEMO

EARTH DATE: 27 August 2397

FROM: Vice-Admiral Kendra Nelligan

TO: Captain Hiromasu Takamura, commanding the star cruiser *Marco Polo*

You will shortly be receiving an official order to add the Dimmlesi mindhealer, Doctor Ixbeth Minegar, to your ship's medical staff. In Earth's current situation *vis à vis* the Great Council, it is imperative that her application for the berth posted by your ship's Supervisor of Medical Services be accepted. We cannot turn down an opportunity to increase our knowledge of an alien species. In addition, this placement aboard the *Marco Polo* may prove personally fortuitous for you. In the wake of last year's misunderstanding with the Nandrians, your successfully integrating the Dimmlesi into your crew can only strengthen the trust that Earth's High Council places in you.

Make no mistake, this is to be treated as a first contact situation, with all the protocols and safeguards that apply thereto. This office has already issued a request for background cultural data to the Galactic Central Archives on your behalf.

The Council was very excited to receive Doctor Minegar's request, as it represents a huge diplomatic breakthrough, possibly leading to further interaction with alien species. Therefore, whatever her underlying purpose may be, you must somehow find a way to make her visit work in

Earth's favor with the Galactic Great Council. Under the circumstances, we have been instructed to exclude the *Marco Polo* from the impending census/relief/evacuation operation for as long as the alien remains aboard.

Speaking as a friend, I have to caution you: not many people in your position get a second chance, Hiro — don't waste this one.

Regards,
Kendra

7

Aboard the *Marco Polo*, Watch Commander Gael Dedrick gazed around the ship's mess, shaking his head in admiration. The quartermaster had outdone herself this time. Red and white streamers looped drunkenly across the ceiling. Snowflake cutouts and asymmetrical foil stars were randomly stuck to the bulkheads. In the corner farthest from the door sat a metal cone nearly two meters tall. It was studded with intermittently flashing lights and topped with a figure crafted out of spare computer parts, meant to represent an angel. A plate of flat cookies shaped like snowmen and bells had been placed on every table. (Some of these 'confections' had tooth marks on them. From year to year, people forgot that the cookies were decorations as well.) And everywhere on the ship, the comm system was sighing out songs about sleigh rides and fireplaces and elves.

All this because it was December on Earth.

Nine standard years earlier, when Ensign Gael Dedrick had been newly assigned to the *Marco Polo*, he had surveyed the crew manifest to see how many Christians were aboard ship and had found nineteen, besides himself. Twenty out of 199. Almost all the rest had designated themselves either agnostic or atheist. Only a handful had declared affiliation with one of Earth's other organized religions. Dedrick knew that other faiths observed holy days in the month of December — he had overheard crew members talking about it. These tended to be private rituals conducted in crew quarters. Christmas, however, was a different matter.

On a Fleet ship, everybody celebrated Christmas, whether they were Christian or not. Christmas was colorful and happy. It was decorations and music and special food served on special dishes. And it was gifts. Once each Earth year, Fleet Control was granted funding earmarked for the transportation of gifts and holiday messages from relatives to the personnel serving aboard Earth's spacegoing vessels. And once each Earth year, over a four week period, the credit units were disbursed. Families in modest circumstances, regardless of faith, were left with no other choice than to send their packages and good wishes in December, turning Christmas on the *Marco Polo* into a month-long shipwide event.

Involuntarily, Dedrick sighed. There hadn't been any Christmas parcels or greetings for him for several years now, not since Aunt Emma had died. Abner's mother had been the last Dedrick left on Earth, and even though she knew Gael blamed her for his own parents' death, she had summarily 'adopted' him shortly after they were gone. At that point, there had been no word from Abner for four Earth years. For the next six years, as Gael worked his way up through the ranks of Earth's spacegoing Fleet, he had received Abner's birthday presents, Abner's Christmas gifts, Abner's share of love and best wishes. Then, on the tenth anniversary of her son's disappearance, Aunt Emma had gone to bed with a mystery novel, a bottle of well-aged scotch, and enough sedative capsules to put her to sleep for good. End of story, end of Dedricks.

There probably weren't more than five crew members who knew the Christmas story well enough to tell it. Gael Dedrick was one of them, but he had long ago decided to keep the truth about Christmas to himself. There was no point in spoiling everyone else's fun by bringing a doomed savior to their party.

His wristcomm buzzed. He stepped over to a wall unit and punched in his identification code to access the comm line:

"Commander Dedrick, please report to the captain in his strategy room right away."

"Acknowledged. I'm on my way."

Three minutes later, he was there. Captain Takamura was in conference with Doctor Deneuve, the Supervisor of

Medical Services. They halted their conversation and looked up as Dedrick entered the room, but only Takamura smiled a welcome.

Hiromasu Takamura's age was indefinable, but it was common knowledge that he had been out in space for more than thirty years, twenty of them spent in the captain's chair. And, adding mystery to his powerful aura of authority, he had somehow managed while out in space to acquire the tough, weathered look of an old salt who had spent half his life on Earth's oceans.

Deneuve, on the other hand, with her short stature and fair, flawless complexion had the smooth, polished appearance of a porcelain doll. Seen side by side, they made an odd pairing.

"Commander Dedrick," said Takamura, waving him closer. "The *Marco Polo* is about to receive a singular privilege. An alien has asked to join our crew."

A guerrilla memory sent Dedrick's heart crashing down into his stomach. "Please, tell me it's not a Nandrian."

"No, it's not a Nandrian," Deneuve cut in. "It's a Dimmlesi. At least, that's what the individual claimed who replied to my posting."

"Claimed?"

Takamura nodded. "According to the Great Council's database, there is no such race in our arm of the galaxy."

"Is Fleet Control aware of this?"

"They are, and I've been informed that our orders stand. We're to add Doctor Minegar to our ship's complement." Takamura shifted his stance and folded his arms thoughtfully. "I don't believe this is a practical joke, although it may be a test. Or possibly a confidence game of some sort. Whatever it is, we have no choice but to deal with it. Doctor Deneuve and I have been attempting to formulate a plan. We decided to ask for your input as well, since you're the one who will be making first contact."

"Me? I—" For a moment, the watch commander couldn't trust himself to speak. Sending a subordinate officer to make first contact was what had triggered the incident with the Nandrians one year earlier. Four crew members had ended up in Med Services with serious injuries. Surely they didn't want to go through that again! Finally, Dedrick cleared his throat and continued in what he hoped would be a calm, professional-sounding voice, "I'm honored, Captain, but with all respect, wouldn't it be more appropriate for the highest ranking officer on the ship to deliver a formal greeting to the alien first?"

"Doctor Minegar has requested that we forgo all ceremony and let her come aboard quietly," explained Deneuve.

All the more reason to wonder about her motives, Dedrick realized.

"Your recommendations, Watch Commander?"

Dedrick sucked in a breath, feeling two pairs of eyes resting expectantly on his face. "Forgoing ceremony doesn't mean we forgo security," he said. "Where are we meeting this Doctor Minegar, exactly?"

"Zekaris Station, just outside Earth space," replied Takamura. "The High Council has forwarded me the coordinates. It's a two-interval journey from here. I've been assured that the only ships docking when we arrive will be the alien's and our own. You'll have to cross the landing deck, meet our new crew member and escort her onto the *Marco Polo* and into this room."

Dedrick nodded. It was doable. "I'll take a security detail with me. Assuming she's traveling alone, two men should be enough."

"Dress them as ordinary crewmen," Deneuve advised, explaining to Takamura, "We don't want to risk frightening her as she steps through the docking portal. They can carry her bags while Commander Dedrick accompanies her on board."

"And have a second security detail waiting just this side of the airlock, to escort us to the strategy room," Dedrick continued. "I'll tell her it's an honor guard."

"Tell her whatever is necessary to avoid the sort of debacle that occurred last year with the Nandrians," said Takamura sternly. "The High Council has indicated that it is willing to forgive that unfortunate misunderstanding, provided we are successful at integrating Doctor Minegar into our crew."

"Aye, sir."

"And, Commander? We know nothing about this alien's culture. Anything at all could be interpreted as an insult, so I want you to be extremely careful around her. Your wording, your body language — everything must be calm and neutral."

"Understood, sir."

Takamura bowed slightly to each of them in turn, murmuring, "Doctor Deneuve, Watch Commander, thank you for your time." Then he spun and headed for the strategy room door.

When it had sighed closed behind him, Deneuve sank into a chair and said wearily, "A moment, Gael, please."

Curious, Dedrick sat down beside her. Deneuve reached a hand into the pocket of her lab coat and pulled out a datawafer. "This message arrived earlier today from Leslie Eberhart's brother Sam. You were right — once the diagnosis of cancer was confirmed, they tried to rescind his Eligibility for medical reasons."

"They tried," he echoed, "but...?"

She smiled. "Whoever your contact is, he's got pull. Once the cancer is cured, Sam gets to stay Eligible for purposes of financial security, consumer options, and health care priority. That's the good news."

"And what's the bad news?"

"They're keeping him on Earth indefinitely. Leslie doesn't know yet, and I dread having to tell her that her brother will have to watch his kids grow up on a commscreen from now on. You know how strongly she feels about family."

Dedrick sighed. Yes, he knew. Eberhart's fierce protectiveness towards those she cared about was the thing that had first attracted him to her. This wasn't a perfect situation, admittedly, but it could have been a lot worse, for both Leslie and her brother. If Sam carried a genetic predisposition for cancerous growths, then Leslie might be carrying it as well. Once the Authority stripped someone of his Eligibility for medical reasons, they could use the rescission as grounds for reviewing the status of *all* his blood relatives. Entire families had been recalled from offplanet postings and restricted to Earth until either their bloodline was cleared or their Eligibility was revoked...

...which, now that he thought about it, might not be such a terrible thing. Interplanetary travel was one hell of an adventure. However, families *needed* to gather in times of stress, to support and comfort one another, and that was hard to do when the Relocation Authority seemed bent on scattering Eligible Humans all over the galaxy. Leslie's two brothers had been posted to colonies at opposite ends of Earth space, where they'd married and were raising broods of little Eberharts. As long as Watch Commander Eberhart wore a Fleet uniform, she would remain, like Dedrick, a singleton in transit. By some miracle, the Eberhart clan had come through Angel of Death almost unscathed. But once all those nieces and nephews had grown to adulthood, the Relocation Authority would separate them and start moving them around, strowing Eberharts across Earth space like seeds blown by the wind. Thanks to Abner and Aunt Emma, Dedrick would never again know the pain of that kind of separation. It was the only benefit, he reflected sadly, of not having any family at all.

"Are you sure you don't want me to tell her what you've done for Sam?" Deneuve asked, breaking into his thoughts.

"Positive."

Deneuve's expression became the portrait of incredulity. "You want her to go on thinking you're a coldhearted bastard who wouldn't lift a finger when she asked you for help?"

Dedrick blew out his breath in a sigh. What he wanted was to remain an anonymous benefactor so he wouldn't end up like Uncle Dennis, constantly pursued by 'friends' with ulterior motives. He was already regretting having confided in the ship's Supervisor of Med Services, but what was done couldn't be undone.

"Until I'm ready to tell her myself, yes, that's exactly what I want. And I don't want anyone else aboard to know about this either. I want your word, Doctor," he added, holding eye contact with her until she finally, reluctantly, nodded assent.

—— «» ——

Ixbeth paused at the top of the debarkation ramp on Zekaris Station and willed her sense hairs — and the fluttering in her midsection — to settle down. There were three Humans waiting for her below. She had sensed them even through the airlock doors, their alien emotions strong enough to pucker the back of her throat. Even when she made herself *drovanoi*, they still managed to get through. Of course, she realized, the Humans were *pritvanu* — unable to control their feelings and therefore spewing them out, like newborn kits. Ixbeth should have remembered this. The docents at the Archives had stressed it often enough. Now she was going to have to find a way to live with it, since her only other option was to return home, abandoning the Reyot Quest...

Weaponless. Powerless. Can't protect. Can't avenge.

...and that wasn't an option at all.

Bracing herself as best she could, Ixbeth studied her welcoming party. The two Humans standing straight and motionless at the bottom of the ramp wore identical brown crew uniforms and appeared to be males. The third, pacing restlessly behind them, was also a male, dressed in the dark blue of an officer.

The scalp beneath Ixbeth's sense hairs began tightening into knots. All three Humans were radiating curiosity mingled with strong apprehension. According to Docent Lankmir, fear in this species usually led to violence. Ixbeth didn't dare run toward them. She wasn't even sure whether she could safely bare her teeth in a smile. Feeling her tail stiffen and her fingerclaws try to extend, she began awkwardly walking down the ramp.

At the first sight of her, the subordinate males squared their shoulders. The officer stopped pacing and, squaring his shoulders as well, stepped forward to block the foot of the ramp.

A growl of warning bubbled up the back of her throat. Stars, what now? Would she have to fight for the privilege of boarding the ship?

"Dr. Ixbeth Minegar? I'm Gael Dedrick, watch commander on the *Marco Polo*," said the officer in Galactic Standard. His accent was clipped and hard, but each word was clearly understandable. "I've been sent by Captain Takamura to escort you aboard. The captain and Doctor Deneuve are waiting to welcome you in the strategy room."

"I requested that there be no ceremony," Ixbeth reminded him.

"And there won't be one, Doctor. This is just a necessary formality, like a thumbprint on a contract."

So, Humans confronted one another in order to exchange names. No doubt there would be numerous such confrontations once she was aboard ship. With an inward sigh of relief, Ixbeth filed the information away. She nodded stiffly to indicate assent and took a closer look at her escort.

Even allowing for the additional bulk of the uniform, Dedrick was much taller and sturdier than the textbook illustrations of Humans had seemed to indicate. This male was gazing slightly downwards at her. He had a cropped dark brown mane, shaped to leave a space around his ears, and equally dark eyes that seemed to capture the hard white light splashing off the station's walls.

Light wasn't the only thing that splashed off the walls. The two crewmen were more curious than fearful by now; however, even after exchanging names with her, the officer was still broadcasting apprehension. How much of it was the Human's and how much was a projection? A 'handy talent to have on a Quest', Krodus had called it. How fearful did a Kularian have to be for the feeling to spill over into another being?

Human emotions tasted a little strange but were nonetheless clearly identifiable. And painfully intense, she noted, suppressing the urge to shake her mane. Kularian mothers kept their litters in the woods until the kits had learned how to mute their feelings and could safely join the community. In a wishful moment, Ixbeth wondered whether that strategy might work on Humans.

The automated cargo transfer vehicle from the Mitradean ship appeared, towing her storage units. The subordinate males immediately took charge of them.

"Our crewmen will deliver your luggage to your quarters, Doctor. Come this way, please." As they walked together, Ixbeth studied Dedrick with a scholar's inquiring eye and the instinctive wariness of a defender. Surprisingly, despite the strength of his emotions, his posture and voice appeared calm. So Humans did possess a degree of control over themselves? Interesting. Even mildly reassuring. Nonetheless, Ixbeth would be the only one of her kind on a ship crewed entirely by Humans. It would take more compelling evidence than this to make her drop her guard.

Impatience. Picking his way through an obstacle course of metal supports and uninstalled conduits, Dedrick remarked tartly, "This is going to be a great hub if they ever get it finished."

Zekaris Station lay just outside Earth space. The transfer point had been designed and built by the Corvou, a hiving race. Its insect-like shape and unfinished interior were typical of their work. However, the Great Council had apparently chosen not to share this knowledge with the Humans.

It was a strange gap to leave in their education, Ixbeth mused. Even she, born and raised on tiny, out-of-the-way Dimmla, knew about the Corvou.

"Actually," she explained to Dedrick, "this is as finished as we're likely to see it. The beings who built it believe that the universe is a work in progress, and that it would be an affront to the Mother of All to complete anything before she did."

Skepticism. "And does this 'Mother of All' ever complete her work?"

"After many years, yes — and at that moment, on their home world, the Mother of All Corvou stops laying eggs. When that happens, the Corvou know they will have one more generation, approximately fifty standard years, to find and finish everything they've begun. If they're successful, then the Mother of All will be pleased and will recreate them the next time she makes the universe."

Still radiating skepticism, Dedrick pursed his lips briefly. "In other words, everyone dies off, leaving the last clutch of eggs, one of which hatches out a queen?"

"Essentially, yes. But the Corvou prefer a more spiritual interpretation of events. I thought your race had organized religions," Ixbeth added uncertainly. Stars, had *any* of the sources on the Archives database been correct about this strange and primitive species?

Bitter amusement. "We still have a few. Mainly, though, we have gods. And people who think they're gods. I'm not sure which is worse."

The silence while Ixbeth digested this observation was uneasy for the Kularian but apparently unbearable for the Human. It increased his apprehension, which in turn worsened Ixbeth's discomfort, and having to walk in order not to outpace her escort didn't help. It was an unnatural gait. Hips and heels were already beginning to complain. How far away could this Earth ship be?

"So, are there religions where you're from?"

Ixbeth debated how to reply, or even whether to reply. The question had been asked in a spasm of nervousness. Dedrick was already regretting having blurted it out. His emotion was a sourness at the back of Ixbeth's throat. Perhaps the best thing to do was preserve the officer's dignity by pretending not to have heard him.

"Excuse me, Doctor," said Dedrick, breaking into her thoughts in a voice even harder than before. "There's something I have to ask. We've been wondering — well, we've been assuming, actually — your reason for signing on — I don't mean to pry, but..."

...but they were curious. Tasting the Human's growing frustration, Ixbeth ignored her instincts and chose to keep her fingerclaws firmly retracted. Clearly, her earlier decision not to respond had been a dangerous miscalculation. Ixbeth's scalp was painfully tight. However, she was on the Quest and needed this ride, Earth ship or not, and that meant she had to defuse this situation before it erupted in violence. Ixbeth longed to shake her mane to release the tension of her sense hairs, but even that harmless movement might be misinterpreted. So she shrugged — a Human gesture she had heard described by Docent Lankmir as 'disarming' — and said, "I needed to travel but have few resources. Your ship needed a two hundredth. It was…convenient." *But it wouldn't have been my first choice*, she added silently

The Humans must have found her words reassuring, for their apprehension lessened. Relieved, Ixbeth felt her tail and sense hairs slowly relax as well. Then she heard one of the males behind her whisper something about a 'big cat' and instantly resolved to find out what that meant. Hopefully, it wouldn't turn out to be an insult.

Stars! They hadn't even boarded the ship yet.

Dedrick's behavior had now contradicted every authority Ixbeth had studied. She almost wished the officer had tried to strike her or had aimed a weapon at her. That would have been a typically Human reaction. But neither his fear nor his anger had found expression in violence.

Had these Humans been specially trained? And if that was possible, did it render invalid all the current information on the species? Ixbeth found herself hoping it did. She would have to interview many more of these aliens before conclusions could be drawn, of course. But then she would be in a peerless position to write the definitive resource text. She might even become an authority herself. This hadn't been her purpose when she signed on originally, but — stars! — what an opportunity now presented itself! To research in her field while fulfilling the Quest. It was perfect.

As the thrill of anticipation pulsed rapidly in her chest, her sense hairs shifted, detecting motion behind her. The two crewmen were closer together now. Her ears angled backward. The crewmen were filled with curiosity and excitement. "Hear it?" she heard one of them whisper.

The officer led them down a long, straight corridor and into an airlock, at last. A moment later they emerged in another hallway, brightly lit but strangely empty, which appeared only slightly more finished than the interior of the station.

Dedrick's aura softened. Ixbeth guessed that they must now be aboard the *Marco Polo*. As the crewmen transporting her belongings moved away down a cross-corridor, two other males stepped out of the shadows and took their place.

Defenders. Instinctively, her fingerclaws tried to extend. These Humans were dressed in gray and wore shoulder patches with the word 'security' on them. There were devices attached to their belts, probably weapons.

"Don't be alarmed, Doctor," Dedrick told her. "It is Fleet protocol, the first time a member of an alien race boards an Earth ship, that an honor guard accompany the visitor to the captain's strategy room."

An armed escort into the presence of the ship's commanding officer. Ixbeth knew better than to imagine that it was *her* safety these males were protecting. Their apprehension joined to what remained of Dedrick's was enough to keep the Kularian's sense hairs rigidly on end, making her scalp unbearably tight and forcing her at last to shake her mane, in pain and in wonderment. Was this how Humans tried to make a good first impression?

"This way," said Dedrick, pointing toward the nearest transport tube door, and Ixbeth nearly sighed with relief. She knew from the deck plans in the information package that the ship was easily two kilopaces long, and that the strategy room was in the command sector, right at the front. She'd been wondering how she would manage to walk there should her 'honor guard' decide it was safer to travel on foot.

As the tube car lurched into motion, Dedrick seemed to reach a decision. "Doctor Minegar, once you've been welcomed aboard by the captain, you may want one of us to give you a tour of the ship," he said. "I'm free after my duty shift, at about twenty hundred hours."

The Human was still uncomfortable in her presence, but becoming more curious than apprehensive now that he was on familiar ground. "I'll remember that," Ixbeth promised.

The tube car let them out almost directly across the hall from the strategy room door. Resuming his official demeanor, Dedrick pressed the enter button and stood aside to let Ixbeth step into the room. There were two beings on the other side of a long table in front of her. As they got to their feet, the guards who had followed her in took up positions on either side of the doorway.

All right, thought Ixbeth, her fingerclaws aching along with her hips, heels, and scalp, she'd been safely delivered to the captain. Now what?

Facing her across the table were a male and a female. The male was only medium height for a Human. He was dark and wiry, with almost no mane, and he wore authority as though it were a cape. Her father would have called him 'rope wrapped in leather'. The female was no stranger to power either. Short, even for a Human, she had deep-set green eyes and a thick yellow mane that was pulled back from her face and twisted into a knot at the crown of her head. She emanated a presence that seemed to energize the room.

Either one could be the captain. Was this a test?

As though overhearing her thoughts, the male rounded the end of the table and briefly dipped his head toward her. "Greetings, Doctor Minegar," he announced. "I am Captain Hiromasu Takamura, and this is Doctor Sylvie Deneuve, our Supervisor of Medical Services. We wanted to introduce ourselves and ask you a couple of questions before you settled in."

Physically, Ixbeth towered over this Human; and yet, she detected no fear in his aura, just immense curiosity and fierce determination. His voice was firm, his brown eyes clear. He was a natural leader of defenders. It was both a surprise and a relief to find one here, among the Humans. "Ask your questions, Captain," she said.

He bowed again and began: "As soon as Fleet Control received your request to join my crew, a copy of your application was forwarded to the Earth High Council, which subsequently requested information about your culture from the Great Council's database. According to the Central Archives, there is no record anywhere of a planet called Dimmla or a race called the Dimmlesi. Can you explain this, Doctor Minegar?"

Ixbeth was stunned. No record anywhere? That couldn't be. The Dimmlesi had been living on their world for thousands of years before the Kularians came across it. Surely other space travelers had discovered it as well. A lush garden planet peopled by a gentle, hospitable race would definitely have been added to the navcharts. And then there was the piloting contract between the Dimmlesi and the Mitrades; it was common knowledge that all such contracts had to be filed with Central Archives. How could there be no mention of the Dimmlesi? It had to be—

"—some kind of error, Captain," Ixbeth replied. "Perhaps a clerical oversight, perhaps a transmission crossover. Dimmla definitely exists, as do the many thousands of beings currently living on it. And they are Dimmlesi, as am I."

"Of course. Forgive me, Doctor," he said, bowing once more. Ixbeth marveled at the consistency of his emotional aura. "It is an irregularity, and protocol requires that we clear it up. Therefore, as a formality, I have Gate-transmitted your image to the Central Archives for verification. Confirmation should be arriving within two standard hours."

Ixbeth's sense hairs stirred, beginning to rise. So much for the cycle of concealment, she thought. The Central Archives was located on Reyi'it, and the Reyota were physically almost identical to Kularians. Well, the Great Presence had smiled on her so far. Perhaps her luck would hold a little longer. Perhaps the under-docent asked to make the identification would be too rushed for time to check the population database and would assume that she must be Reyot, and that the Humans, being a primitive and inferior species, had simply misread her application. But then the question would become, what could possibly make a Reyot want to join the crew of a Human ship? Ixbeth let her breath out in a sigh. The next two hours were going to feel very long.

Meanwhile, her own curiosity had been aroused. "If you were suspicious of my identity, Captain, then why did you permit me to board your ship?"

A sudden medley of tastes splashed the back of her throat: guilt, dread, undirected resentment, and, permeating everything else, an overpowering desire to *know*. Exactly what Ixbeth herself had been feeling for the past three intervals as she prepared for this quest. It appeared they had a lot in common, she and this Human.

"I was certain there must be a simple and logical explanation," he replied.

He was lying. Did she care? She decided she didn't.

"Besides," he added, with a brief smile that revealed perfectly even white teeth, "I'm an explorer. The unknown holds a great attraction for me."

This was the truth. A being like Takamura would happily spend his whole life on a quest. Hopefully, hers would not take that long.

"Doctor Deneuve would like a turn with you now, since she will be your superior in Medical Services. I must return to the bridge. However, if you don't mind, the guards will remain here. I'll notify you as soon as I receive the response from Central Archives." Takamura bowed again, holding the position a few seconds longer this time so that Ixbeth felt compelled to bow back. Then he left the room.

Takamura's aura had apparently overlain Deneuve's. Ixbeth tasted its metallic tang the moment the strategy room door slid closed behind him. The female was anything but serene.

"Doctor Minegar," said Deneuve, gesturing toward the chairs on Ixbeth's side of the table, "please sit."

Ixbeth took a close look at the way the seats were constructed and realized that they hadn't been designed to accommodate a tail, not even a short, stubby one like hers. Deneuve had reached the same conclusion. "I'll have to get the quartermaster to make some modifications for you," she said, deliberately pulling out a chair and lowering herself onto it. Testing her, no doubt. Ixbeth selected the chair facing Deneuve's and turned it sideways before sitting down.

Mild satisfaction, but also resentment, which Ixbeth found unsettling. This was the first actual hostility she had encountered aboard the Earth ship, and it was emanating from a female Takamura had identified as her superior. According to Docent Lankmir, female Humans were much more volatile than the males, much quicker to anger, and they tended to inflict much crueler punishment. This was not, she reflected with some trepidation, the most auspicious way to begin a working relationship.

A beat, then, "I'm going to be perfectly honest with you, Doctor Minegar," said Deneuve. "You were not my first choice to fill this post. Fleet Control snapped you up because you were the first non-Human ever to express an interest in serving on an Earth ship. They call it a diplomatic breakthrough. Now they're pressuring my captain to pressure me to add you to my staff, just because you're an alien, and that doesn't sit well with me. Not because you're an alien. I've worked with aliens before and look forward to doing so again. But I happen to be responsible for the quality of health care aboard this ship, and I need to know that everyone I am depending on to maintain that quality is both competent and fully qualified. Any failure by any member of my department ultimately rests on my shoulders. So, you see, my concerns in this matter are not personal, but professional.

"To be blunt, I have reason to question your qualifications. You say you have completed five years of study at an alien institution, but you have not received any sort of degree?"

"The Archives on Altera does not award special titles, except to docents," Ixbeth explained. "I have, however, been evaluated repeatedly over the course of my studies and have scored excellent levels in all disciplines."

...five years wasted, training to do nothing....

Everything about Deneuve stiffened, including her voice. "I see. And I suppose there's no way to obtain a transcript of these scores to attach to your application? As a necessary formality."

Ixbeth tasted the Human's doubt and apprehension and chose to remain silent. Despite her protestations, there was a personal dimension to this fear, meaning that Deneuve would probably not be satisfied with a printed record, even if it were possible to obtain one.

"I didn't think so. All right, then. As a courtesy, we shall continue to call you Doctor Minegar. However, before I give you any responsibility to go with that title, I need to be certain that you can handle the job. Here's my problem: I have to assume that you've obtained all your information about Humans from non-Human sources. At best, it's out of date. At worst, it's totally incorrect.

"I need someone with current knowledge who is familiar with Human psychology to administer and interpret a battery of tests. Clearly, you don't fit that description. That means I'm going to have to educate you as well as train you; and because there are many demands on my time and energy right now, I need to be selective about where I invest them. You've arrived without credentials, without references, without a publishing history in your field. So tell me, Doctor: what special talents or qualities do you possess that would make you an asset to my department?"

Ixbeth took her first full breath in what seemed an age, letting it out slowly as she considered her options.

The Human had held nothing back. In responding to her question, Ixbeth knew she ought to be equally honest. And yet....

Common wisdom held that Humans were happiest when sharing physical closeness without an emotional connection. As Ixbeth now knew, Humans were incapable of making themselves *vanoi* — they could only choose not to vocalize or demonstrate their emotions. And since Humans had no way of perceiving unexpressed emotions, they truly believed that such feelings were safely concealed from others. Alone with a shipful of *pritvanu* Humans, Ixbeth was already in significant physical discomfort. Did she really want to stir them to rage or terror by letting them know how emotionally transparent they were to her? Just thinking about the torment that would result was enough to stiffen her tail and make her heart pound in her ears.

In that moment, she heard Tal's voice at the back of her mind.

You need the mental discipline, it whispered urgently.

Stars, no! This was impossible. She had rejected his offer of bonding, and yet he was here!

"Well, Doctor?" Deneuve prodded.

Shaking out her mane and deliberately relaxing her tail, Ixbeth replied, "I can't tell you. I mean, I don't know enough yet about Humans even to surmise what qualities you might consider valuable or desirable. But I was hoping to learn."

Satisfaction. Surprise. Deneuve leaned back in her chair. "Well, well, well," she said softly. "All right, Doctor, assuming we get the right answer from the Central Archives, welcome to Med Services."

The Human's aura had calmed considerably. Evidently, Ixbeth had passed the test. But how? Had Tal reached through her mind and done something to influence Deneuve's feelings?

"I don't want to sound ungrateful, Doctor, but— Why?"

Grim amusement. And something else. Determination? "Let's just say I like your attitude. A former teacher of mine, Nayo Naguchi, once stated that it's possible to learn something from every being and every experience one encounters in life. Humanity may have more to learn than many of the other races in this arm of the galaxy, but I refuse to believe that we have nothing to teach others. You obviously share that philosophy. I think you'll fit in quite well. Let's begin the preliminary briefing."

Ixbeth was confused. "Don't you want to wait until my identity is confirmed?"

"Not necessary. I'm a very intuitive person, Doctor Minegar, and I trust my instincts." Deneuve leaned forward, bracing her arms on the tabletop. She was all business now — Ixbeth tasted the change in her aura. "You've received the data package, I trust? Well, the individual who prepared it left out a few items. On this ship, Medical Services comprises four sections, not three: Trauma, Surgery, P and R — that's Prevention and Rehab — and Counseling, each with its own section head. I'm the Trauma head, as well as the Supervisor to whom the others all report. While I'm training you, and as long as you're working on the psych testing assignment, you'll be reporting directly to me as well. When that project is completed, you'll join the Counseling staff as an intern psychologist and receive further training from the Counseling head, Doctor Marchenko. Clear?"

Swept along in the Human's energy wake, Ixbeth could only repeat, "Clear."

"I'll have the quartermaster hunt up a couple of men's size tall uniforms. They'll be altered, of course, to accommodate your tail. And I'll find you a lab coat with an extra long vent in back," Deneuve went on briskly, counting off items on her fingers. "Doctor Marchenko will have to work up some sort of neuro-psych profile on you for the medical database. The ship's cook has cleared a storage locker in the galley for any Dimmlesi foodstuffs you may have brought with you. As for the crew: we've had very little contact with alien races and none at all with members of your species, so curiosity is running high. For the first interval or so, you may have to field some very personal questions."

Regret. Ixbeth frowned. "Personal?"

"Regarding mating practices, hygiene, and various other things that in Human society would normally be considered private. If the Dimmlesi have no taboos about discussing such matters with strangers, then fine. Otherwise, feel free to report anyone who oversteps the bounds to one of the watch commanders. Predictably, the rumor mill went into overdrive when we first got word an alien would be joining the crew, so there are some half-baked ideas floating around that you may wish to dispel — or may not," Deneuve added with a sudden grin. "Sometimes, remaining a bit of a mystery can work to your advantage. You should be warned, however, that Humans love a mystery and won't leave it alone until they've solved it — or think they have."

"Thank you," said Ixbeth. "I'll consider that my first lesson in Human psychology."

"You'll need quite a few more before you're ready to tackle this assignment. Do you have any questions while we're waiting for your clearance?"

Ixbeth had one. And she was certain that Deneuve would be completely honest with her. "I overheard one of the crewmembers call me a 'big cat'. What does that mean?"

"It means you bear a physical resemblance to an animal native to Earth." Ixbeth's silence in response to this made Deneuve just as uncomfortable as Dedrick had been earlier. Unlike the watch commander, however, the Human healer was not moved to frustration. She simply felt compelled to continue talking. "Depending on the location of its natural habitat, a cat might be a small domesticated creature kept as a companion, or a large, very effective predator. We have extensive data on both varieties in the ship's InfoComm system. Once you're cleared for access, you might want to look them up."

Now Ixbeth's curiosity truly was piqued. And her apprehension. Companion or predator — which of those two impressions had she made on the crewmen sent to meet her? More to the point, which one would keep her safe in this alien place?

8

Beneath Lania's *frantic fingers, the grass tore easily, parting like a curtain. Leaves rustled urgent warnings in the forest behind her. Abner was getting closer. She should have known — should have known! — someone that angry wouldn't stay in the ground. In seconds she had a hole large enough to step through — but there was a barrier!*

Forcing down her panic, she remembered the button.

He was wheezing air in and out of his lungs now, filling the clearing with the smell of decay. Tears blurred Lania's vision as she groped in the hillside next to the door.

Found it! She slammed her palm against the hard little knob, nearly fainting with relief when she heard the click and low rumble of the metal slab moving aside. Just as Abner emerged from the trees, she hurled herself through the grass curtain, found the second button on the other side, and closed the entranceway again, hearing her father's howl of frustration as the door sealed shut between them.

Her hand felt wet. She looked down and saw that it was covered with blood. Blood was suddenly everywhere. It dripped from her fingers and splashed on the floor. It painted her clothing, turning it stiff and black. It raced down the walls to join the dark puddles already forming around her feet. And from it rose the smell of death, a suffocating perfume that hung in the air for a moment and then settled gently over her like a shroud.

She couldn't move her arms or legs. She opened her mouth to scream, but it filled with blood—!

Lania sat up in bed with a gasp, clutching her perspiration-soaked blanket to her chest. Daylight poured into the cave, showing her the smooth grayness of its curving walls and floor. There was no blood. She had been dreaming. And yet, the faintly sweet smell still lingered in her nostrils.

Then she remembered. With a feeling of dread, Lania put two fingers to the place between her legs. The fingers came away sticky and red.

Not again!

She flung the blanket aside and scrambled out of bed, but it was too late to save her improvised mattress. Disgusted, she rolled up the grass-filled sheet, took it outside, and shook it out. Then she carried it down the hill to the stream.

Lania knelt beside the cool rush of water. She had no soap, but it didn't matter. The stain was fresh and the sheet was eager to be rid of it. In a matter of seconds, the soft fabric was clean again.

After spreading the sheet on the taller grass to dry, Lania could tend to herself, as Rose had taught her to do. She stepped off the bank where the water was knee-deep and sat down carefully in the stream, legs apart, letting the current soothe her body while the warmth of the sun caressed her shoulders.

In a few minutes she would return to the cave. That wasn't what it was, of course, but once she'd parted the concealing grass curtain and located the door-opening mechanism, the empty gray room inside the hillock had certainly *looked* like a cave.

There were other spaces as well in Abner's ship. An inner door led to a short hallway. Here Lania had found a bedroom, a storage room stocked with supplies, a small, strangely-equipped area that she guessed had something to do with food, and a place labeled 'head', whose function she didn't entirely comprehend either.

Across the passageway from the head, however, was the place that called out to her. It contained lustrous brown panels set into the walls, and a swiveling chair tucked into the crook of a matching brown counter. Everywhere she looked in this room, Lania saw buttons, dials, gauges, and small flashing lights. They were pretty, but they weren't what had first pulled her through the door, and they weren't what kept her coming back.

Each time she entered, Lania caught her breath, feeling her entire being resonate with the power that lay sleeping just beneath that countertop.

She had sensed the same quiet pulsing in some of the items Abner had brought back from the colony's supply dome. She hadn't understood it then, but now she knew why she'd been so irresistibly drawn to touch them: the power inside them was alive. Power lived in the objects that Abner had locked up in the tool shed, and a lot more of it lived in the ship. That power could protect her. All she had to do was wake it up.

She could do this. Lania had found enough food packets in the supply dome to feed her for years. She'd also found a small talking device named Tooter that promised to teach her to read, among other things.

There was a safe way for her to leave Dedrick's Planet. She would just have to be patient and take things one step at a time.

9

Dedrick reported to the strategy room as ordered and found Takamura once again deep in conversation with Doctor Deneuve. This time, the doctor was the one who glanced up and smiled as the watch commander walked through the door. Takamura looked as though he had just found vinegar in his pudding.

"Captain?"

"We've received confirmation from the Central Archives. According to the Prime Docent herself, Doctor Minegar's ancestors most likely belonged to a faction of the Reyota that left Reyi'it centuries ago to found a colony and were never heard from again. If she's right, then they evidently did reach a suitable planet but for some reason were unable to contact their home world. She figures that they must have named their colony Dimmla and themselves the Dimmlesi, and the reason no one has ever heard of them is that none of them went back into space. Until now."

"But you're not satisfied with that explanation?"

Takamura leaned back in his chair, frowning. "It's a logical enough theory, I suppose. It may even be true. However, when a Human submits a routine request for information, the Prime Docent is the last person one expects to hear from. The fact that someone that important is involved tells me there has to be more to this situation than meets the eye. I don't know who Doctor Minegar is, but she's clearly someone who matters, at the highest levels. And that naturally raises the question: Why choose an Earth ship?"

Dedrick and Deneuve exchanged sober looks. "To hide?" they said, almost in unison.

"It makes sense, Captain," Dedrick pointed out. "All of it. She told me she *needed* to travel. That was the word she used.

And we were *convenient*. And—" He paused uncomfortably. "Let's face it, an Earth ship is the last place anyone would think to look for an alien."

"I hope you're wrong about her," said Takamura. "Otherwise, we could be headed for something quite unpleasant and potentially embarrassing — again! Believe me, I would much rather leave Doctor Minegar on Zekaris Station and let the politicians deal with her. However, Earth High Council has specifically ordered us to welcome her into the crew, regardless of her intentions. And that is what I want you both to find out, as soon as possible.

"I need to know what Doctor Minegar is doing on my ship, preferably *before* her presence puts us all in harm's way."

———— «» ————

Waiting in her cabin, Ixbeth stared around her in dismay. According to the two security guards who had brought her here, she had been assigned standard crew quarters. A pallet, a chair, a work table, a light screen. Whatever else there might be was hidden away behind sliding wall-panels. Every surface was smooth and straight and synthetic — and lifeless. There wasn't a leaf or a stone or a splinter of wood to be seen.

Ixbeth could understand an absence of natural materials in the working parts of the ship. But surely beings far away from home would wish to surround themselves with as much 'home' as possible, especially in a sector designated 'community' and set aside for relaxation activities!

Ixbeth glanced at her two storage units, stacked in a corner of the tiny room, and sighed. Even on the Quest, looking ahead rather than over her shoulder, she had brought with her as much of Dimmla and Altera as her mass-allotment would permit. Unfortunately, there was little point in unpacking. If the Central Archives could not validate her identity, the captain would undoubtedly order her put off his ship immediately.

And what would she do then? Alone, without transportation, with only her most precious belongings to barter for passage, what *could* she do?

Impulsively, she opened the larger unit and pulled out the meditation blanket Tal had made for her. He'd given it to her the first time she'd left home for Altera. It was woven to show a portrait of Tal on one side and an image of Ixbeth on the other, joined back-to-back on the blanket the way they'd been in the womb. Protecting and completing each other. Ixbeth wrapped herself tightly in Tal's gift with his image facing outwards. If ever she needed her litter-twin watching her back, it was now.

Tal always said that the Great Presence allowed nothing to happen without a purpose. If that was so, then why conceal the existence of Dimmla? Was there an oracle on some other world speaking to the Dimmlesi? Had it ordered them into hiding, perhaps? Would it someday send an army of Dimmlesi on a quest like hers?

Somehow she doubted it.

A gnawing sensation in her belly reminded her how long it had been since her last meal. Ixbeth opened the other unit, the one Dallia had packed for her, and found a feast: slices of dried *eliban* with the tough red rind left on, fresh *porrets*, plenty of *drithra*, an airtight container of *bokhara* leaves — enough to brew at least a year's worth of hot *caranth* — and, of course, a supply of her mother's famous bread, seasoned with herbs and crunchy with whole grains.

Ixbeth plucked a *porret* out of the storage unit and took a bite, savoring the sweetness of its flesh as she settled pensively onto the narrow Human pallet. She had always been a non-Believer. And yet...

What if Tal was right and the Great Presence really was guiding her progress toward truth? And what if it was Avo'or's will that the Humans assist her on that journey? *There* was a thought. Popping the rest of the fruit into her mouth, Ixbeth arched her spine and snugged the blanket around her shoulders. What if it *were* Avo'or's will?

What if every being in the galaxy was ultimately doing what Avo'or wished, and the only difference between a Believer and a non-Believer was the amount of coercion required to influence that person's choices?

A loud buzzing noise startled her to her feet, fingerclaws extending as the meditation blanket crumpled to the floor behind her. There was someone outside her cabin, broadcasting a strange mixture of emotions. Ixbeth could taste them right through the bulkhead.

"Doctor Minegar?" called an uncertain voice through the small round speaker on the wall beside the door. "I have a message from the captain, and one from Commander Dedrick. May I come in?"

——— «» ———

He'd promised her a tour of the ship, and that was what she would get. As Dedrick waited for Doctor Minegar to join him in the corridor outside her quarters, he mentally mapped out their itinerary, beginning with the science sector, then moving forward toward the bridge.

Commander Dedrick was by now a practiced tour guide, having regularly been assigned by Captain Takamura to show off the *Marco Polo* whenever civilian passengers were aboard. He enjoyed talking with visitors about the workings of the ship. It was a genetic trait, he suspected — his father had had a gift for conversation too, especially when the discussion turned to something he loved.

As if summoned by the thought, Leslie's face appeared in Dedrick's mind's eye. He felt his stomach tighten and tried to banish the image with a violent shake of his head. The last thing he needed right now was this kind of distraction.

Eberhart was mad as hell at him and making sure he knew it. She hadn't spoken more than a dozen off-duty words to him since he'd turned down her request to help her brother. She was civil towards him on the bridge and pointedly professional whenever they teamed for assignments, but that was all. It was as though she had pressed a reset button, taking them back to a time before they'd gotten to know each other, when neither one of them believed they could even be friends, let alone lovers.

And now her emotions were sinking hooks into his mind at the worst possible time, and his inability to shut them out was making him mad as well. He needed to get himself under control, he reminded himself sternly. Takamura wanted to know what Dr. Minegar was doing aboard the *Marco Polo*. That was Dedrick's mission right now. That was what he needed to focus on.

There would be more than two angry people aboard ship if he didn't.

—— «» ——

The Earth vessel *Marco Polo* carried a crew of 200, including Ixbeth now that her identity had been confirmed by the Prime Docent at the Central Archives. Whoever this Yorell Enne was, her word was apparently sufficient to open doors and shut down objections half a galaxy away. Perhaps Avo'or was on Ixbeth's side after all. Perhaps the Earth ship would even turn out to be the 'world wandering' of the prophecy…?

No, she decided. Quests weren't supposed to be that easy.

Ixbeth had had ample time to study the deck plans provided in the data package. Even before her tour with Commander Dedrick, she had known that the ship consisted of three distinct sectors. The science sector was by far the largest, a dome-studded cylinder twelve decks high, framed at its bottom by a circle of thrusters. Projecting from the top of the cylinder was the long hexagonal community sector. And attached to the front end of the community sector, looking like the thick stub of a kit's stylus, was the command sector, with the bridge located on its upper curve. All the parts of the ship were tightly linked together by a Personnel Transport System of interconnecting tunnels with passenger cars running through them.

What the data package hadn't prepared her to see — and what Commander Dedrick had fairly waxed poetical over during the tour — was the warren of passageways that ran vertically as well as horizontally between the innermost and secondary bulkheads. Besides providing rapid access to a multitude of boards, grids, and exposed tubes and pipes, this multi-hulled design made the *Marco Polo* significantly smaller on the inside than it was on the outside.

Aesthetically as well, the ship's interior came up short, Ixbeth thought. The color scheme — if it could be called that — was shades of gray, brown, and a muddy green Dedrick called 'olive drab'. Drab was the right word for it. There were red, white, and silver decorations in the 'mess hall', but they apparently signified a religious celebration and would soon be gone. That was a shame. No intelligent being ought to be expected to live and work in such depressing surroundings.

Including herself. Immediately after receiving the captain's welcoming message, Ixbeth had unpacked the larger of her storage units. Putting up the wall-cloths and grooming glass she'd brought from home hadn't exactly transformed her quarters, but it was a beginning. She would find other things that pleased her and add them to the décor. And when she was done, she'd promised herself, the barren little cell would be a memory.

Ixbeth wrapped herself in her meditation blanket and sat down on her pallet to mull over the problem of Watch Commander Dedrick. Doctor Deneuve had instructed her to report any crewmember 'overstepping the bounds' to a watch commander. But what if the individual being intrusively personal *was* a watch commander?

To be fair, Commander Dedrick had been an excellent tour guide. For the entire two hours, he had been outwardly pleasant and polite, despite the frustration that progressively darkened his aura as she deflected question after question about her actual reason for being aboard his ship. Clearly, her earlier response had not satisfied him, and he was determined to solve what he perceived as a mystery. If he believed she was lying, that could explain the ongoing resentment she had been sensing from him; or there could be another reason for him to dislike her. Asking him directly might reveal what that was, but it would also let him know that Ixbeth was able to sense a concealed emotion. Not a wise thing to do at this point, she decided.

Meanwhile, some of the things Dedrick had said that day stuck in Ixbeth's mind. A star ship was like a living creature. The command staff was its brain. The crew was its blood. The medical team headed by Doctor Deneuve kept the crew healthy and enabled them to maintain the ship. And Ixbeth was now part of that team, working to keep the heart of the *Marco Polo* beating steadily so that two hundred people could continue to live in the vacuum of space.

Unbidden, the words of the prophecy came to her:
...and a machine with the heart of a child.

The Humans had been the last of the known races to venture into space. Figuratively speaking, that made them the children of the galactic community. And by that definition, couldn't any Earth ship be considered a machine with the heart of a child?

No. She was reaching. The prophecy was abstruse, but not that abstruse.

Ixbeth sighed and glanced longingly at her work table, still the only other furniture in the room besides her 'bed' — the Human word for a pallet — and a single chair, which had been crudely modified to make room for her tail. The table's left pedestal held an InfoComm unit. The computer's ports were a row of narrow slots in the shiny brown tabletop. And beside them, looking lost and alone and obviously incompatible, sat her datacube. Ixbeth had downloaded the history of the Children of Kula'as onto it before boarding the ship to Zekaris Station.

She was certain she needed to know more about her people's past before she attempted to interpret the prophecy. She'd brought the datacube with her so that she could study what was on it. But first, she would have to find a way to link the cube to the InfoComm unit in her quarters. She knew she could do this — Evin Lurrlo had been a better docent in many ways than the three who had been assigned to her at the Archives. Still, it wasn't a task she relished. The ship's computer system had been designed by Humans. Like its creators, it would probably turn out to be far more complicated than it appeared.

She paused, waiting for a caustic remark from Tal's voice in her mind, but it was silent. Perhaps she'd only imagined his comment in the captain's strategy room. Part of her devoutly hoped so, because that would mean Tal had kept his word and not bonded with her against her will.

The rest of her huddled briefly into the blanket he had made her, saddened by the thought of having left him so far behind.

—— «» ——

"All things in the universe resonate," Evin Lurrlo had once told her. "And our Kularian senses are attuned to those resonances. That is how we can detect motion around us, and how a trained technician can determine when and which part of a computer is not functioning properly. Technology is all about harmony. When all the parts of a machine are resonating in harmony, the machine will operate efficiently. If even one part creates disharmony, the machine will break down. Perhaps quickly, perhaps slowly, but inevitably, it will stop working. With practice, you should be able to identify a source of disharmony, even when something appears to be functioning perfectly."

In the five years that Ixbeth had spent on Altera, Lurrlo had seen to it that she got plenty of practice. (His feelings for her had been sadly transparent.) But they'd been working with Kularian technology, and this InfoComm unit was a Human device. Would anything that he'd taught her work here?

The light screen was dark. The computer inside the work table was drawing minimal power. Ixbeth ran her fingers lightly over the port slots, maximizing her senses as Lurrlo had trained her to do, and detected something faint but familiar. Of course. This device would be in harmony with the ship, since they shared a primary power source, and Ixbeth had been sensing its ambient resonance for several days now. Keeping one hand on the computer, she carefully reached out the other toward the datacube. There was bound to be some disharmony, which her heightened nervous system should feel as a very mild — *shock!* Ixbeth's hands leaped away from both devices. For several long, painful seconds, she could feel every nerve in her body tingling.

This wasn't going to work. The two technologies were much too alien to each other. No amount of fine-tuning would create harmony between them if they were joined. But — stars! — she needed to know what was on that cube! It wouldn't take her long to read the information. Perhaps a series of adjustments could delay the inevitable breakdown, just long enough for a single rapid scan?

There was only one way to find out.

10

"Are you fond of games, Doctor?"

Startled by the abruptness of the question, Ixbeth stared into Deneuve's eyes. Her fingerclaws had automatically extended. Quietly, she retracted them again. On the other side of the gray metal desk, the Human healer gave no sign of having noticed the defensive reflex.

Medical Services was a maze, and Doctor Sylvie Deneuve had her office in one of its remotest corners. The first time Ixbeth had stepped into the tiny, pale green room, she had been certain she'd misread the deck plan. It was hard to believe that this was the work space of someone as important as the ship's Supervisor of Medical Services. Stars! It wasn't even as large as her 'standard crew quarters' aboard ship.

"Humans have various ways to exercise," Deneuve was explaining. "Many of them involve games. I was wondering: do the Dimmlesi play any games for amusement or relaxation?"

"Dimmlesi don't relax by competing with one another. They prefer to create beauty and meaning with their hands."

Eventually, the Human would drop her chatty façade and reveal what was really on her mind. Deneuve's emotional aura was tough and turbulent today. Ixbeth quickly reviewed her activities of the past eighteen days aboard ship — the research, the interviews, the staff meetings, the guided and self-guided tours, and the several times when walking had become too painful and she just *had* to break into a run, scattering Humans in her path. Most recently, there had been the unfortunate experiment in the virtual reality room. Could that be what this was about? Finding something harmless for her to do in her off-duty hours?

"So they're artists? Do they paint? Sculpt?" Deneuve persisted.

Ixbeth smiled faintly. By purposefully arranging the elements of nature, rotating crops to create both sensory and nutritional harmony, even teaching living trees to speak with the shapes of their branches, the Dimmlesi had turned their entire world into a work of art. The Human word was pale and inadequate, like Human understanding, but it would have to suffice. "They sculpt," she replied, her thoughts turning involuntarily to the spirit tree on the road to Turvanen.

Destiny. *Rachjab* trees lived virtually forever. Overnight, that one had died. Had the Oracle's prophecy been the lightning that killed it, forcing it to reveal its message of hope at the start of the Quest? Tal would say it was; he didn't believe in coincidences. If he was right and there was a powerful intelligence arranging every detail of the universe—

—blackened branches stretching toward the stars. Helplessness. Rage!

Deneuve cleared her throat, dragging Ixbeth back into the moment. "I had several reasons for asking you to come here today, Doctor," she began.

Discomfort. Ixbeth shook her mane and waited 'for the shovel to kiss the ground', as her father would say of a situation like this.

"There's a rumor going around," Deneuve continued. "No, not a rumor — sorry, bad choice of words — an opinion. It was expressed by a senior officer in the hearing of several crewmembers, who immediately began passing it along to other officers and crew. This morning it reached me. I would like to head it off before the captain hears about it, and to do that I need the truth from you." Deneuve took a long, steadying breath before continuing, "Apologies, but I must be blunt. Doctor Minegar, what are you doing to the ship's InfoComm network?"

For a moment Ixbeth was speechless. Then something clicked into place in her mind.

"Could this have to do with the computer in my quarters? It wouldn't read my storage medium. I attempted some modifications. Did I breach a protocol? There was nothing in the data package prohibiting—"

Intense relief. "Of course there wasn't," said Deneuve. "That's because the bright light who assembled the package forgot that it wasn't going to a Human. This was our mistake, Doctor Minegar, not yours. Every Human child grows up knowing how to use the InfoCommNet. As a result, many basic instructions and warnings are routinely omitted in order to conserve transmission energy.

"The first rule of the Net is that the InfoComm unit must be left online. Taking it offline triggers an alarm on somebody's status board, requiring that a technician be sent immediately to make repairs. Lieutenant Mbuku is the best Engineering Specialist in the Fleet. He's very proud of having kept this ship running smoothly for the past four standard years. And when you lit up his board three times in one six-day period and each time refused entry to your quarters to the technician sent to fix the problem..."

Large swallows small, small corrupts large, Lurrlo had taught her. Ixbeth had gutted the computer's ports, spreading components all over the tabletop. The InfoComm unit used polarized light, precisely directed, to create data streams. Nothing else about this machine was even remotely similar to the devices on Altera. Ixbeth had improvised like mad, adjusting polarities, buffering connectors, retraining microlenses, in a fruitless search for a resonance pattern both technologies could accept, even if only marginally, for a brief time. *Small corrupts large*. She had taken the unit offline while she worked, to protect the ship's internal communications network from the resulting disharmony, and had carefully put things back the way she'd found them when she was done. And this was her thanks.

"...he naturally assumed that I was attempting sabotage."

"No, I don't think he really suspected you of sabotage, or he would have gone directly to Captain Takamura. I think he was just very frustrated and blowing off steam, and unfortunately, he happened to be overheard. I'll drop correcting statements in a few senior officers' ears and squelch this thing before it goes any further. So, what is the data storage medium that your unit can't read?"

Powerful curiosity. Ixbeth felt her scalp contract and chose her next words carefully.

"It's a datacube containing some personal research, and despite my best efforts, it appears to be completely incompatible with the ship's systems."

"Mbuku would love a challenge like this. To solve your decoding problem while learning something about an alien technology...!"

Ixbeth opened her mouth to protest, then shut it again. She, with her understanding of Kularian devices, had tried and failed three times to access the information on the cube. Mbuku was trained in Human technology. What if his understanding provided the missing key?

Together, victory.

"Would there be any harm in letting him try?" Deneuve persisted.

Good question. At worst, he might corrupt the cube, making it unreadable. But — stars! Without a decoding device it was unreadable anyway.

At best, however, he might actually succeed in unlocking the data, giving her a greater understanding of the history of her people and possibly ensuring her completion of the Reyot Quest. If there was even the smallest chance, she knew she had to take it.

"No harm," she agreed. "But it must not go online, and I have to monitor—"

Concern. "It won't explode, will it? It's just a simple storage device?"

Small corrupts large. These Humans had such limited sensory abilities. Was there any point in making them aware of the danger that disharmony posed to every system on the ship? Yes, she decided. They needed to approach the cube's otherness with respect.

"Not that simple. It is capable of drawing power," Ixbeth finally pointed out. "If it is incorrectly attached—"

Mild impatience. "All right. He won't be happy, but I'll explain that the two of you have to work on this together. And the next time Mbuku sends you a tech...?"

Ixbeth sighed inwardly. She'd forgotten about that. "I'll open the door and let him in."

Deneuve couldn't imagine what a concession that was. For a Kularian surrounded by *pritvanu*, privacy was not a negotiable luxury — it was a necessity.

Several times each day, tail rigid and scalp in knots from the ceaseless clamor of uncontrolled Human emotions that filled the rest of the ship, Ixbeth retired to her quarters for a standard hour of relative relaxation. Some of those feelings still bled through, of course. Not even metal doors and double bulkheads could block them entirely. But there was an enormous and painful difference between tasting them at the back of her throat and feeling them tighten the muscles beneath her sense hairs. In her quarters, Ixbeth often watched a Gate transmission from Earth or delved into the ship's databases, blessing whatever Human custom it was that prevented anyone from disturbing her solitude.

Meanwhile, there hadn't been a sound out of Tal the whole time. He had evidently respected her wish to embark on the Quest alone. Ixbeth hoped that he was missing her as much as she missed him.

"I know you've been exploring the ship," Deneuve continued briskly. "That means you must have been acquainting yourself with the crew as well. In that regard, is there anything you feel the need to discuss before we move along to the main business of this meeting?"

There was, but Ixbeth was unsure how to express it without sounding petulant. Deneuve seemed to sense her dilemma. Instead of pushing on to other matters, she waited patiently for Ixbeth to find the right words. "Commanders Dedrick and Eberhart," she said at last. "Is there some reason for them to dislike me? Or each other?"

Sadness. "It isn't you, Doctor. There's a lot going on in their lives right now. It's left them both feeling frustrated and a little bit mad at the world."

Ixbeth waited in silence. As before, Deneuve felt compelled to explain.

"Up until several intervals ago, Gael and Leslie were what we Humans call 'an item'. There was considerable attraction between them, but something happened and they had a disagreement. A misunderstanding, really. Anyway," she concluded with a sigh, "they broke off the relationship and are no longer a couple."

"But they would like to be?"

"I'm sure they would."

Ixbeth was confused. "What is preventing them?"

"It's complicated."

Of course, it was. Everything about these Humans was a puzzle to be unraveled, a minefield to be traversed.

"The important thing for you to know, Doctor, is that their resentment is not directed at you."

"According to Doctor Marchenko, undirected anger is an early warning of mental instability," Ixbeth pointed out. "Are Commanders Dedrick and Eberhart at risk of failing their rescreening?"

"I doubt it. The anger is justified in this case and sure to be short-lived. Leslie and Gael are both exemplary officers and solid professionals. They know how important it is not to let personal feelings interfere with their working relationships." Sudden suspicion. Her brows knitting, Deneuve cocked her head and continued softly, "We all do, Doctor. Earth ships are cramped for space, so we have to make a special effort to control our negative emotions. Of course, an extremely intuitive individual could still sense those emotions and feel uncomfortable around them, correct?"

Ixbeth inhaled sharply. "Doctor Den—!"

"You know, I happen to be highly intuitive myself. Often, I sense things about people, things that I can't prove and therefore am not required to report. Captain Takamura is more impressed by facts than by rumors or idle speculation. However, this sort of intuition has been known to serve us well as we update the crew's neuro-psych profiles. In fact, the more sensitive one is to the emotional vibrations of others, the more effective one will be at determining each subject's true state of mind. When I asked you two-and-a-bit intervals ago what special talents or qualities you possessed, this was precisely the kind of thing I meant."

Ixbeth stared at her in bewilderment. Had Deneuve just said—?

There was no clue in the Human's aura. And once again, Deneuve cleared her throat and barreled ahead, all business, giving Ixbeth no time to reflect on what she had just heard. "Earth High Council and Fleet Control have a standing policy regarding ship's personnel. It's quite simple. They have to be our very best people, or they aren't allowed out into space. And they have to keep on being our very best people, or they aren't allowed to stay out here. Every crewmember on every Earth ship is an ambassador, representing our race to the rest of the galaxy. That's the first reason why we have to rescreen each entire crew every couple of years and keep their medical and neuro-psych profiles up to date.

"As for the second: On a science-exploration craft like this one, mission time is measured in standard years," Deneuve continued. "Being crammed together on a ship for that long is very stressful for Humans, even with the SPA."

Ixbeth repressed a shudder. She knew all about the Shared Programmable Activities room. During her neuro-psych session, Doctor Marchenko had taken one look at the way her legs were constructed and had prescribed virtual cross-country running for stress management. The projections were ultra-high definition, he'd promised her. Extremely responsive programming. It would feel just like racing through a field back home. The prospect of being able to run whenever she wanted to had been irresistible. Once tucked inside a user suit and plugged into the console, however, Ixbeth had realized immediately what a dreadful mistake this was. The energy surrounding her was in disharmony with her resonance pattern. *Large swallows small.* Heart bursting, vision failing, muscles twitching almost out of control, she had tried to strip off the suit without first disconnecting it from the program, managing only to stun herself nearly unconscious. And so, Ixbeth's first — and last — SPA experience had landed her in Rehab for half a day while her nervous system recovered, along with everyone else's.

"The SPA can be very realistic — for Humans," Deneuve added. "At some level, however, we remain aware that it's a deception. Sooner or later, tempers fray, moods start to swing, and eventually composure snaps."

Interesting. Subconsciously, Humans did understand the principles of resonance.

"So, we need to test to find out who's starting to — fray? —and take measures to resolve the situation before it can become critical."

"Correct. We can't let any individual's personal problems affect the operation of the ship. That's why it is very important not to let anyone skip an update. Not even a watch commander." Deneuve handed her a datawafer from the stack sitting beside the computer screen. "Commander Dedrick is your assignment. This is his file, containing all his background and the results of his previous screening for comparison."

Ixbeth frowned in puzzlement. "But I thought you said I would need a lot more training."

"You will. But this is a busy ship and he's one of the busiest officers on it. I figure it's going to take at least seven or eight standard intervals to get him to come in for testing, so I'm giving you a head start."

11

"**This planet Dimmla** sounds like a paradise," Takamura commented after reading Deneuve's and Marchenko's uploaded reports. "A beautiful home world, a large and loving family... Makes me wonder even more what could have forced her to leave all that. Now, Doctor," he added, swiveling his chair and leaning forward to rest his elbows on the desktop, "I want to know what you *didn't* put in there."

Deneuve took a deep breath and began: "First, she actually read the data package Fleet Control sent her, and she is anxious to follow all of its rules."

"That could be good or bad," he grumbled. "Next?"

His tension was contagious. Consciously relaxing her shoulders and settling back in her chair, Deneuve continued, "It makes her physically uncomfortable to be around Humans for extended periods of time. Marchenko made note of it while conducting her neuro-psych session. Apparently, we give her headaches. It could simply be an allergy, but I have reason to suspect she might be empathic."

That got his attention. "How empathic?"

Deneuve shrugged. "Hard to say. Even if she agreed to take them, none of our tests are normed for alien species. I'm classified highly intuitive, but I would estimate she's at least an order or two of magnitude above that."

"Which could also be good or bad," he observed, frowning, "depending on how self-aware she is. Let's assume the worst. Is there any chance that her discomfort could drive her to physical aggression?"

"Doctor Minegar? I doubt it, Captain. If she were going to tear Med Services apart, she would have done it right after the incident in the SPA room."

But Takamura shook his head. "I wouldn't be so quick to let my guard down, Doctor. Have you seen her claws?"

"In brief glimpses. She seems very self-controlled."

Still frowning, Takamura pointed out, "*Seems* being the operative word. Commander Dedrick has had no luck at all getting information from her. So, Doctor, it's up to you. Besides waiting for Mbuku to crack the code on that mysterious alien datacube, what next?"

"I've assigned her to conduct the psych rescreening of Commander Dedrick."

A startled pause, then, "Are you sure that's a good idea?"

"In the give and take of a rescreening, information comes out about both parties. It's the nature of the beast. She wants to do a good job, so she'll be focusing on getting Gael to reveal himself. I know how Marchenko has been coaching her. If she wants Commander Dedrick to open up, she'll have to open up as well."

"And these sessions are recorded?"

Deneuve grinned. "Always, Captain. It's standard procedure."

He nodded approvingly. "And Commander Dedrick is on board with this?"

"I've decided not to tell him about it."

"That's probably for the best," he conceded. "As I recall, he wasn't exactly cooperative with Doctor Marchenko the last time. What did he accuse him of — 'reopening old wounds and rubbing salt in them'? It will be interesting to see how Doctor Minegar fares with him."

—— «» ——

It took sixteen intervals of pursuit before Ixbeth was able to corner Watch Commander Dedrick and drag a commitment out of him.

By then it was common knowledge all over the ship that the 'cat woman' was an empath, and that Human emotions gave her headaches. Humans sometimes got headaches too, Ixbeth found out, from stress or hunger. She suspected that a Human tension headache was nowhere near as painful as the ones these Humans were giving *her*. Still, the fact of her suffering created enough sympathy to dull the crew's natural resentment at losing their emotional privacy, and for that she was grateful. She harbored no illusions about fitting in on this ship, but at least she could get on with her job.

She was determined to do it well.

As promised, Deneuve had put her through rigorous training involving lectures, readings, case studies, and the viewing of innumerable recorded psych sessions. Ixbeth had also observed over a dozen current rescreenings by Doctor Marchenko before being allowed to conduct one of her own. The subject, a well-adjusted male tech, had passed with flying colors. After that, Deneuve had put her to work on the least problematic cases, letting her build the skills and confidence she would need to handle the most challenging member of the *Marco Polo*'s crew: Watch Commander Gael Dedrick.

Over the past one-third of a year, Dedrick had made and then forgotten or canceled appointment after appointment, offering endless apologies and excuses. Ixbeth found his emotional aura strangely mixed: anger, regret, anxiety. Judging from his record, Dedrick was a fine officer, with nothing to fear from a fitness evaluation. She assumed he must be reacting to the idea of its being conducted by the 'cat woman'. In his place, Ixbeth knew she would probably feel the same way. That was why, initially, she'd been patient with him; however, even Kularian patience had limits.

Doctor Minegar wasn't authorized to impose official sanctions, but, as Deneuve had once suggested during a briefing, there was nothing to stop her from threatening them. According to his file, Dedrick was a very intelligent man, 'smart enough to know which side of the door was out', as Krodus liked to say. And that was the side the commander would be facing, Ixbeth decided, if he didn't keep his next appointment with her.

Learning that Commander Dedrick was on his way back from a surface mission, she waited for him just outside the Decontamination Unit, then fell into step beside him as he emerged. He was very tall for a Human, with long legs that devoured nearly a meter of deck with every impatient stride.

Thank the stars, he was hurrying, making it easier for Ixbeth to pace him. Dedrick stared stubbornly ahead, refusing to acknowledge her presence. Meanwhile, his emotional aura was becoming stormier by the second.

Before either of them had spoken a word, Ixbeth could feel the muscles of her scalp contracting. This was going to end with a headache — a bad one — but she couldn't allow him to put her off any longer.

"Commander Dedrick," she said, letting her voice rise on the last syllable.

He halted at the tube stop and jabbed the call button with his thumb. Still not making eye contact with her, he remarked briskly, "I don't have time to chat, Doctor."

"Good," she replied, matching his tone, "because neither do I. This is important."

The tube car arrived then and they boarded it together. Dedrick's displeasure was a sourness at the back of her throat as Ixbeth reached across him, punched in the destination code for the bridge, then hit the express button.

This conversation would require privacy.

"You're overdue for your psych rescreening," she pointed out once the car was in motion.

Annoyance. "Doctor, my duties aboard this ship—"

"—are directly dependent on your continuing to hold the rank of watch commander aboard this ship."

Surprise. And — amusement? He threw her a disbelieving look. "Are you attempting to bully me, Doctor Minegar?"

Ixbeth felt a pang of disappointment. Admittedly, intimidation being a tactic she had never tried before, she could probably have executed it better. Nonetheless, from what she had read in his file, Dedrick should have responded more seriously to any implied threat to his career, regardless of its source.

Resisting the urge to shake her mane, she recomposed her facial expression and replied evenly, "Of course not, Commander. I'm merely stating a fact. Since your duties as watch commander leave you no time to be rescreened, and a successful rescreening is a prerequisite for remaining out in space, it appears you have three options."

Rising anger. She'd struck a nerve. And her scalp was knotting up, giving her the promise of a crushing headache.

Never mind, she told herself. *This is progress. Keep going.*

"First, you can accept a reduction in rank to one with less responsibility. That will permit you the time for rescreening and keep you out in space. However, with the demotion on your record it's highly unlikely that you will ever come under consideration for a captaincy."

Shock. Indignation. Dedrick glared at the control panel as though wishing it dead. He was probably wondering how she could even suggest such a thing to a career officer.

The pain was bad enough now to blur her vision. It took an effort to focus her eyes. *Keep going!*

"Second, you can continue being too busy, a decision that will force Doctor Deneuve to become involved. Whether she orders you to come in for rescreening or simply recommends that you be rotated back to Earth, your career in space will effectively be over."

Sorrow. He was realizing that she was right.

Ixbeth dragged in a lungful of air and willed her senses to clear. *Just another few moments. Keep going!*

"Third, you can meet me in Med Services tomorrow morning and get this rescreening over with, so we can both turn our attention to other things," she concluded, wincing at the raggedness she heard in her own voice.

Resignation. Dedrick's broad shoulders sagged as he let out his breath in a sigh.

By the time the car door opened onto the bridge, Ixbeth's head felt as though two spikes were being driven through it in opposite directions, and an appointment for the following day had been made that Commander Dedrick was certain to keep.

—— «» ——

Later on, Ixbeth sat in her quarters, shaking her mane and wondering wearily how well Tal would be faring in her place. Did the mental discipline that he had worked so hard to acquire include a technique for shielding a Kularian mind from 199 *pritvanu*? Silly question. Of course, it must.

The headache was finally fading. As Ixbeth's scalp muscles relaxed, she closed her eyes, savoring each ripple of relief. No, she decided, shielding her mind was not the major problem. Ignorance was her problem. She knew more about Dimmlesi customs and holidays than she did about the traditions of her own people. Stars, at this point she knew more about the *Humans* than she did about her own people!

It wasn't for lack of trying — she and Mbuku had spent many intervals and had taken every approach they could think of to the problem of the unreadable datacube, but without success. Her senses had been inundated by the Human engineer's bitterness and frustration as he kept insisting that the cube must have been damaged somehow. Ixbeth knew better, but chose not to comment. Small corrupted large, not the other way around. Disharmony was disharmony. Still, the result was the same: Ixbeth was no closer to the meaning of the prophecy than she had been before. What if it were referring to a Kularian or Reyot myth that she had never heard of? What if the key needed to unlock its meaning were a knowledge of the orbits of Kula'as and its sister planet, Reyi'it?

And if it were, how, by the blessed stars, was she supposed to find out that information away from Altera, during a cycle of concealment, and stuck aboard an Earth ship?

As if all that weren't bad enough, Ixbeth had discovered that Humans weren't *pritvanu* only during their waking hours. They continued to broadcast their emotions — and sometimes their dreams — as they slept!

Stars be thanked, none of the Humans' nightmares generated the same agonizing terror as the ones she had endured back on Dimmla. One dream, however, could have come from the Oracle. It was filled with hatred — toward her! Each time this dreamer's venom invaded her awareness, Ixbeth couldn't get rid of it. For days afterward, it nested in the corners of her mind, fouling the back of her throat, stiffening her tail at odd moments, and causing her fingerclaws to try to extend.

There was someone on the ship who secretly wanted to torture and humiliate her. This crewmember hadn't yet been rescreened, she was certain — that much anger and loathing would have stood out like a beacon during a neuro-psych session — and as time passed, she found herself dreading more and more the prospect of encountering the Human across her desk.

Ixbeth was torn. She knew that she ought to be reporting this situation to Deneuve, that Marchenko could probably help her deal with it. But she also knew what she could expect if the Human crew ever learned that 'the cat woman', the stealthy alien who could reach into their minds and steal their emotions, was now breaking into their sleep and sampling their dreams.

No, she decided, she would have to find some way to resolve this problem on her own.

—— «» ——

It was the same recurring dream he'd had as a child, image for image and word for word, and why it had chosen now to resurface, Gael Dedrick couldn't begin to guess.

He was seven years old and at a carnival of some sort, strolling the grounds with Abner and Aunt Emma. As they rounded a corner, little Gael spotted a wrinkled old crone standing motionless beside the open flap of a large, midnight blue tent. She wore a fringed shawl and a head scarf, both the color of blood, and gold hoop earrings large enough to brush her shoulders. At first he thought she was a likeness placed there as an advertisement or a decoration. Then she turned her head to look straight at him, her piercing dark eyes deep as wells, and next thing he knew, he was inside her tent and she was reading his future.

After a second he realized that Abner was there also, standing beside him, absolutely still.

The old woman looked at Abner, and then at Gael, and then she stared into a crystal ball for what seemed a very long time. She shook her head, as if she couldn't believe what she'd seen in the crystal ball, and took out a strange deck of cards. She arranged some of them in a pattern, face up on the table, and studied them carefully. Then she shook her head again, still having difficulty believing what she was seeing.

Finally she spoke, in a voice that crackled as if with interference of some kind. "Two angels from a fiery world ... one to damn and one to save ... one to bring and one to take away ... one to rise and one to fall ... deaf and blind but angels both."

Gael felt his limbs grow heavy. The weight of his arms dragged him down to the ground. When he next opened his eyes, he was lying on his bed, staring at the ceiling of his cabin with the fortune teller's words echoing in his mind.

12

As Gael Dedrick was finishing his breakfast and wondering for the hundredth time just how long it was possible for one Human to remain angry with another one, Leslie Eberhart stalked up to his table in the mess hall and demanded, "Why the hell didn't you tell me you'd changed your mind about helping Sam?"

"How long have you known?"

"Answer my question first."

He paused for a breath, directing his gaze at the unfinished toast on his plate. In fact, he would have preferred that she never find out what he'd done. But he was too much of a realist to think that such a thing was possible aboard a Fleet ship.

"I didn't tell you because I didn't do it for you."

"What?" Stunned, she dropped into the chair facing his.

"I did it for Sam. You made me aware of his situation. I wasn't going to commit myself until I was certain I could deliver, so I did a little research, made my decision, and pulled some strings. Anonymously."

"But you let me think—! And then you let me go on thinking—!"

"You chose to think," he pointed out quietly. "There's a difference."

Her eyes were bright with unshed tears. "It was still a rotten thing to do to me, Gael."

"I know, and I'm sorry it was necessary."

They were tears of anger, he realized as she got to her feet, composed her features, and said in a voice that could have cut glass, "And I'm sorry you believed it was necessary, because you were wrong. Just ask yourself how you would have felt if Sam had been your brother and someone you'd come to trust and care about had treated you this way."

And with that, she wheeled and walked away.

Dedrick heaved a philosophical sigh. "You're welcome," he murmured.

——— «» ———

Ixbeth strode through the triage area and past the row of Trauma cubicles with their modesty curtains standing open.

First watch was three standard hours old, and this part of Medical Services was quiet and empty. However, they were orbiting a carbon-based planet on which scientific teams were in the process of being deployed. According to Deneuve, scientists exploring a new world tended to look everywhere except where they were going. In another hour, two at the most, casualties would begin arriving from the planet's surface. Rarely serious, these tended to be mostly allergic reactions, cuts and scrapes, and the occasional bone fracture. The Med Services staff were ready for them. A regen unit and a trauma kit had been broken out for each of the eight cubicles.

Med Services was still a maze, but now it was a familiar one. Ixbeth continued walking past a darkened operating room and around the vault-like safelab, made a quick left turn down a cul-de-sac, another at the first doorway, and was in her office.

It was actually a small meeting room next to Deneuve's office, a gray box with a square gray metal table and two gray metal chairs, and it suited a neuro-psych rescreening rather well. Giving a subject nothing interesting to look at forced him to turn his gaze inward. In this unprepossessing corner of the ship, armed with detailed instructions from Doctor Deneuve and pointers from Doctor Marchenko, Ixbeth had already successfully rescreened almost a third of the crew. At 1115 hours this morning, it would be Commander Dedrick's turn. She had spent so much time preparing for this interview that it felt almost like a Docent's evaluation.

It should have made her anxious. And yet, even knowing that a headache would undoubtedly follow the session, Ixbeth found herself looking forward to it. The blood of hunters must be flowing in her veins, she reflected — the long and difficult pursuit of this particular subject had whetted her appetite for him.

Dedrick arrived at the scheduled time and took his seat across the table from her. His gaze scanned the room, briefly pausing on the sensor unit in the corner, then returned to study her face with an intensity that instantly tightened her scalp.

Gael Dedrick was a powerfully built male with rugged features and a commanding air. Ixbeth had noticed this about him the first time they'd met, but their contacts since then had been either brief or full of distractions, giving her no opportunity to truly appreciate his physical qualities. Until now. Now they were alone together with nothing to focus on but each other, and Ixbeth was sensing his almost Kularian maleness and becoming uncomfortably aware of her twitching right ear, and of her tail pressing stiffly against the back of her chair. Each time she met his gaze, it was all she could do to still the vibration in her chest.

His eyes were mesmerizing. The irises were almost black, and simultaneously shone and smoldered as though fashioned from *incharna* stones. Reluctantly, she broke eye contact in order to call up the first set of questions on her handcomm screen.

Ixbeth took as deep a breath as she could and willed her voice to sound confident and professional.

"Are you ready?" she asked.

"Fire away, Doctor."

She tasted apprehension. His right thumb was worrying a ring he wore on the same hand. He needed to be put at ease.

Thank the stars, her role in these interviews was well rehearsed. Her heart pounding in her ears, she cleared the screen and sat back in her chair with what she hoped would be interpreted as a friendly smile. Begin with 'safe' questions, Marchenko had taught her. It was best to give the subject some information about herself before asking for any back. "I was a little envious of you yesterday, Commander."

Curiosity. "Oh?"

"You were returning from a surface mission. I trust it went well?"

"We accomplished our objective," he replied.

"It's so crowded aboard ship. I would very much like to visit the surface of a planet sometime, just to have the room to run. Back home on Dimmla, my brother and I would run everywhere, never walk. Did you get to run down there?"

A smile. It was a start. Then he shook his head and tilted it to one side, and she was reminded of Tal. Swallowing hard to clear her throat, Ixbeth almost missed Dedrick's answer to her question: "I was assisting with a mineralogical sampling, Doctor. You don't run with rocks in one-point-eight gravities."

"What about on Earth? You were born there, correct? Did you enjoy running when you were younger?"

"Running, baseball, tennis — I used to enjoy a lot of things."

"And now?"

"Now I take long hikes in the SPA room."

"Do you regret going out into space?"

"Not for a standard second, Doctor. Do you regret coming aboard the *Marco Polo*?"

Startled by the question, but even more by the intense curiosity behind it, Ixbeth heard herself reply, "At moments. But this has been a very educational experience."

Satisfaction. Dedrick relaxed visibly in his chair, and Ixbeth finally understood what had just happened. A Human had crept up on the 'cat woman' and stolen some information from *her* mind. Now they were on even terms. The interview could proceed.

"Tell me about your family, Commander," she said.

Impatience. The dark eyes flashed, and Ixbeth felt her scalp contract. Had she misread his mood somehow?

"Doctor, I've been rescreened seven times. Everything I could possibly tell you about my family is already in my file," Dedrick pointed out.

No, she thought grimly, it wasn't. "Your file says that you're a nephew of one of Earth's Supreme Adjudicators, Dennis Forrand. A very important person, I gather. What is it like having someone like that in the family?"

Dedrick chuckled mirthlessly. "Ah, the late great Supreme Adjudicator. If he's important enough and knows it, he isn't really *in* the family — he wears it like a suit of clothes. When I was growing up, that was how he treated us. Like fashion accessories. He expected us to make him look good, and stuffed us in the back of the closet if we didn't. That's the reason I'm out in space. When my cousin Abner began constantly getting into trouble, Uncle Dennis clapped us both into the Fleet training program. I liked it and stayed. Worked my way up the ranks, and here I am."

It was a practiced response to a question he'd heard many times before. This time, it wouldn't suffice. This time, Ixbeth decided, they had to dig deeper. A lot deeper. As she settled once more into her professional persona, the questions began to come automatically. "Why do you suppose your cousin began getting into trouble?"

Annoyance. Anxiety. He'd answered this question in the previous rescreening as well, but the response had been flagged. Sense hairs rising, Ixbeth watched with interest as Dedrick's features composed and recomposed themselves several times. Sorting through possible answers, no doubt. Or being forced to speculate on something he would rather not think about, or perhaps taking a different perspective on a matter that hadn't crossed his mind in a long time.

Exasperation. Finally, he blurted out, "Abner was spoiled, Doctor, given whatever he wanted whenever he wanted it. He never had to work for anything in his life, so he figured he should never have to. Anyone who said no to him he found a way to hurt. And Uncle Dennis saw to it that he never had to take responsibility for his actions."

"He protected Abner?"

"Actually, he was protecting himself. Abner seemed bent on dragging the Forrand name through the mud. Adjudicators whose names are constantly popping up in the tabs tend to have short careers. And his career was all Uncle Dennis had going for him. So, I sincerely doubt whether anything he did was ever purely for Abner's benefit."

"Still, it sounds as though he spent a lot of time and effort getting your cousin out of trouble," Ixbeth observed evenly, despite the anger beginning to knot the muscles of her scalp. "Did *you* ever need his time and effort?"

Dedrick uttered a shocked syllable. "Never," he declared. "If I'd so much as asked him for a favor my mother would have killed me."

It was a figure of Human speech, Ixbeth reminded herself. Nonetheless… "That's a little drastic, isn't it?'

"Not if you knew my family, Doctor Minegar."

"Really? What were your parents like?"

Ixbeth already knew quite a lot about the Dedricks and the Forrands. That two brothers had married two sisters, one the oldest and the other the youngest in her family, and that each pairing had produced a singleton son was a matter of public record. That the middle Forrand sib, Dennis, had never married or reproduced was also on Earth's database, along with information about the unfortunate traffic accident in which he had lost his life, three Earth years after Abner Dedrick had fled into space and disappeared.

"My mother was older than my father, and she definitely ran things around our home," Dedrick recalled. "She was strict, maybe a little too strict, but only because Aunt Emma let Abner walk all over her and Uncle Carl. *They* could raise a delinquent if they wanted to, she used to say, but any child *she* produced was going to be a stand-up citizen. I think her proudest moment was the day I graduated from officer training at the Fleet Academy."

And, whether or not he was still happy as a Fleet officer, he had been striving to keep her proud of him ever since, reflected Ixbeth. Sadly, she was very familiar with this particular family dynamic.

"What about your father? Was he supportive as well?" she asked.

The anger abated somewhat. "He was a musician and songwriter, a pretty good one. I don't know how he felt about my choice of career, but I do know he hated any kind of confrontation. He always deferred to my mother when it came to what he called 'domestic details.'"

"It sounds as though *you* were one of those domestic details."

Dedrick leaned back thoughtfully. "I guess I was."

"How did your mother get along with her sibs?"

Puzzlement. "Sibs? You mean her brother and sister?"

She nodded.

"When I was younger, it was friendly enough, I guess. The Dedricks and Forrands got together for holidays and birthday celebrations, things like that. Then Abner's dark side emerged, and relations became a little strained."

"Just a little?"

"When I was about nine years old, Abner broke one of his toys that I'd been playing with and slashed my arm with it. The injury was serious enough to require regen at the local hospital. My mother hardly spoke to Aunt Emma after that. When it came out that I hadn't been his first victim, or his last, she pretty much cut off Uncle Dennis as well, for pulling strings to prevent Abner from getting what was coming to him. My mother had high moral standards," he concluded, "and she didn't forgive easily."

"So you never saw your cousin again after he injured you?"

Dedrick flashed a brief grin. "Not in the presence of our mothers, anyway. Our fathers still got together from time to time, and Dad would sneak me out to go low-grav bowling or have lunch with Uncle Carl and Abner. Abner could be a lot of fun as long as he was getting what he wanted."

"How do you suppose he felt about his uncle constantly 'pulling strings' for him?"

Anger surged back, sweeping away every other emotion. "I don't think it was what Abner wanted," he said, with emphasis on the final word.

"Commander, are you blaming your uncle for what has happened to your family?"

Raising a hand to massage her temple — a symbolic gesture, she knew, but it seemed to help — Ixbeth met Dedrick's gaze again and swallowed hard. His eyes were smoldering, generating enough heat to raise Ixbeth's body temperature as well. She could practically feel internal organs beginning to melt. Fortunately, he'd chosen to answer her question. She wasn't sure she could have framed another in its place.

"I don't have to. Uncle Dennis's will was a *de facto* confession of guilt. Uncle Carl had already gotten a divorce and an offworld posting, in that order. Without her big brother to cling to, Aunt Emma turned to my parents. A year later my mother got tired of Emma's whining and decided it was time to put some distance between them and her. The Relocation Authority had revoked Emma's Eligibility for health reasons. My parents were still Eligible, however, so they took an offworld posting on one of the colonies. Several intervals after they arrived, so did Angel of Death. Within a year, Uncle Carl and my parents were all dead of the plague. Five Earth years ago, my aunt died of a drug overdose. So, regardless of who's to blame, the bottom line is that I'm the only Dedrick left," he concluded.

At last, thought Ixbeth. They'd uncovered the root system of the poisonous plant. Just another few tugs would expose it to the air, where it could be examined briefly and then thrown away to die. Ixbeth and the other students had joked about this analogy after hearing Docent Quibbo use it in class, but it described Commander Dedrick's case to perfection.

"The only Dedrick?" she echoed. "What about Abner?"

"The last time I heard any news of him was about nine standard years ago. According to the Gate 'casts, he vandalized a laboratory on Thrygg and then disappeared. The Thryggians screamed bloody murder, tried to get him extradited — but of course it was all moot, since nobody knew where he was. Shortly after that, the plague hit, and everybody was too busy dealing with Angel of Death to give much thought to Abner Dedrick. Including me. I have no idea where he is right now or whether he's still alive, and I've no desire to locate him."

Clearly, Commander Dedrick was his mother's son. And yet...

Regret. The *incharna* eyes had stopped smoldering, and Ixbeth realized with a pang that despite his protestations, Dedrick, a singleton, had no real wish to abandon his last living relative. If she could bring that out, help him recognize how unreasonable his mother's expectations were in this situation—

Suddenly aware of his gaze once more trained curiously on her face, Ixbeth returned to the moment. She'd already lined up the questions in her mind. The next one stepped obediently into her mouth. "Knowing that there are only the two of you left, if Abner were to walk into this room right now, what do you think you would say to him?"

Ixbeth had to ask this question in order to validate the previous ones. It was unfortunate, for Dedrick instantly began radiating displeasure at the thought of meeting his cousin again. As he prepared his response — something sarcastic, no doubt — the knotted muscles of her scalp continued to throb painfully, forcing her at last to shake her mane. Had the Humans figured out yet what that signified? she wondered. Or did they believe it was just another point of similarity between her species and those lazy Earth lions she'd viewed on the ship's database?

At that moment, the wallcomm beside the door emitted a beep.

"Commander Dedrick, please report to the captain on the bridge!"

Relief. Dedrick shrugged. "Something urgent must have come up. Sorry, Doctor."

He was lying about being sorry, but Ixbeth let it go. "We can resume day after tomorrow, same time," she told him, making a mental note to find out whether there really had been an emergency on the bridge.

13

"Thryggians? Out here?" Ixbeth was dumbfounded.

Returning to Med Services for an afternoon rescreening appointment, she had walked unsuspecting into what appeared to be a frantic bout of cleaning. Every storage compartment stood wide open while medical staff with handheld sensors removed and scanned each item, then checked it off on a list. The entire department was being taken apart, dusted off, and put back together. Ixbeth tasted weary determination emanating from all around her.

Except where Doctor Deneuve was standing. Deneuve was livid. Busily coordinating the effort from behind the P and R unit's nursing station, she said grimly, "Yes, Thryggians. They established a synchronous orbit above us, punched through our shields, and scanned us from nose to thrusters, focusing especially on the science sector and on this department. Claimed to be looking for stolen property. Clearly, they found none. But now we'll have to recalibrate every regen and diagnostic unit. And God knows what that energy beam has done to all our stem cells and vaccines, culturing media, blood elements…! Damn them, they're supposed to be scientists, and they're behaving like pirates!" she declared, throwing her hands in the air.

Impotent rage. The Thryggians seemed to inspire this emotion in others. Ixbeth had tasted the same metallic tang at the back of her throat the day Evin Lurrlo had announced to the docents and students on Altera that he'd finally managed to put the fragments of data together from the Central Archives — more than thirty standard years after the empaneling of the Galactic Tribunal.

"Here. I took a snap from the visual record of the encounter. Behold," the Human said, emphatically punching keys to access the databank, "the mighty star ship that was able to do this to us."

Ixbeth stared in dismay at the image that appeared on the screen. The ship looked like a parody of a spacegoing vessel, like something hastily assembled out of spare parts and junk. Roughly ovoid in shape, it traveled narrow end first and was randomly studded with appendages. Patching was clearly visible on its hull.

As Deneuve continued to fume, a shiver crossed Ixbeth's back, stiffening her tail. "Did they actually identify themselves as Thryggians?" she demanded urgently. "Did the transmission originate from their ship? Was it recorded by this one?"

"Yes, yes, and yes, of course. Why?"

"Because that transmission is evidence. If the Thryggians are out here, it's in defiance of a planetary confinement order imposed by the Great Council fifty standard years ago. Their fleet was destroyed, and they are forbidden space travel of any kind."

Puzzlement, becoming apprehension. "But we worked with the Thryggians for years after the first outbreaks of Angel of Death. They offered to help us trace the contagion vector, and we accepted. We knew there was a ban on travel to their home world, but this is the first I've heard of their being forbidden to leave it."

Ixbeth didn't know what to reply to this. The Children of Kula'as had been out of touch with the Great Council for ten generations, except for the tiny bits of information Lurrlo managed to steal from the Central Archives. Perhaps the Council had warned its member races only, purposely omitting the 'barbaric Humans'. And the Kularians, of course, who had all 'mysteriously disappeared'. The community on Altera would still be living in ignorance of such momentous events if their Guardian of Light hadn't been determined to keep the local Archives abreast of what was happening in the galaxy.

Dread and remorse. "We've been trying so hard to obey the Great Council's laws. If our collaboration with the Thryggians has made us accomplices to some sort of criminal activity—! Oh, sorry," she added, as the 'cat woman' sighed and pressed a hand to her temple.

A moment later, Ixbeth was able to reply, "You're not the evildoers, Doctor. The Thryggians are. They're on trial. The Tribunal has been in session for decades, moving from planet to planet to hear all the evidence against them. So don't be surprised if they behave like pirates, because that's what they are. This 'stolen property' they claim to be looking for is probably something that can incriminate them."

Sorrow. Her lips pressed tightly together, Deneuve shook her head. "Now *I'm* getting a headache. I think you'd better find Captain Takamura and tell him everything you know about the Thryggians."

Ixbeth nodded, grateful to be leaving Deneuve's vicinity but all too aware of the gaps in her own knowledge. Everything Ixbeth knew about the Thryggians might not be sufficient to protect the Human ship if the pirates returned. And they probably would return, she realized, to do more than scan now that the *Marco Polo*'s transmission log could be used against them at the Tribunal. As she pressed the call button at the tube stop, Ixbeth couldn't help remembering the words of the prophecy.

Life out of death. That could mean survival of a disaster — or of an attack. Ixbeth's fingerclaws tried to extend as she visualized once again the snap she had seen of the Thryggian ship. One of those had effortlessly punched holes in the Earth ship's shielding. What sort of damage could more than one do? *Bodies flung, broken....* Ixbeth shivered.

A machine with the heart of a child. Only if that heart were made of stone. The Thryggians lived and breathed scientific inquiry, caring nothing at all for the lives they disrupted or destroyed in the process. That was why they were on trial.

Together, victory. Over the Thryggians? One could only hope.

———— «» ————

It was not a good day to be highly intuitive and in the presence of Hiro Takamura.

The captain of the *Marco Polo* stalked back and forth behind his desk as Deneuve sat fidgeting in the seat in front of it.

"It can't be a coincidence," he stated, "that shortly after a secretive alien comes aboard, the Thryggians violate house arrest to go in search of stolen property."

Deneuve was incredulous. "You don't honestly believe she's a common thief, do you?"

"Of course not!" declared Takamura. "Whatever Doctor Minegar is, she is not common. Influence has been exerted to ensure her acceptance among us, I'm not sure I even want to know by whom. And our own planetary government has charged us with keeping her safe. I asked her straight out whether she was the reason the Thryggians were here, and instead of giving me a simple yes or no, she suggested that *they* might be the reason *she* was here. Speaking in riddles! There is definitely something strange going on." Rounding on Deneuve, he added, "Have we found out anything further about her? Besides the fact that she knows more about the Thryggians than our friends on the Galactic Great Council have seen fit to tell us?"

Deneuve shook her head.

Takamura's deskcomm chose that moment to beep, and he leaned over to thumb the control.

"Captain," said Leslie Eberhart's voice, "the Gate transmission you authorized has been sent to Fleet Control, recommending an all-ships warning about the Thryggians."

"Thank you, Commander. Hopefully, no other Earth vessel will be caught unawares by those pirates."

Struck by a sudden thought, Deneuve mused, "What if she's a spy, sent by the Great Council to find out more about us?"

Takamura scowled, his disgust almost palpable. "I doubt it, Doctor. You spy when there's reason to believe the truth is being withheld. Earth High Council is so eager to please right now that it would hand over our entire databank, along with specimen Humans for dissection if the aliens requested it, no questions asked. If Doctor Minegar is a spy, it isn't for the Galactic Great Council."

For a moment, as they both considered the unsettling implications of Takamura's final statement, there was silence in the room.

"Then what if they sent her for a different reason?" Deneuve offered. "The Council must know that the Thryggians are criminals, but they can't take any official action against them until the Tribunal has finished gathering depositions, so—"

"—so they send us an empath who is prone to migraines, and who withholds information about the Thryggians until they have already come and gone?"

Deneuve shrugged, out of ideas.

The captain sighed then and sank down onto his chair. "I have a feeling that events are beginning to converge on us, Doctor, events that could very well hinge on the intentions of our alien guest. Keep monitoring her, please. I am not fond of surprises."

PART V

First Contact: Planet MF-307

Sylvie Alaine Deneuve (b. 2351 C.E. – d. 2479 C.E.) was the youngest of three daughters born to Raymond and Celestine Deneuve on Paradis, an Earth colony later wiped out by the Angel of Death plague. She returned to Earth in 2369 C.E. to study medicine at the University of Toronto in Lakeshore Ontario Urban District, completed residencies in paediatrics and immunology at the prestigious Hospital for Sick Children, and became the youngest person ever to serve as the Head of Medical Research at King George Hospital in London. In 2386 C.E. she was seconded to the Disease Control Task Force on Angel of Death, where her bold research methods were instrumental in the development of an effective vaccine against most strains of the plague virus. In 2391 C.E., Deneuve requested reassignment to a deep space exploration vessel. She was subsequently posted to the *Marco Polo* as Supervisor of Medical Services, where she served with distinction for eight years before being implicated along with Commander Gael Dedrick in a case of data tampering. Although cleared of all charges, she resigned her commission in order to become Docent of Human Studies at the Archives on Kula'as, a position she held until shortly before her death.

— *Sic Transit Terra, An Unauthorized Planetary History*
(2673 C.E.)

Fleet Control Headquarters, Earth

MEMO

EARTH DATE: 21 February 2399

FROM: Vice-Admiral Kendra Nelligan

TO: Captain Hiromasu Takamura, commanding the *Marco Polo*

It is my happy duty to inform you that while conducting a census on planet MF-307, the Fleet ship *Vasco da Gama* discovered a survivor of Angel of Death. She appears to be a relative of one of your officers, Watch Commander Gael Dedrick. Therefore, effective immediately, the *Marco Folo* is ordered to alter course for MF-307 to pick her up.

The long version of your orders is attached, along with a copy of the *Vasco da Gama*'s report.

You will note that the census has also confirmed the death of Abner Dedrick. Please convey our deepest sympathies to your watch commander on the loss of his cousin.

The quarantine on MF-307 is being relaxed solely to permit the removal of Ms Dedrick to your ship. Please ensure that your landing party takes appropriate precautions while onplanet and especially when making contact with the subject. Your Medical Services staff should be instructed to give highest priority to determining whether she is infectious and how she managed to survive the plague. We are pre-authorizing immediate Gate transmission of this information to Disease Control on Earth.

Good luck and godspeed, Hiro.
Kendra

14

Captain Takamura waited for Ixbeth and Deneuve to settle into chairs facing each other across the table in the strategy room. Then he sat down himself. Ixbeth tasted apprehension, despite the smile teasing the corners of his mouth.

"This is a mission briefing, Doctors," he told them. "A young relative of Commander Dedrick was found alive on a world thought to be plague-dead. We have changed course in order to pick her up."

Ixbeth straightened in her seat.

Life out of death, said Tal's remembered voice inside her head.

"Naturally, Commander Dedrick has submitted his application for temporary guardianship to Fleet Control. I am confident it will be accepted."

"And of course, you'll want us to check the young lady over when she arrives on board," said Deneuve, nodding.

"Both medically and psychologically. Doctor Deneuve, Fleet Control would like you to determine precisely what it was that kept her safe from Angel of Death. And Doctor Minegar, this girl has spent the past standard year living all alone with nothing but traumatic memories for company. I asked Doctor Marchenko which of his staff would have the best chance of initiating her emotional recovery, and he recommended you."

Ixbeth's hand went automatically to her temple. Headaches, dreams, and now this. He couldn't know what he was asking.

Regret, mingled with determination. No, she amended, he knew what the cost might be — or thought he did

Life out of death...

"We'll keep a close eye on her, Captain," Deneuve assured him.

"I want you both involved from the beginning," said Takamura. "You will accompany Commander Dedrick to the planet's surface to pick up his cousin, and you will continue monitoring her for the whole time she is on this ship."

Ixbeth swallowed the growl rising in her throat. In Human society, cousins were either the offspring of sibs or the offspring of cousins. From what she knew about Gael Dedrick's family, there was only one way he could have a young female cousin. "Captain, is this young one the daughter of Abner Dedrick?"

Takamura nodded. "That is the presumption. Abner Dedrick and his partner died of the plague, as did the entire population of the colony on MF-307, approximately one year ago."

"So there isn't actually any genetic proof that the child is Abner Dedrick's offspring?" Deneuve asked, frowning.

"Correct, Doctor. That is why the guardianship is only temporary. The Relocation Authority requests that you add the girl to their files and, in the process of creating the necessary records, that you determine whether in fact she is genetically related to the Dedrick or Forrand family. If she is not, then Commander Dedrick will have a decision to make." Pausing, Takamura sighed quietly. "It won't be easy for either of them, I'm afraid. This girl is a child, no more than thirteen or fourteen Earth years old, and Gael has been on his own for a long time."

And what about the girl's otherness? Ixbeth wondered. Humans feared otherness, and this young one would be a walking anomaly. Her very existence on that world was astonishing, inexplicable. Plague-dead meant that the entire planet had been exhaustively scanned and no large carbon-based life forms — the only ones Humans were interested in — had been found. As long as the girl was proven to belong to Commander Dedrick's family, the crew would nonetheless accept her. But if it turned out that she was not genetically related to one of them, what would happen to her? Would the Humans form a pack and carry her off to be destroyed, like the males in attendance at a Kularian birth? Ixbeth felt her fingerclaws begin to extend and placed her hands out of sight below the level of the table.

"We can set up a support network, something he can fall back on," Deneuve was saying, "arrange for the sorts of activities that might appeal to an adolescent, as well as companionship, supervision, that sort of thing. We should probably also warn anyone who might come into contact with her about the possibility of emotionally disturbed behavior and give them pointers on how to deal with it. All this will need to be in place ahead of time, of course."

Sudden apprehension. Deneuve shifted uneasily in her chair. "Sir, does Commander Dedrick know about our assignments?"

"He will. And he will cooperate."

Life out of death, Tal's remembered voice repeated quietly, *dealing out death*.

Ixbeth felt a chill beneath her fur. Abner Dedrick had sired a daughter, and she had survived the plague, a destroyer of worlds. Otherness unexplainable. If this young female had been raised to have Abner's attitudes, if she had inherited his violent nature, or, worse, if she had survived Angel of Death by taking it inside her own body, then her problems might be disastrous for all of them. Should Ixbeth speak out? Takamura's aura was becoming somber. No, she decided. Otherness was enough for the Humans to deal with right now.

———— «» ————

Family. Dedrick rolled the word around in his mind, considering its implications as he read over the reports on planet MF-307. Data Management had forwarded not only the final census information but also any status reports from the colony that mentioned the Joneses. A video clip had been surreptitiously recorded while Abner and his alleged daughter were burning and burying some deceased settlers. It showed him grabbing and shoving the girl as he told her in a voice that sent shivers of recognition down Gael's spine, "This is *my* planet, Dedrick's Planet, and don't you forget it!"

In a way, it was comforting to know that Abner hadn't changed. It meant that Gael's decision to put emotional distance between himself and the rest of the Forrand-Dedrick clan had been the right call. Family had played havoc with his state of mind for most of his early life. In fact, he mused, since emotional stability was a prerequisite for Eligibility, it was a wonder any of them had been allowed even to keep that designation once Dennis Forrand had died.

For years Gael Dedrick had lived comfortably within the structured embrace of Earth's spacegoing Fleet, unencumbered by family ties. He had watched his immediate circle of friends shrink as he moved up the ranks and the Fleet reassigned his newly-promoted fellow officers to hubs or other ships. Gael was outgoing and never lacked for companionship, but he understood that each new friendship came with a high probability of loss. Over time, he had learned precisely how much of himself he could invest in these relationships to protect himself from the pain of losing them. But now family was back, upheaving his well-managed life like the cat that refused to stay away in an old Earth song, and Gael suddenly found himself on shifting emotional ground. How did he feel about this unexpected change to his ordered and orderly existence? He wasn't sure. There was probably a way he was *supposed* to feel, but he wasn't sure what that was either.

All he knew was that Abner had died, leaving behind a child that Gael was expected to share his life with, take responsibility for, and protect, because that was what family members owed to one another. That much he'd learned from Leslie Eberhart. Well, if there was one thing Gael Dedrick was good at, he decided, it was doing his duty.

—— «» ——

Ixbeth stood outside the door to Commander Dedrick's quarters, staring at the enter button as she tried to compose her thoughts. She had put off this meeting as long as she dared, but she couldn't procrastinate any longer. His cousin would be aboard in approximately two standard days. If their efforts to help her were to have any chance of success, then they both had to be able to focus on her needs.

Unfortunately, Ixbeth wasn't able to focus very well on anything right now. For the past three days she had been feeling feverish, and there was an itch she couldn't scratch, deep beneath her genital fur. Every male on the ship seemed to be giving off a musk that made her light-headed and threatened to dissolve her leg joints. She couldn't sit still. Stars, she could barely stand! In a word, with exquisitely cruel timing, Ixbeth had slipped into *disvan*, her first time ever in the absence of other Kularian females.

Twice before, she had been *disvanu*, and her friends had gathered around her and connected emotionally with her to bleed off the worst of the effects. They'd told her what friends always told an unpaired female at such a time: "We're doing this to help you keep a clear head." It was a gross understatement. Experiencing the full force of the ancient imperative for the first time in her life, Ixbeth now realized that if they hadn't done it, she would have rushed out and mated with the first male she found, just to make *disvan* stop. That was what she wanted to do right now. Forget the cycle of concealment. Forget the Quest. If there had been any other Kularians on the ship, she would have been partnered for life three standard days ago.

The worst part was, she should have known it would happen. *Disvan* was the oldest compulsion in the universe. How foolish to assume that it could only be triggered by one of her own species! The first time she'd felt the warmth of Gael Dedrick's eyes kindle an answering flame inside her, the first time she'd admitted to herself that he was attractive, she should have remembered that this was how the process began. There was no shutting *disvan* down once it had started, even when the male who had inspired it was Human and therefore not a suitable mate. Ixbeth would simply have to suffer with it until it had run its course, lasting roughly five days.

Stars, this was unbearable! She could feel panic rising. Her fingerclaws wanted constantly to extend. And with Commander Dedrick's young relative coming aboard, could the timing possibly have been worse?

Ixbeth had cut back her rescreening schedule on the pretext of needing time to prepare for the young one's arrival. Deneuve hadn't commented yet, but she was intuitive enough to have noticed that something was wrong. And now Takamura was expecting Doctor Minegar to meet and work closely with the same Human male who had inspired this

— this *change* in her, at the same time as she was trying to fulfill the prophecy and save her people from extinction.

Avo'or had to be laughing himself silly.

Well, thought Ixbeth grimly, she might as well get this over with. She took a steadying breath and pressed Commander Dedrick's enter button. After all, what was the worst that could happen?

The door slid aside for her almost immediately.

This was the first time Ixbeth had seen the interior of a command-level officer's suite. Dedrick lived in a single, relatively spacious room decorated in cream and shades of gold, with designated areas for working, eating, and entertaining company, and a screened-off area for sleeping. The furnishings she could see from the doorway were few and simple, but they were all made of polished wood and reflected an individual's tastes. Ixbeth's eyes feasted hungrily for a moment on the commander's warm, dark slab of a desktop and matching armchair, then moved to a painting she recognized, hanging on a nearby wall.

She had seen the same artwork, depicting a sunny field of blue and yellow flowers, in one of the ship's databases several intervals earlier. Ixbeth had been searching for a picture she could have the quartermaster reproduce and frame for her, and had paused on the image because it reminded her of Dimmla.

What she was looking at now was not a copy. It was the original, created in the early twenty-second century. Beautiful things practically emanated the feeling that had gone into their production. Ixbeth could taste—

Stars, no! A sudden wave of heat seemed to set her genital fur on fire. Reflexively, her hands flew between her thighs, a second before it occurred to her that Commander Dedrick had to be somewhere in the room. These were his quarters, after all, and his spoken command must have let her in. Ixbeth froze. Sense hairs erect, she straightened slowly and stole careful glances over both shoulders before turning back around. Thank the stars, he hadn't seen her. She would have to exercise much stronger self-control from now on. Either that or lock herself in her cabin until *disvan* was over.

Several heartbeats later, once more trusting herself to speak, she called out, "Commander?"

"Over here."

Ixbeth followed his voice to the far side of the sitting area and saw a muscled arm wave to her, apparently from inside a section of bulkhead. Curious, she drew nearer.

"I'm cracking open a sleeping module for Lania," he explained.

"Lania?"

"I think that's her name. It's what the colonists called her in their reports to the Relocation Authority." He swung one leg over the threshold, keeping the other inside the bulkhead. "This is supposed to be a breeze. Just unlock a wall panel and replace it with a sliding door. That's what the quartermaster told me, anyway."

His voice and muscles straining, Dedrick wrestled the door into position.

The nipples on Ixbeth's belly tingled and hardened as another wave of warmth suffused her body. She gasped softly, then pressed a hand to her stomach and rubbed a slow circle, thankful for the stiff fabric of her lab coat.

Dedrick touched a switch beside the door and stepped out to admire his handiwork. At once, the ceiling panels inside the module began to glow. "I wanted to see what this place would look like with two people living in it instead of just one."

Ixbeth peered over his shoulder and saw, in a long narrow space, a stripped single bed, two empty wall-nooks, and a built-in wardrobe. Her heart sank. This wasn't a room — it was a cell even smaller and starker than her own had been when she'd first arrived on the ship.

She paused, weighing a more diplomatic approach before finally blurting out, "Commander, this adolescent Human female has had an entire planet to herself for over a standard year. You can't suddenly ask her to live inside a—" *A tiny box*, she'd been about to say, but thought better of it. "—a space this small. She'll revolt."

"At first, maybe," he replied gruffly. "Then she'll adjust. We all had to adjust. Don't forget, most of this area will be shared." He gestured toward the desk, the sofa, the dining area. "It isn't as though I plan to keep her locked up in there, you know."

"I'm afraid you may have to convince her of that. You'll be a stranger to her, after all."

Grim amusement. "Actually, I won't, Doctor. My father and Abner's were identical twin brothers, and Abner was born less than a year after I was. When we were younger, people had trouble telling us apart. I've often suspected that that was why Uncle Dennis tossed us both into the Fleet program: he wanted to make damn sure he got Abner."

Premonition washed over her. Twins were halves of a whole, one male and one female soul, complementing each other. Kularians considered same-gender twins to be an aberration, a single soul divided between two bodies. Apparently, the Humans let such a litter live. So Abner's father and Gael Dedrick's father had been same-gender twins, and now their singleton offspring, each the fruit of half a seed, were physically similar as well?

And if Abner had been as cruel to his daughter as he'd been to his cousin—!

"You're going to scare that poor young one out of whatever wits she has left," she told him, fighting to keep her voice steady. "She'll think you're Abner, risen from the dead."

"I know. I've been thinking about how to introduce myself so that doesn't happen." A pause, then, "I'll let you and Doctor Deneuve know once I've made my decision. Is there anything else I can do for you?"

His words conjured an image before her mind's eye that instantly tightened her loins and stiffened her fur. Stuffing her hands into the pockets of her lab coat, Ixbeth cleared her throat and said, in as professional a voice as she could muster, "You know that Captain Takamura has assigned us to Lania's case."

A flare of resentment, quickly smothered. Ixbeth swallowed reflexively to clear the unpleasant taste from the back of her throat. It was a symbolic gesture, like the hand to her temple. The taste would last as long as his resentment did. "Yes, he told me. Actually, he ordered me."

"I'm sorry about that, Commander. But I've been getting things ready for her and I wanted to bring you up tc date." *Busy. Stay busy. Focus on details.* Ixbeth pulled cut her miniscribe and paged forward to the list she'd made. "Ensign Park has agreed to be her tutor, Crewmember Topsias to orient her and guide her around the ship, and Ensign Bailey to supervise her recreational activities. When you're on duty, of course. And whenever you need a break.

"And there's me as well. Once we've completed a full psychological assessment, I'll be closely monitoring her adjustment to life aboard ship."

"Well, it sounds as though you have everything completely under control," he remarked.

She jammed her hands back into her pockets. *Oh! If only he knew!*

For a long, silent moment, Ixbeth stood staring into Gael Dedrick's face, punching the insides of her pockets and sifting her thoughts.

"I've suspended your rescreening," she offered, "so that we can focus on your cousin."

"That's probably a good idea."

"Commander, if you ever need to talk, or if there's anything else I can do for you...?" Ixbeth heard herself utter these words and was appalled. *Disvan* must be dissolving her brain. How could she hope to help that traumatized young female if she couldn't even help herself? The slightest movement of clothing against fur was sending shock waves through her entire body. Any moment now, the bottoms of her pockets would give way under the pummeling of her tightly-curled fists.

Those *incharna* eyes were devouring her again. "Are you all right, Doctor? You look kind of tense."

She wanted to laugh. Tense? Tense didn't begin to describe what she was feeling at that moment. "I'm fine," she told him, not surprised that he didn't believe her. "I'd better go now."

Gael Dedrick's curiosity and bemusement followed her out the door.

15

Lania pulled the wagon steadily up the slope from the rockbed. It wasn't a steep incline. She only had to be careful to avoid the ruts and dips in the path and keep the wheels turning until she reached the top, where the road leveled off just beyond the first burned-out homestead.

The nightmares had finally subsided. Abner's spirit was back in the ground where it belonged. And once she'd been able to get a full night's sleep and could think straight, Lania had come up with a plan to keep him there.

Once every seven days during the warm season, she followed the stream down to the lake. The round stones that lined the shallows came in different sizes and several deep shades of gray. She collected enough to cover the bottom of the wagon and then pulled it back along the path to where Abner was buried. And once every seven days, after dumping another load of stones onto his grave, she felt a little more securely in possession of Dedrick's Planet. She had decided not to rename it. After all, Lania reasoned, she was a Dedrick too.

There was a fresh, moist breeze off the lake this morning. She turned her face into the redolent mist and inhaled deeply. Over time, the planet had replaced the sickly aroma of death with its own strong perfumes — the water rose and jezebel that grew along the shores of the lake, and the pleasantly sharp scent of ripe creamberries wafting from the field beside the ship.

Abner had never let Lania or her mother pick the berries. At season's end, he would go out each day with two large buckets and bring them back brimming with the tart-tasting fruit for Rose to compote. She cooked them together with ice apples, which would otherwise have been unbearably sweet.

And she always knew just how much fruit would be needed to feed her family through the coming year.

The cool season was beginning. If Lania were still farming, she would have to plant her below-ground crops now. And she would have to lay in a supply of firewood to keep her warm at night, and harvest all the fruit and wild nut trees, and store the baskets in the shed.

Soon the night temperatures would dip lower and the sun would lose the strength to bring them back up. The ground would chill her bare feet. All the flowers would disappear. The water rose blossoms would tumble from their stalks and blacken the surface of the lake with their withered remains. The jezebels would close their fiery orange and purple petals and go to sleep. The burrilweed would grow dry and brittle, scattering crisp little shards at the touch of each passing breeze.

The grasses never changed, of course. They stiffened a little in the cold nights, but they endured. Endurance had always been the key to survival on Dedrick's Planet.

Finally Lania reached the top of the slope. The narrow road stretched out before her, following the crest of a ridge from which she could see almost every homestead site in the settlement. Cleansing fire had reduced them all to little blackened heaps. Automatically, she glanced across the stream and identified the ruin that had once been her mother's home.

Minutes later, she was there.

Lania stopped and stared in horror. It looked as though something — or someone — had dragged itself out of the middle of the rubble, heading in the direction of the forest.

Impossible.

All at once an icy hand was at her throat, cutting off her breath. Then a bolt of terror shot through her, and Lania dropped the tongue of the wagon and ran. Gasping and wild-eyed, she raced through the forest, over the hills, beyond the thicket to the clearing, to the hillock with the opening in its side.

Sweating and shivering, she staggered through the door of her cave and collapsed on the floor beside her computer.

"Oh," she moaned, every breath sharper than a knife in her ribs, "oh, please, help me..."

The computer screen blinked on.

WHAT IS WRONG, LANIA?

"They're here — someone — I don't know," she sobbed. "They're here."

WHO IS HERE?

"I don't know!" she cried, nearly choking on her own voice. "But there are cinders and ashes lying all across the front of my mother's house. Maybe it's Abner's ghost."

YOU SAW HIS GHOST?

"No, of course not," she sighed, her heartbeat beginning to slow at last. "I'm just worried because someone else is here and I don't know who it could be."

Promptly, the computer screen repainted:

ALIEN VISITORS

DISEASE CONTROL AGENTS VERIFYING THE STATUS OF THE COLONY

ATMOSPHERIC DISTURBANCE

SEISMIC IRREGULARITY

The computer went on to list several more possibilities, but Lania's attention was riveted on the first line, as her lips formed the word she could not bring herself to pronounce aloud.

Thryggians.

Abner had threatened Rose and Lania so often with that word. He had made a point of telling them both that the Thryggians weren't done with them yet, that the aliens were out there, searching every planetary system for Rose and her offspring.

And now someone else was on Dedrick's Planet. Nowhere was Lania safe anymore, not even on this beautiful, deadly world that her father had claimed as his own.

She had to get away. The ship. The control room had eyes and ears now. Her computer would give it a brain, with luck also a soul. Time was running out. She couldn't wait for this ship to finish waking up on its own. If the computer couldn't make it want to protect her, her life would be over the moment she was found. And she had fought too hard for her freedom and had sacrificed far too much to let that happen.

Nobody — not Abner, not the Thryggians — was ever going to own her again.

16

Commander Dedrick was an experienced pilot. He set the short-hop vehicle down gently in an open field about a hundred paces from the coordinates supplied by the ship's computer.

Seen from orbit, planet MF-307 was a small green ball wearing a belt of fluffy clouds around its equator. Seen close up, it was a fairytale landscape of lush green hills and valleys, sparkling streams, and thick stands of trees, some with rubbery, funnel-shaped leaves.

The countryside seemed to be holding its breath, waiting for birdsong, for the chattering of tree rodents. It would wait forever. This world was plague-dead. There were lethal toxins in the soil and the water. Nothing was safe to eat here. Nothing was safe to touch. Only the plants and one young female had survived.

Life out of death.

Ixbeth shuddered. There were several good reasons for her not to be on the planet's surface when first contact was made, but Captain Takamura had given his order and that was that.

The rescue team numbered five altogether: Commander Dedrick, Dr. Deneuve, Ixbeth, and a pair of security officers. They were all wearing bright yellow envirosuits to prevent their coming into physical contact with anything that might be carrying Angel of Death's toxins. The security backup had been additional protection ordered by Takamura. Emotionally disturbed people were unpredictable. The girl might have a weapon.

Or she might *be* a weapon.

Life out of death, dealing out death.

Ixbeth shuddered again.

At least Commander Dedrick had conceded that his resemblance to his cousin Abner made him a poor choice for first contact with the girl. Deneuve was the smallest, had a Human face, and was therefore the least threatening member of the group. As she stepped through the thicket into a clearing with a large grassy hillock at its center, the others hung back, concealed by a stand of heavy-boled trees.

At first, Ixbeth tasted only hopefulness and anxiety — Deneuve's. Then, amazingly, a young Human female appeared. She seemed to step right out of the hillock, parting the grass as if it were a curtain. Barefoot, Lania was closer to Ixbeth's height than Deneuve's, with a thick fall of dark brown hair that partly concealed the shoulder straps of her green coveralls. Her face was angular, her eyes as dark and challenging as Dedrick's own. Ixbeth had only a moment to take this in, for all at once:

Defiance! Fear! They hit her like hammer blows, the second Lania and Deneuve locked eyes. Then, her scalp already in knots, Ixbeth gasped as she was hit again, this time by possessiveness and hatred.

Unmistakably, this was Abner's offspring.

Concern. "What is it?" whispered Dedrick, crouched behind a neighboring tree.

Ixbeth pressed her lips together and carefully shook her head. It felt precariously connected, as though any sudden movement might tumble it off her shoulders. The base of her tail was aching as well. And *disvan* wasn't helping. It was distorting her senses, making the young one's emotions taste odd.

From a reassuring distance, Deneuve was introducing herself to the girl and explaining in a calm, gentle voice why she'd come. It wasn't working.

"She's not going to cooperate," Ixbeth whispered back through gritted teeth.

Then Deneuve mentioned the word 'guardian'.

Lania sidled away from the hillock and glanced behind her. Suddenly dizzy, Ixbeth laid a hand on the corrugated tree trunk to steady herself.

Pity and frustration. Ixbeth swung her gaze and found Dedrick's *incharna* eyes trained on her face. His expression was strained. His emotions were crisp and definitely Human. Lania's were not. *Disvan* had nothing to do with it.

At that moment the girl's terror exploded inside Ixbeth's head. Tears streamed down her cheeks as she leaned helplessly against the tree. This wasn't right. It shouldn't be happening.

"Go back and tell them you couldn't find me," Lania was shouting at Deneuve. "I don't need any guardian! I belong to myself!"

"All right, that's enough," Dedrick growled, and he charged into the clearing.

The child's panic when she saw him was more than Ixbeth could absorb. She cried out and sank to the ground, dimly aware of Humans galloping past her.

Lania was running away. Too slowly, as the distance between them increased, the vise that felt as though it had been crushing Ixbeth's skull loosened its grip.

She sensed Deneuve at her side, Dedrick hovering anxiously.

"She's barely conscious," Deneuve told him. "At least her pulse rate is back on the scale."

Guilt. "We shouldn't have brought her here. The risk was too great. I should have questioned the captain's orders."

More guilt. "No, I should have belayed them. I knew better than anyone what could happen, and I have the authority to countermand. *Merde!* Her pulse is back up."

Life out of death, dealing out death...

...to Ixbeth? Had the prophecy been warning her of danger? The danger of undertaking a Reyot Quest without the necessary training? Thank the stars she was *aisvanu*, then, more sensitive to the male who had inspired it and less sensitive to anyone else.

Ixbeth lay on her back, staring up at a distant green and blue blur. She heard the sound of someone moaning in pain and realized dully that it was her own voice.

Tal had been right. She should have let him bond with her before she left Dimmla. He had been trying to persuade her when he let her sense how badly he wanted to join her on the Quest. Ixbeth had reacted badly to the pressure. But she should have known her brother better. Tal loved her. They were halves of a whole. He might occasionally go against her wishes, but he would never act against her best interests.

Tal, I was wrong. I wish you were here to help me. Ixbeth conjured her brother's face into her mind's eye, visualizing his blunt features, generous mouth, unruly red mane.

I am here, whispered his voice, *and I'm glad you've finally come to your senses.*

You're here? You're real?

Yes. Together, victory, my sister.

A tide of joy swelled Ixbeth's heart. Tears of relief joined her tears of agony.

There are corners of your mind where the pain can't reach, whispered Tal. *Let me guide you there.*

His eyes were softly glowing amber pools, waiting to envelop her in warmth and peace. With a grateful sigh, Ixbeth surrendered to their pull. She tumbled down, into a dark, silent place of perfect tranquility. There, free of pain at last, she let herself be rocked gently to sleep.

—— «» ——

Lania was near the top of a rubberleaf tree, somewhere in the forest. She had no memory of crossing the stream, but the legs of her coveralls were wet. She had no memory of climbing the tree either, but there she was, desperately hugging a topmost branch as tears burned their way down her cheeks.

There were footsteps approaching. Lania clung even more tightly to her perch and concentrated on breathing as slowly and silently as possible. Her coveralls were green. As long as she didn't move, maybe the intruders would think she was part of the foliage.

The footsteps stopped directly beneath her. She squeezed her eyelids shut and gritted her teeth, willing whoever it was to keep on walking.

"Found her!" called a man's voice. Then she heard him sigh deeply. "Come on, little lady. This game is over. I'm not going anywhere, and you can't stay up there indefinitely."

Lying motionless on her branch, Lania swallowed a sob.

"Come on down," he told her, his voice sharpening with impatience. "Nobody's going to hurt you." A pause, then, "Don't make me climb up after you," he warned. When she didn't respond, he added in a barely audible mutter, "Gawd, I *hate* climbing trees."

Her arms and legs were beginning to ache. Lania lay as quietly as she could, her vision clouded by tears.

"I can see you, you know," he pointed out.

She heard more footsteps and voices approaching.

"Well," he concluded, "since you won't come down here, I guess I'll just have to go up there."

Lania's branch shivered with his climbing. A moment later, she was shivering too. She could feel her grip loosening, her body peeling away from the tree like old bark. She lifted her head and peered over her shoulder. His eyes locked onto hers. They were the eyes of a predator closing in on its prey...

...and in that instant her mind fled inward, leaving behind it a hull of meat and gristle that tumbled senselessly through lashing layers of branches before landing with a sharp crack on the forest floor. She felt a wave of agonizing pain. And then she retreated further, to the deepest, most peaceful corner of her being, where nothing could hurt her anymore.

——— «» ———

"Okay, first things first. To whoever finds this voice log: the ship and everything aboard her belongs to me."

Of course it did, thought Gael grimly. Abner had been like a black hole practically from the moment he was born. Everything was coming to him and nothing was given up once it was in his possession. And God help anyone who tried to steal from him, as the Thryggians had apparently learned the hard way.

Strictly speaking, it was not Gael Dedrick's responsibility to listen to the log from his cousin's disabled ship But if Lania was Abner's daughter, then her life on MF-307 couldn't have been easy. If he was to help her, Gael needed to find out as much as possible about her past. And so he'd uploaded a copy of the log to his personal compupad before turning the file over to the *Marco Polo*'s Communications Officer.

Even before the playback began, Dedrick had known it would be difficult, even painful to listen to. Abner's voice speaking for just a couple of seconds on the settler's vidclip had sent a mortal chill through him. Memories had resurfaced that made it hard for him to sit still. They'd both been children back then, and Gael had had a mother determined to protect him from Abner's abuse. What, he wondered, had Lania had?

There was only one way to find out. Abner had routinely blamed everyone but himself for whatever went wrong in his life. If anyone had gotten in his way on MF-307, he would have ranted about it in his log. Gael would have to review every excruciating minute of the recording, for Lania's sake, and pray that when she came out of her coma there would actually be something he could do to help make her world right.

——— «» ———

Slowly the darkness parted, and Lania became conscious again. First she was aware of the weight of her body, of lying on her back on a warm, yielding surface. Then she felt the pressure of something gripping her arm, and the sensation of the arm being stuck with pins. She moaned and tried to pull free, but that only increased the pressure and the pain.

"*Ssh*, lie still." A cool hand was stroking her forehead. For a second, Lania thought it might be her mother's. And then a scalding wave of memories flooded her mind, bringing tears of rage to her eyes.

Rose was dead. Abner had killed her. Lania had been sure he was dead too. But she'd been wrong. Somehow his malevolent spirit had survived and taken form once again. And then he had waited patiently, choosing the cruelest possible moment to snatch away her hard-won freedom. And he'd taken her — where? Where was she? Lania reached out with her senses. There was a strange smell in the air, an odor like tater-alc. And a sound, a barely-heard purring of distant machinery. And power. It resonated inside her like the power she'd awakened in her father's ship, only these vibrations felt different somehow.

"You're safe, Lania," said the suddenly familiar voice. It was the yellow-haired woman, the doctor. And she was lying. If Abner was nearby, Lania was anything but safe right now.

Cautiously she raised her eyelids, just enough to see where she was. What she saw was a room like her cave, but much larger. The outer walls were gray and shiny, and the ceiling was crisscrossed with narrow metal pipes that stuck into the walls instead of curving down along them. And there were other, transparent walls that divided the room into cells, each with a bed and a chair and nothing else — and Lania was a prisoner inside one of them.

The doctor leaned over her, blocking her view. Lania heard another voice murmuring something. "Good! I'll be there in just a minute," the doctor replied. "I thought she was stirring. I guess I was wrong. However, her readings are back up to normal, so it's just a matter of time now. I'm programming the regen unit to release the arm once the bone is seventy percent mended. With luck, she'll be awake before then."

Soft footsteps receded. Then there was silence.

Lania waited several long minutes to be sure she was alone, then glanced in the direction of her left arm. It was extended at right angles to her body and trapped inside a large metal sleeve, from shoulder to wrist. So this was a healing device? It was much too slow. With a sigh, Lania reached inward with the fingers of her mind and found and held her focus. Then she gathered the energies of her being and poured them into her injured arm in a cool, soothing stream.

A short while later, the device unclamped. Lania pulled her arm free and flexed it experimentally. Seventy percent didn't feel good enough to be usable. Once she had escaped from this little room, she would hide somewhere and finish the job right.

The transparent walls were a lot stronger than they looked, and the door had some sort of mysterious locking mechanism. The only way for her to leave her cell, Lania soon realized, would be if someone released her. She was safe here, all right — until Abner came and picked her up.

Had she only dreamt about killing him? Was she dreaming now? No, she decided, he was real, and just as mean as she remembered him. She would need two good arms when he walked through that door. She had made herself a promise and she would keep it, no matter how many times she had to kill him. If necessary, she would do it with her bare hands. But first she needed a safe corner in which to heal.

There wasn't enough room under the bed, so she settled for tucking herself into the narrow space between it and the chair. Lania leaned her back against the wall, drew up her legs, and wedged her arms as close to her body as possible. Then she closed her eyes and gathered all the energies of her being once more, assuring herself, *This shouldn't take long.*

—— «» ——

Ixbeth swam slowly to the surface of her mind and reached out, sense hairs registering a small, warm presence beside her — no weapons, a negligible threat. Only then did she become aware of a slightly yielding surface beneath her, a faint chemical smell in the air, and the soft, pervasive humming of engines. Concern. Frustration. Relief. A strange mixture of emotions, but very Human. She must be aboard the *Marco Polo*.

Warily, Ixbeth opened her eyes and rolled onto her back. The first thing that slid into focus was Deneuve's smiling face. Then, pale green walls and ceiling, with pipes crisscrossing overhead.

A moment later the itching was back as well. Ixbeth's hands searched for pockets to punch but found none. Stars!

"Welcome back," said Deneuve. "Do you know where you are?"

"Medical Services. Rehab?"

"Good guess. Now, can you tell me where you've been for the past four hours?"

"Four hours?"

"That's how long you've been unconscious. Commander Dedrick has been buzzing me every ten minutes to ask about you. You scared him half to death. You scared us *both* half to death," scolded Deneuve. "What happened down there?"

Ixbeth wanted desperately to tell her, but it was impossible. She and Tal were still in a cycle of concealment. "I ... found a way to escape from the pain."

Dismay. "By putting yourself into a coma?"

"Actually, it's more like jumping into a hole and pulling it in after you."

Deneuve sighed. Tasting her growing impatience, Ixbeth fell silent. "And how are you feeling now?" asked Deneuve. "Sit up and tell me, is there any dizziness, blurred vision, weakness in your limbs?"

Obediently, Ixbeth levered herself up, moved her arms and legs, then took a deep breath and expelled it slowly. "I'm fine, Doctor. Could I have my lab coat, please?"

Life out of death...? Tal reminded her gently.

I know! Don't push.

"So, besides being empathic, members of your race have the ability to render themselves unconscious at will?" Despite the sharpness of Deneuve's voice, there was no real anger behind her words.

"Not at will, Doctor. I had no idea I could do that until it happened. I apologize if it caused you concern."

"Concern? My concern is how to present this to the captain. He's already displeased over the outcome of the rescue mission. I'm sure he'll have a few choice things to add when he reads the follow-up reports. In the meanwhile, my diagnosis for your data chart will be that you passed out from the intensity of the pain," Deneuve decided. "Your alien physiology responding to extreme stress will be the probable explanation for all the depressed readings on my instruments."

"Depressed readings? How depressed?"

"Near cessation of heart, lung, and brain activity. If you were a Human patient, I would have described your condition as imminently morbid and ordered a death vigil. But since you're an alien, apparently even to yourself, I'm just going to record this and move on." Deneuve cocked her head then and demanded, "Did you pick up a skin irritation on that planet?"

"No. Why do you ask?"

"When Humans fidget like that it means they're itching."

Ixbeth sighed. It appeared that *disvan*, like her ability to taste emotions, could not be kept secret for long. "It is a kind of itch, Doctor, but this is not a skin irritation."

Sudden dread. "When did it start?" When Ixbeth hesitated, confused by what she was tasting, Deneuve snapped, "This is serious, Doctor. I need to decide whether to put you into Isolation. When did it start?"

Given her current condition, Isolation might not be such a bad idea, Ixbeth reflected. Then Tal shot her a jab of disapproval and she replied, "It began five days ago, and it should be over any time now."

Puzzlement. "Why didn't you come into Med Services, then, for—?" Deneuve broke off as comprehension dawned. "You're in heat," she declared. Then, to Ixbeth's amazement, the Human burst out laughing.

"There's nothing comical about this, Doctor."

"No, of course not," Deneuve acknowledged, struggling to regain her professional composure. "But, *mon dieu*, I was having visions of some unknown strain of the plague being brought aboard ship and wiping us all out. And to discover that it's just—! I'm sorry. To you it's not *just* anything. But sometimes, when we're nervous or we feel that we've had a very narrow escape, Humans will laugh. There's no disrespect intended." About to giggle once more, she turned the spasm into a cough, then cleared her throat and inquired with a smile, "Are you terribly uncomfortable?"

Ixbeth could feel Tal's urgency tugging at her thoughts. "It's nothing I can't manage. What about the young one, Doctor? Is she aboard?"

Sorrow wiped away the Human's grin. "She's in Isolation with a regen unit on her arm and a concussion. To get away from the security detail, she ran into the woods and climbed a tree. One of the men climbed after her. He says he never touched her. She just closed her eyes and fell eight meters to the ground. Broke her left arm in two places and knocked herself out. Last time I checked, she was still unconscious. Head trauma is a serious injury for a Human, Doctor Minegar. It could be a long time before she wakes up."

We can't wait, Tal whispered.

Ixbeth had to agree with him. "Nonetheless, would it be permitted for me to look in on her? She's my patient too."

Suspicion. Her lips pursed, Deneuve saved Ixbeth's chart and cleared the screen. "You know," she began, "since you came aboard ship, I've seen your reactions to all kinds of Human emotions. Some of the rescreenings you've done must have been quite painful for you. But I've never seen you as incapacitated as you were earlier today by that child. You're quite right — we share the responsibility for her. That means we should be sharing information about her as well. So tell me, Doctor Minegar, is there something I should know about *our* patient? Or perhaps there's something I should know about *you*. Are the effects of your condition more serious than you're letting on?"

For a moment Ixbeth debated with herself, and with Tal. Finally she said, "It wasn't me. Her emotions were more forceful than anything I'd had to deal with before."

"Have you any idea why?"

"It's only a suspicion."

A flare of annoyance. "Come on, you're a scientist. Hypothesize."

"It's just an instinct, Doctor. Her emotions tasted different. Not like Human feelings. I'm sorry I can't be more clear about this, but..."

Deneuve sighed and shook her head. "It's all right. What you sensed could be the reason she survived the plague. We'll just have to continue testing her and see what develops. But, considering how her emotions affect you, are you sure it would be wise for you to—?"

"No, I'm not. As a healer, however, I owe her my best effort."

The grin returned to Deneuve's lips, if not to her eyes. "In that case, *Doctor*, you're discharged. You know where the Isolation Unit is. Go put on a lab coat and visit your patient. I'll inform Commander Dedrick that you've recovered. More or less."

Your superior is right, you know, Tal warned her. *If you walk in there unprepared and the young one is conscious, she'll only flatten you again.*

Ixbeth paused outside the Isolation Unit door, sensing overwhelming fear and rage on the other side. Even with the blunting effect of *disvan*, it felt as though her scalp was trying to peel itself off her head.

Tal, tell me what to do!

You need to project a different emotion into her. You can do this, Ixbeth. With practice, you'll be able to do it at will. What do you want her to feel?

I need her to trust me.

Then you need to trust yourself, totally and implicitly. You can only project an emotion that you feel yourself. Do you honestly believe that this young female embodies part of the prophecy?

Yes, I believe she does.

Then do you trust the oracle that chose you to receive it? Do you trust your own commitment to the Quest? Heart-sister, do you trust yourself as much as I trust you to carry it out?

It rippled into her mind then, a gentle spreading warmth like loving hands caressing the very core of her awareness — Tal's trust in her, given without reservation. Ixbeth opened herself and let the emotion blossom within her. It filled her completely, calming and strengthening her. At once, the pain in her head subsided to a dull, barely noticeable ache.

This is our shield, Ixbeth, whispered Tal. *It protects us from the emotions of others and it bonds us in pairs, mate to mate and brother to sister, as it has always done. As it will continue to do until our people are no more.*

Anxiety. "Are you all right, Doctor?"

Ixbeth turned to face Deneuve and smiled. "Yes, I'm fine. The patient is awake. Let's go talk to her."

Entering the Isolation Unit, Ixbeth found the source of the rage and terror that were thickening the air all the way to the Trauma room. Lania crouched on the deck beside her bed like a wounded animal gone to ground. She had made herself as small as possible. And her eyes, those *incharna* eyes, drilled right through the transparent walls of her prison and fastened unblinking on Ixbeth's face, glaring defiance.

Life out of death…

…must be fierce to survive. You are not her enemy, Ixbeth. Just keep your shield strong and do as I instruct you.

Puzzlement. Annoyance. "That regen unit must be defective," remarked Deneuve. "It's programmed not to release until the bone is seventy percent mended."

"Perhaps it *is* seventy percent mended, Doctor," Ixbeth replied. Maintaining eye contact with the cornered girl, she sank slowly to her knees.

Reach out to her, Ixbeth, with your mind and your heart. You are filled with trust in yourself. Share what you are feeling. Think of the fire bugs, their swarm a ribbon of golden light. Imagine their glow penetrating this barrier, illuminating the darkness between you, entering her body. Picture the light filling her heart with trust and confidence, forcing out every other emotion.

At last, the young girl's brow smoothed, her lips parted, her limbs relaxed. Her body released its tension in a sigh. Ixbeth heard its echo behind her and realized that Deneuve must have been holding her breath. *Incharna* eyes blinked curiously, as though awakening from a dream. Not until Lania reached out voluntarily to press her hand to the barrier, however, did either female speak.

"I am Ixbeth. I am a Dimmlesi."

Wonderment. "Can I touch you?"

Deneuve now crouched at Ixbeth's side. Tasting amusement, Ixbeth murmured to her, "Is this normal behavior for an adolescent Human girl, Doctor?"

Deneuve murmured back: "No, but these aren't normal circumstances. Don't be alarmed, Ixbeth. Just keep her calm as long as you can. Hello, Lania," she said brightly, speaking in conversational tones once more. "I'm Doctor Deneuve. Do you remember me?"

A flare of anger. Yes, Lania remembered betrayal very well.

"You're in the Medical Services department of our ship," Deneuve continued. "There was an accident on the planet. You were badly hurt, so we brought you here to heal."

Skepticism. "And once I'm healed, will you send me back home?"

"You mean back to the planet? That isn't my decision to make, I'm afraid."

"It's *his* decision, isn't it? My guardian." Lania spat the word out as though it were something foul-tasting that she had unexpectedly found in her mouth.

You're the only one she'll trust, sister. Say something, Tal urged.

"On my world, guardians are called by a different name," Ixbeth told her. "We are called defenders, and our duty is to protect our community. In each family, parents and older sibs have a duty to protect the youngest ones, but if a young one has no family, then a defender is assigned to care for that child. You have been alone and without protection for a long time—"

Fear. "Then will you be my defender? Please?"

Ixbeth gazed a question at Deneuve.

"All right," Deneuve decided. "Doctor Minegar can be your defender, on one condition."

Dread. "What condition?"

"That you let Commander Dedrick be your guardian as well."

Tasting the child's growing defiance, Ixbeth added quickly, "Just because two people look alike, that doesn't mean they *are* alike. Once you get to know Gael Dedrick, you'll realize how different he is from Abner."

Uncertainty. "*Gael* Dedrick?"

"Your cousin. Abner is dead," Ixbeth assured her.

Mild skepticism. "Well ... all right, then. Maybe."

"If we've settled this little matter," Deneuve cut in, "then I must ask the defender to step aside while the doctor examines the patient."

"I'm fine now," Lania protested. "I'm healed."

"That was a nasty fall you took, young lady, so if you don't mind, I would like to verify your condition for myself. Would you get up onto the bed, please?"

Watching Deneuve suit up to enter the Isolation cubicle, Ixbeth couldn't help sharing her concern. At the moment, Lania trusted her defender, and she had more or less agreed to keep her fingerclaws retracted around Gael Dedrick. But what would happen if he began barking orders at her again? Would she launch another barrage of fear and hatred? And then there were the medical anomalies: the disappearing concussion, the alien-tasting emotions, and the broken arm that had apparently knitted in a matter of hours.

Ixbeth sighed and pressed her fists deeply into her lab coat pockets.

"You know, I would have bet anything that you would end up on a Trauma table yourself when she woke up," Deneuve murmured drily. "So what happened? No, don't tell me. You discovered another of those special Dimmlesi talents that you were unaware you had, right?"

"Am I now a mystery to solve, Doctor?"

Ironical amusement. "Maybe later, when I have some spare time." In a whisper, she added, "I don't know how you did it, but I'm really glad you found a way to reach her."

How were you able to do that? Ixbeth wondered as she rode the Personnel Transport System to her quarters. *You heard me calling you in my thoughts, all the way from Dimmla. But I rejected the bonding.*

According to the Dr'rava Kula'as, every Kularian is a latent telepath, Tal explained. *Normally, there are two ways to establish a telepathic bond. The first is by mating. The second is with a litter twin. In the womb, twins share consciousness through the soul cord. When it dissolves, shortly before birth, it leaves the kits with pieces of each other's consciousness in their minds. We've always been bonded, Ixbeth. Only our common desire was required to activate the connection. That is why I've trained so hard in the mental discipline. I'm a level nine adept now. With the help of the brotherhood, we should be able to remain connected, sharing thoughts and feelings, no matter how great the distance.*

That was what you meant when you said nothing would be done without my consent, wasn't it? But why did you talk as though—?

I had to make you aware of the possibility. We cannot desire what we don't know exists.

No. We can desire it, my brother. We just cannot say its name.

Ohe'elu, Tal whispered.

17

Lania spent most of the afternoon in Isolation, undergoing tests. Finally Deneuve discharged her, satisfied that she posed no medical risk to the ship's personnel, and Ixbeth took her via the PTS to Commander Dedrick's quarters. Dedrick was on duty. She and Lania would have the place to themselves for the next several hours.

Thank the stars!

Lania had been serious about wanting to stroke Ixbeth's fur. Since they were alone in the tube car, Ixbeth decided to permit it. Lania's touch was quite gentle. If Ixbeth hadn't been *disvanu* she would probably have enjoyed the sensation. As it was, she thought she could feel stitches giving way at the bottom of her lab coat pocket.

At the end of their tube car ride, Lania stood in her cousin's living area, gazing about her in wonderment. Ixbeth carefully sampled the girl's emotional aura — and was astonished. No corrosive guilt. No self-loathing. No despair. No death wish. None of the emotions that Ixbeth's research into sole survivor syndrome had prepared her to encounter. In fact, the young one's aura contained very little emotion of any kind. It was almost as though she were muting her feelings. Was that possible?

Ixbeth did it routinely, of course, even among the Humans. It was the first social skill any Kularian kit learned. But it was a *social* skill, acquired and practiced in the presence of others who were *vanu*, and that was the second impossibility in Lania's situation. She was the sole survivor of a Human colony, and Humans were by definition emotionally unconnected. Down on the planet's surface and in the Isolation cubicle, Lania had spewed out fear and anger uncontrollably. They'd struck Ixbeth like a volley of weapons fire. And suddenly these feelings didn't exist? There was something very unusual going on here.

Ixbeth tried again to taste her emotions. Mild anxiety, some curiosity — these were to be expected when one was among strangers in totally unfamiliar surroundings. But where was the fear of meeting her 'guardian' again? Where was the anger at being uprooted from her home? Where was the frustration of being demoted to child again after living on her own for an entire standard year? Human or alien, Lania couldn't be a sentient being and not be experiencing these to some degree. No Kularian projection of trust could obliterate them entirely.

Among Ixbeth's errands of the morning had been a visit to the quartermaster with a last-minute list of supplies to be delivered to the commander's suite. It had taken almost an hour to make the vacant sleeping module look like a proper bed chamber, but Ixbeth would have gone to greater lengths if necessary, to prevent a repetition of what had happened on the planet.

"This is the common area. Over here is your private space," said Ixbeth, gesturing toward the sliding door in the wall. "You may find it a little cramped at first, but you'll get used to it."

Curiosity. Lania stepped past her and began investigating her new bedroom, registering a mixture of pleasure and sadness when she found the wardrobe containing half a dozen changes of clothing.

"The quartermaster had those in stock," Ixbeth explained. "We had to guess at your size. If they don't fit or are not to your liking, she can order different ones for you."

Resignation. "They're all right."

"No, they're not," Ixbeth decided. "Draw up a list with all your favorite colors, and I'll take you foraging later."

Delight. A gasp of recognition.

"Lania, what—?"

But the child had already raced back to the common area. She stood there for a moment, her gaze searching the room.

Growing excitement. "Is one of those mine?" she asked, pointing at the computers on the commander's desk.

"Yes. Commander Dedrick ordered it brought aboard and installed for you. Go on," Ixbeth urged. "Test it out."

Poking around the clearing after Deneuve and her two patients had returned to the *Marco Polo*, Dedrick had discovered Abner's sprint craft concealed inside the hillock, and Lania's pallet, tool kit, and computer in its cargo bay. The supply lockers were filled with emergency food packs. The console in the control room had been opened up and rewired in ways that defied engineering logic. The computer was wired crazily too. Once it was aboard the *Marco Polo*, Mbuku wanted to repair it; but Dedrick had overruled him, reasoning correctly that it was more important to respect Lania's ownership of her possessions at this point than to have another working computer on board.

Mixed emotions, hard to identify. Slowly, Lania circled the desk. She halted half a meter away from the commander's large wood and leather chair and glanced questioningly at Ixbeth.

Recalling what Dedrick had told her about Abner, Ixbeth thought she understood the girl's hesitation. "Your father didn't like sharing his possessions."

Lania shook her head, her surfacing memories of wrath and hatred potent enough to bring Ixbeth's shield back up. So the emotions were there after all. Ixbeth wasn't sure whether to feel relieved or concerned.

She calmed herself as Tal had taught her and began projecting. "Lania, listen to me. Commander Dedrick is not Abner. He has some things that are all his, and he expects that you will have some things that are all yours. The rest are for sharing, like this desk and chair. Go ahead," she repeated. "Sit down. It won't bite you."

Lania trusted her defender, but just barely where her guardian was concerned. Cautiously, the young one sat. "Computer on."

GOOD MORNING, LANIA

Ixbeth's heart leaped. Mbuku had sworn up and down that this device did not and could not function. Lania had built it herself, assembling and wiring it in apparently random ways. It couldn't dissipate heat energy and it was only marginally compatible with the only available power sources. That disharmony alone should have prevented it from operating. Nonetheless, Dedrick had insisted that the Engineering Specialist hook the computer up exactly as they'd found it. To say that Mbuku had not been happy about this would be a gross understatement. He had left Dedrick's quarters shaking his head, utterly convinced that the 'mutant computer' was nothing but a fire hazard.

He should have been right; and yet, not only was the computer functioning, but even from a distance, Ixbeth could sense that all its parts were resonating in harmony.

An answering vibration began inside her chest. This was a bridge between technologies, like the one that she had earlier been attempting to create in order to read the information on her datacube. Ixbeth had failed, but Lania had not. Somehow, this child had used alien principles and Human-made parts to build herself a voice-activated computer that recognized her and addressed her by name but wouldn't work for anyone else.

Otherness unimaginable.

Life out of death, dealing out death.

Could that be why Avo'or had put her here? Were she and these Humans unknowingly on the same quest for truth?

Lania found her datawafers, selected one, and thrust it into the computer's drive slot.

"Read and execute program," she instructed it as Ixbeth sidled behind her for a better view of the screen.

WHAT WOULD YOU LIKE TO PAINT?

Sudden melancholy, unexpectedly strong but still manageable. Homesickness, Ixbeth guessed. "Landscape. Show me backgrounds."

Obediently, the computer quartered the screen. In each quarter Ixbeth saw a different kind of terrain: mountain, prairie, forest, marsh. And in each quarter of the screen the sky was dark and it was raining.

Lania touched the quarter containing the prairie. "Maximize this one," she continued. "In the foreground, a little girl. Six years old. Green blouse, white lace collar. Short yellow hair. Petting a pony. A gray and white pony with a shaggy white mane."

The screen refreshed to display what Lania had described. The little girl had a sweet, round face. And she was crying — standing in the rain, stroking the neck of an animal, and crying. Ixbeth's throat grew hot and tight as she let herself be drawn into the sharing of emotion. At the same time, her thoughts were racing. This couldn't be happening, shouldn't be possible, but there it was, in full and dreary color. Lania had never specified tears. Her sadness had clearly been picked up by the computer and incorporated into the image.

A machine with the heart of a child, Tal confirmed.

The door buzzer sounded. Reluctantly, Ixbeth called out, "Come in!"

A young woman in brown fatigues walked into the commander's quarters with a confident smile on her small, heart-shaped face. This was Alex Topsias, the youngest member of the *Marco Polo*'s crew, arriving right on schedule to take Lania on a tour of the ship.

Ixbeth introduced the girls to each other, carefully noting Lania's reaction to meeting someone who looked about her own age. Alex was unfailingly cheerful and optimistic, and today her mood appeared to be contagious. In the moment before Lania shut down the program to go on her tour, Ixbeth couldn't help noticing that the image on the screen had changed. It had stopped raining.

A machine with the heart of a child.

Lania had built this computer. The only way she could have made an emotional connection with it was by investing it somehow with a piece of her own consciousness. But was it possible to bond with a machine?

Yes, in a way, came her brother's response. *In ancient times, our people used their mental skills to operate a range of technological devices. Even today, members of the brotherhood can project more than emotions. They can use their minds to move objects, open and close circuits, even alter wavelengths and frequencies. I've seen it done.*

But those are Kularian talents, Tal. This child—

—is not Human, despite her appearance and what the others wish. She hurls her emotions to disable the enemy, like an ancient defender. She put herself into a healing sleep earlier, and that comes straight out of the Dr'rava Kula'as. After ten generations of concealment, we must look beyond appearances to find Kularian blood, my sister. But you cannot tell them about her without revealing your own heritage. They must discover her otherness on their own.

I know. And her emotional connection with the computer, is that an ancient Kularian skill as well?

Tal paused uncomfortably. *I'm not sure what it is. Be careful, Ixbeth, please. If this computer is the machine of the prophecy, it could be extremely dangerous.*

A machine with the heart of a child, she mused. Children were impulsive, unpredictable. And if this one had Lania's heart, then it probably shared her past and all her feelings as well. The anger. The resentment.

Life out of death, dealing out death, Tal reminded her.

And a tearful girl standing in the rain. Her brother's apprehension mated with her own, sending an icy trickle down Ixbeth's back.

——— «» ———

"I know where Angel of Death originated and how it was carried, and so does every other patient who left Thrygg that day."

Captain Takamura halted the playback and reclined in his chair with a sigh. "Plague dogs," he said, so softly that he might have been talking to himself. "It's a very primitive form of biological warfare, Mister Dedrick, used in ancient times on Earth. Animals were deliberately infected and then set loose in the enemy's territory to spread as much disease as possible among the civilian population. It tended to be quite demoralizing."

Seated across from his captain, Dedrick leaned forward, his expression taut, his jaw muscles working. "Are you saying the Thryggians were waging undeclared war, sir?"

Takamura shook his head. "No, I think your cousin got it right and they were simply using the strategy to set up an experiment, cleverly orchestrating it to circumvent their house arrest. In fact, it's quite likely that this sort of activity is the reason they're currently facing an interplanetary tribunal." He paused, a faint smile tugging at the corners of his mouth, before continuing, "An interplanetary tribunal that should include Abner Dedrick's testimony, wouldn't you agree? That was his original purpose in recording it, after all. And I think it's fitting as well that he be remembered for something positive, since he did save the Earth."

In response to Dedrick's quizzical stare, Takamura pointed out, "He stayed away from it."

—— «» ——

Lania followed Alex out of her guardian's quarters to the unmarked tube door at the far end of the hallway.

As they waited for the tube car to arrive, the other girl gazed sadly at her and said, "Commander Dedrick told me that your parents died of the plague. I'm sorry for your loss."

Not knowing how to answer, Lania shrugged. Clearly, people who lived in perfectly normal families assumed that everyone else did too.

"How long did you live down there?" asked Alex.

"Always."

"I envy you," Alex sighed, "being able to stay that long in one place. I was a space brat. My parents were divorced and posted to different hubs, so I got passed back and forth a lot. What did your people do?"

"We grew our own food, fixed things when they broke — just lived, I guess." *In pain*, she added mentally, *plotting to kill the monster and escape.*

The tube car door slid open then, and Alex ushered Lania inside.

"I think we'll start ... there," said Alex, pressing a sequence of numbers on the keypad.

As the tube car began to move, Lania glanced sideways at Alex, noticing the slender figure inside the brown and beige uniform, the thick tousle of short dark hair, the determined angle of the other girl's chin.

"How old are you, anyway?" blurted Lania.

Alex gave her a lopsided grin. "Now, that's a matter of some debate around the ship. According to my service record, I'm twenty-three Earth years old. But there are times when I feel much younger than that. And other times when I feel a whole lot older."

The tube car was moving steadily sideways. "How long is this ship?" Lania wondered aloud.

"A couple of kilometers, nose to thrusters. But it's not that far to the Arboretum."

The car paused, changed from horizontal to vertical motion, and climbed for a few seconds before changing back, this time catching Lania by surprise and nudging her momentarily off balance. Alex, she noticed, had kept her legs braced the whole time and didn't even sway.

"And what is an arbor — arbo—?" essayed Lania, just before all sideways motion stopped and the tube car door slid open.

Alex's reply was a smile.

They stepped out into a broad gray corridor. ARBORETUM, said the large sign on the double doors facing them.

"Come inside and find out," teased Alex, pressing her thumb to the button beside the doors.

As they sighed apart, Lania looked beyond them and saw a forest. Just like the one she had left behind on Dedrick's Planet, it had trees and vines and clumps of thick shrubbery.

"Are they real?" she whispered hopefully.

Alex's grin widened. "Come inside and find out," she repeated.

Lania took a deep breath and entered the woods.

Walking on something that looked and felt like a spongy, fragrant forest floor, the girls strolled past trees of every description. Doctor Deneuve had given Lania shoes to wear. Impulsively, she kicked them off.

She stared around her, at leaves and needles of every color, at berries and nuts and odd-shaped seedpods that nestled and perched and dangled overhead. Lania remembered the crunchy sweet pepperels she had gathered last year — and would be gathering right now if the commander hadn't come to gather *her* — and her mouth filled with longing to savor the wild fruit just once more.

She stopped and ran her fingertips over the rough bark of a tree that reminded her of the rubberleafs back on her home world. Lania broke off a chunk of the bark. It was pale and sticky on its underside, and she brought it to her nose and inhaled deeply, willing the smell of the sap to match her memories — but it didn't. It was just sweet and a little musty. With a disappointed sigh, she dropped the piece of bark on the ground at the foot of the tree.

"I saw that!"

Lania's breath caught in her throat. She whirled, ready to duck a blow, but the owner of the voice wasn't standing at her elbow as she'd thought. He was a dozen meters away, a wiry man with sharp features who repeated shrilly as he strode toward them, "I saw that! Don't deny it! I saw what you did to my *Novis Novis Gangliaris!*"

Stunned, Lania could only watch him approach, his white lab coat flapping around his knees at every step. When finally he stood face-to-face with her, she realized that they were almost exactly the same height. But he was an adult, she reminded herself with a shiver of familiar dread, and he obviously owned these trees.

"Well?" he prompted sternly. "You've trespassed in a botanical laboratory and willfully damaged an irreplaceable specimen. What do you have to say for yourself, young lady?"

Lania swallowed hard. She couldn't see a weapon on him, but that didn't mean he wouldn't punish her if she said the wrong thing. "I thought it was just a forest," she offered, her voice little more than a tremulous whisper.

He made a rude sound. "Aboard a star ship?"

"Professor Tam," cut in Alex. "This is Lania Dedrick, Commander Dedrick's ward. She just arrived aboard ship this morning."

He cleared his throat with a loud ha-*rumph*. "And that's supposed to make a difference?" he snapped.

"The commander suggested I bring her up here, just for a short while," said Alex, trying again. "He thought she might be a little homesick."

Tam's eyes narrowed thoughtfully. "All right, all right," he finally conceded, throwing his hands up in surrender.

"Walk around if you like. Only remember that this *forest* consists of specimens I've spent a lifetime collecting from many different planets, none of which I'll probably ever visit again. So I don't want anyone carving or plucking or *climbing* them. Do you understand?"

"Yessir," said Alex, nudging Lania with her elbow.

"Yessir," she echoed soberly.

A smile flickered briefly at the corners of Professor Tam's lips. As he turned and walked away, Lania suddenly felt very strange.

It began as a gentle vibration deep inside her, a tingling on its way to becoming an itch that flowed like a current through every part of her body. It buzzed maddeningly when it reached her ears. It made sparks dance inside her eyes, her nose, her mouth. It prickled her skin and made her limbs feel as though they were shrinking to little nubs. Lania floated gently to the ground, dimly aware of large shapes looming over her. And then everything winked out.

—— «» ——

Sitting in Deneuve's office, Ixbeth stared in disbelief at the medical readout on the screen.

"This can't be right," she protested. "According to this, almost every bone in her body is broken."

"*Was* broken," Deneuve corrected her. "Those are all old fractures. The reason they show up so clearly on the scan is that none of them were healed by regeneration. There were five units in that agricultural colony — it's standard medical equipment, included in every first aid kit. Every space vehicle is required by law to carry at least one. And yet, Lania told me she'd never seen a regen unit until today.

"I checked for bone disease or mineral deficiencies — any pathological condition that would increase her susceptibility to skeletal fracturing — and I found none." Deep sadness and rage. The creases around Deneuve's mouth were more pronounced than Ixbeth had ever seen them. "This image is proof that Lania must have suffered regular, severe beatings by an adult, someone who either denied her medical attention or was in a position to prevent her from receiving it."

As Abner's name hung unspoken between them, Ixbeth felt a chill touch her soul.

"Have you shared this with Commander Dedrick?"

Deneuve nodded. "He's been listening to the log his cousin Abner left on the sprint ship. It's the diary of an abuser. He manipulated them both, tormented them, isolated them. They weren't even allowed to talk to any of the colonists. Forget 'sole survivor syndrome' — we're into a whole other set of problems here."

"By both, do you mean Lania and her mother?"

Deneuve visibly composed herself before answering. "Her name was Rose. She was a fellow patient at the Thryggian medical research facility. When Abner escaped he took her with him. It wasn't a relationship, Ixbeth. The log makes it clear that he considered her to be his property, and we both know how Abner treated his toys. She became pregnant with Lania shortly after planetfall." Deneuve's voice faded to a harsh whisper. "Damn him! They were alone on that planet for years. Lania couldn't possibly be anyone else's child. And yet..."

"And yet?"

"Her DNA. It has more in common with yours than it does with Abner's."

Kularian blood? Ixbeth paused to fortify her emotional shield. "You mean it isn't Human?"

"It may have been Human to start with. Now I'm not sure what it is. I found additional chromosomes and unidentifiable gene groupings in all her body cells. At a guess, I'd say this could be the reason she survived exposure to Angel of Death. There isn't a trace of the virus or its toxins anywhere in her system. If I'm right, the big question is, how? If she inherited the immunity, then one or both of her parents should have survived the plague. If she mutated *in utero*, then whatever caused the mutation should have affected her parents' genes as well, giving them the same protection. But if her parents both died of the plague, then how—?" Sudden suspicion. Ixbeth could almost hear puzzle pieces clicking into place in the Human's mind. "*If* her parents died of the plague," Deneuve repeated thoughtfully. "Abner and Rose's remains are buried on the planet below us. It wouldn't be that difficult."

"Are you thinking of performing an autopsy?"

"Not yet. For now, all I need is a DNA sample from each of them, to confirm that they were in fact Lania's parents. Even if they were cremated first, some mitochondrial material should have survived inside bone fragments. Captain Takamura is planning to send a tech team down to check out the sprint craft. Maybe I can get them to—" Deneuve's next words were cut off by the blaring of a klaxon. Sharp annoyance. "What now?"

A strange wave passed over Ixbeth then, an almost tickling sensation that raised all the fur across her shoulders and caused her fingerclaws to try to extend. It also detonated the frustration that had been simmering inside Deneuve. "I don't believe this," she spat. "Where did you say that tribunal was in session, Doctor? I'd like to testify against those pirates myself."

So that was a Thryggian energy beam? Ixbeth hadn't even felt it the first time. Her reaction to Commander Dedrick's maleness had evidently been much stronger than she thought.

The deskcomm buzzed, startling both females. "Medical emergency coming into the Trauma room, Doctor," announced a male voice. "It's Lania Dedrick. She's unconscious."

PART VI

The Battle

Star cruisers *Marco Polo, Vasco da Gama, Magellan,* and *Columbus* formed the backbone of Earth's Deep Space Fleet. Designed to be self-sustaining over long periods of time, these vessels were staffed and equipped with the very best Earth had to offer. Their original ongoing mission was to discover sites for future colonization, make contact with other sentient species, and explore and chart the unknown reaches of Earth space. After the first outbreaks of Angel of Death, however, the star cruisers were pressed into emergency service, enforcing quarantines on plague-stricken planets and making food and supply drops to the colonists trapped on those worlds. By 2398 C.E. the plague had run its course in our arm of the galaxy, and the entire fleet was mobilized for a mop-up operation called Census/Relief/Evacuation. This translated to mass funerals on planets where there were no survivors, and food and medical supply drops to survivors awaiting processing and relocation. Records indicate that of the 58 colonies established prior to 2384 C.E., 24 were completely wiped out, at a cost of over 1.5 million lives.

— *Sic Transit Terra, An Unauthorized Planetary History*
(2673 C.E.)

Fleet Control Headquarters, Earth

MEMO

EARTH DATE: 10 March 2399

FROM: Matthew Freeman, Chief of Security

TO: Vice-Admiral Kendra Nelligan, Operations

ENCRYPTION LEVEL: Highest

Further to the Gate messages received from the *Marco Polo*, *Magellan*, and *Columbus* and forwarded to the Galactic Great Council on 26 February 2399:

We have received a prompt and patronizing reply to our request for assistance. The full version is attached, but the gist of it is that we're on our own. The 'flying egg' profile doesn't match anything Thryggian in the Central Archives databank. Therefore, until we can provide incontrovertible evidence that the unknown craft claiming to be Thryggian and harassing our ships in Earth space are actually being flown by Thryggians, the Great Council chooses to treat the matter as Earth's internal problem, while no doubt watching carefully to see how we handle it.

Personally, I would have no qualms about making an omelet out of those flying eggs and serving them up on a platter at the next session of the Great Council. If history is any indication, however, Earth High Council will almost certainly take a different view. Please keep that in mind when composing your next all-ships bulletin.

Best regards,
Matt

18

Alex Topsias was on the verge of tears. She had frozen, making it necessary for Doctor Tam to initiate the distress call from the Arboretum, and her feelings of guilt hung like a fog in the Trauma room.

Curiosity. Deneuve had drifted over to stand beside Ixbeth. "Lania's awake. I think she's going to be all right," the Human remarked. "She still doesn't know what hit her, but Commander Dedrick is with her right now, giving aid and comfort. Or trying to. What about Alex?"

"Alex will understand as she gets older that Humans learn from making mistakes."

Sadness and regret, quickly suppressed. "You mean *if* she gets older. Out here, some mistakes are more permanent than others. I've done some checking: while everyone aboard ship felt the Thryggian beam pass through, Lania was the only one it affected this way."

Disharmony, thought Ixbeth, recalling her ordeal in the SPA room.

"I can't help wondering why," Deneuve continued. "If they were looking for inorganic items, then none of us should have been affected, Human or not. If their sweep was meant to identify organic materials and they'd adjusted it to disregard Humans, then you and Lania should both have passed out."

Purposeful disharmony, Ixbeth amended. The young one had clearly been targeted. Detected. As soon as they realized this, the Thryggians would be back in force to take her.

To try, came Tal's urgent whisper. *They mustn't succeed. The Humans mustn't let them.*

Life out of death, she reminded him, *dealing out death. The child is a defender.*

Tal didn't reply to this, but she could taste his anxiety as a lingering sharpness at the back of her throat.

Meanwhile, Deneuve was murmuring, "This makes no sense. I must be missing something."

Ixbeth paused for a moment, sampling Deneuve's exasperation as she debated how best to respond. There was going to be a battle, one the Earth ship could easily lose. Given too little information, the Humans would underestimate the enemy and overestimate their chances. Given too much information, they might panic and freeze. Like Alex Topsias.

Together, victory.

"The Thryggians are geneticists, mainly," she said at last. "They like to experiment with the nucleic materials of other species. The reason they're on trial is that they have apparently never bothered to ask permission."

Deneuve stared at her for a long, tense moment before speaking. "You already know what I'm going to find when I analyze those mitochondrial DNA samples, don't you?"

"No, but to use your own words, Doctor, I'm a scientist, and I can hypothesize. In a genetics experiment, each introduced variant would have to be tagged in some way, to make it traceable from one generation to the next."

Deneuve was nodding her agreement. "That means the same markers should be present in Abner's and/or Rose's DNA as I detected in Lania's. All right. But that still doesn't—" Dawning horror. An audible intake of breath. "Yes, it does. *Mon dieu!* That's why she was the only one affected by that beam. And now that it's found her—!"

Warned by a sudden bitterness in her throat, Ixbeth stiffened her emotional shield just as Deneuve's outrage exploded into the room. "*That* was the stolen property the Thryggians were looking for?" the Human sputtered. "Please, tell me those pirates wouldn't actually claim ownership of a Human child!"

Of course they would. She was the offspring of Rose, the original stolen property, snatched by Abner Dedrick when he escaped from their home world. And they would fight to take her, destroying the Earth ship if they had to — but the Humans didn't need to know that yet.

"I wish I could tell you with certainty what to expect, Doctor, but I can't," Ixbeth said with a sigh. "As you have so often said to me, we need to take things one step at a time."

Impatience. "Yes, of course. First I need those samples from the surface, *stat*," Deneuve muttered. "If I can prove Lania's a Dedrick, Captain Takamura's path will be clear; and no matter what happens, the High Council will have no choice but to back him up."

Two hundred on a world, life out of death, and the machine with the heart of a child. All the elements for victory are here. Do you trust the prophecy, Ixbeth?

Deneuve's intuition was impressive, Ixbeth reflected as the Human bustled out the door. Soon she would have her proof and so would the Galactic Tribunal. Abner Dedrick had vandalized a laboratory before fleeing Thrygg, probably right after discovering what the Thryggians had done to him. It was, ironically, a textbook Human response.

Several minutes later, Deneuve returned to the Trauma room from her office, radiating frustration. "Captain Takamura won't authorize a separate mission," she fretted, "and he won't permit the tech team to bring any organic materials aboard the ship. Even though the virus isn't airborne, Disease Control has placed this planet under strict quarantine. He says the tech team is bending the rules already by going back down to investigate the sprint ship, and he doesn't want to press our luck. *Merde!* We have to be certain, Doctor. Intuition and probability are not good enough." Guilt. Dread. Deneuve glanced in the direction of Rehab. "Do you think Lania knows anything about the Thryggian experiment?"

Ixbeth repressed a shudder. What little she had learned about Abner at this point made her sure of one thing, at least: Lania would know about the Thryggians whatever Abner had seen fit to tell her, no doubt to instill fear so that he could control her more easily. Ixbeth raised and fortified her mental shield before following Deneuve through the doorway.

Lania had regained consciousness in Rehab and found an anxious Commander Dedrick sitting beside her bed. Although she visibly shrank away from physical contact with him, the young one was not as terrified as she'd been before. Either his evident concern for her well-being had short-circuited her fears, or Ixbeth's earlier projection of trust had had secondary effects. Or perhaps both. It didn't matter. Ixbeth remained just inside the door, unable to hear the words of their conversation but sampling their auras with a certain degree of professional satisfaction. After all, a major stumbling block to the young one's emotional recovery had been surmounted, and her defender hadn't even had to be in the room at the time.

Deneuve had paused to appraise the situation as well. "Marchenko was right about you," the Human congratulated her quietly. "Now stay close, and be ready to work your magic."

Deneuve stopped at the foot of Lania's bed, permitting Ixbeth to stand beside it, opposite Commander Dedrick. Her loins tightened only briefly as their eyes met. Either *disvan* was finally subsiding or another *vanu* was absorbing some of its effects.

Tal?

Not a chance, he declared. *Not now, not ever.*

"Hello, Lania," Deneuve began. "How are you feeling? Better?"

The girl nodded, her emotional aura guarded. Clearly, she could sense that something unpleasant lay at the end of this conversation. Ixbeth inhaled deeply, reminded herself how much she trusted these two Humans, and began projecting.

"We think we know what happened to you in the Arboretum," Deneuve continued. "I just need to ask you a couple of questions to be sure."

Lania glanced to her cousin for reassurance before nodding again, Ixbeth noted. The projection must be working.

"This is the second time the *Marco Polo* has been scanned by the same alien race. We know who they are, and we also know that you were the only one affected by the beam." Deneuve's expression tightened, along with her voice. "Lania, I promised you earlier that you would be safe aboard this ship, and you will be. We're all going to keep that promise. But we need to confirm something. Did you ever hear your parents talk about a place called Thrygg?"

Abject terror. Ixbeth gasped aloud as it sliced through her projection like a spinning blade.

"Thryggians?" she whispered, her lips forming the word twice before any sound came out. "The Thryggians are here?" Lania scrambled backward on the bed. Evading the two pairs of hands that had reached out to comfort her, she pressed herself defensively against the wall. Her gaze darted around the room, found Gael Dedrick, and locked onto his face. "Put me back!" she begged him. "This ship won't protect me. It has strength but no soul. I can feel it. Please! Put me back in the other ship!"

Confusion. The commander's *incharna* eyes swung questioningly from Ixbeth's to Deneuve's and back. "Is she talking about that disabled sprint craft on the surface?"

A machine with the heart of a child. Help me, Tal. I have to focus.

Slowly, Ixbeth sank onto the bed. The truth was very close. She mustn't frighten it away. "Lania, does your computer have a soul?"

"Yes," came the murmured response.

"It shares your feelings. It cares about you."

The Great Presence made his children out of stars, so they would have souls that could share the emotions of others.

"Yes," Lania whispered.

"And the ship on the surface, where you were living, did you give it a soul too?"

She shook her head. "I woke it up."

"Did it shelter you before, from energy beams like this one?"

The young one hesitated. "I — I'm not certain. It never told me."

Faintly aware of minds and voices suddenly clamoring around her, Ixbeth gazed into the face of 'life out of death' and said in a low, urgent voice, "It knows how to protect you from the Thryggians, doesn't it?"

Lania stared back and replied slowly, "I don't know if it knows how, but it wants to."

Evin Lurrlo had once told Ixbeth that it was the dream of every technician to create a computer with higher-order thinking skills. "Everything resonates," he had said. "We sense movement because the air resonates. We sense the emotions of others because the energy inside the brain resonates and our nervous systems are attuned to its various patterns. Just imagine, if the energy inside one of these devices could be made to match the resonance patterns of a living brain making complex decisions while experiencing sadness, or joy!"

All at once, Ixbeth knew the truth, or part of it. *Together, victory.*

"It's not the computer," she breathed excitedly. "It's the ship. The whole star-blessed ship!"

Alarm. "Doctor Minegar, what are you talking about?"

"Is the tech team down on the planet yet?"

Bewilderment. "Possibly. I'm not sure," stammered Dedrick. "Why?"

Ixbeth's chest began vibrating. She was so filled with elation that it took an effort of will not to project it. "Tell the captain, they mustn't modify the sprint craft. It's a template for bridging technologies."

"What?"

"Commander, I know how we're going to defeat the Thryggians," she told him. "With Lania's help, we're going to give the *Marco Polo* a soul."

------ «» ------

"All right, Commander. What's this all about?"

Ixbeth had tasted Takamura's impatience even before the enter buzzer sounded outside the door to Dedrick's quarters. Now he blew into the room like a storm-laden wind, followed closely by Lieutenant Mbuku. Sitting behind the desk, Lania took one look at the Engineering Specialist's stern face and stiffened in her chair.

"As you so urgently requested, I instructed the inspection team not to disturb your cousin's ship while conducting their damage analysis," Takamura announced. "Meanwhile, Mister Mbuku has shown me the preliminary report from the surface. His word for what the techs have found down there is 'spaghetti'. He estimates that his people will need at least one interval, possibly two, to make the sprint craft spaceworthy again, since it appears that someone has done quite a thorough job of disabling it."

"Lania wasn't disabling it, sir," Dedrick told him. "Not deliberately, anyway. She was converting it."

Skepticism. "Like she converted the computer?" challenged Mbuku, crossing his arms over his chest.

"I don't fully understand this myself, Captain, but I have seen Lania operate this computer. It may not be a technology we're familiar with, but it works. She can give you a demonstration if you'd like to see for yourself, sir."

"And then we can get her to pull scarves out of people's ears, or saw someone in half," Mbuku cut in. "I can't believe any of you would let yourselves be taken in like this!"

Anger. Dedrick was glaring at the engineer, his expression darkening ominously.

Fear. Before Lania could bolt from the room, Ixbeth took a deep breath and began projecting for all she was worth.

"Let's assume for the moment that what you've seen is not an illusion, Commander," said Takamura, frowning. "So the computer works, and it shares a rather unorthodox technology with the sprint ship, which may or may not work. I still don't see the relevance of all this to our current situation."

"Lania was found alive on a planet declared plague-dead. Somehow, three separate high-intensity sensor scans all managed to miss her. Everyone is calling it some kind of miracle. But if we think about it, it becomes obvious that she must have been shielded from those orbital scans, most probably by a technology alien to our own."

"Go on," said Takamura, clearly intrigued.

"The only alien technology on that planet right now is inside the sprint ship. Lania talks about it as though it's alive. It 'wants to protect her'. And Doctor Minegar believes that if we can install this same technology aboard the *Marco Polo*, we may be able to protect ourselves when the Thryggian pirates come back."

"Does she?" Takamura seemed to notice Ixbeth for the first time. As his eyes briefly widened, she tasted the smoky-sweetness of his satisfaction at the back of her throat. "And do you have any hard evidence to support such a belief, Doctor?"

"Not yet, Captain. But you have well-trained technicians down there and well-equipped scientists up here. Once your people have analyzed and tested their findings, we should have a much better idea of what Lania's 'spaghetti' can do."

Takamura's lips curved slowly into a grin. "Yes, we should. Mister Mbuku, have your team transmit their data directly to Doctor Hesl in the Field Physics laboratory."

"But, sir—!"

"Tell them to work as quickly as possible, Lieutenant, around the clock if necessary. If this alien technology really is stronger than our own, and if we can find a safe way to implement it, I want to have a surprise waiting for the Thryggians the next time they drop by."

Mbuku's face twisted, as though he could taste the sourness his disgust created at the back of Ixbeth's throat. "Yes, sir." He threw Lania a venomous look before turning to follow his captain out of the room.

That venom had a disturbingly familiar flavor to it. Like something out of a nightmare.

—— «» ——

"You were right!"

Startled by Takamura's pronouncement, which he'd jubilantly delivered from the threshold of her office, Deneuve leaned back in her chair. The fact that the captain had come looking for her in Med Services was in itself unusual. The smugness that now played across his normally inscrutable features made this visit doubly intriguing.

"When Doctor Minegar hinted to me earlier that the Thryggian pirates might be the reason she was aboard, she wasn't simply refusing to answer my question," he continued in a calmer voice, settling into the other chair in the room. "I don't know how she knew we would encounter them — it's possible that they had been harassing ships all over the galaxy and Earth space was simply their next logical target. In any case, whether acting alone or as an agent of the Great Council, she is clearly on a covert mission to foil the Thryggians."

"And that she chose the *Marco Polo* to carry out this mission...?"

He straightened perceptibly in his seat. "That was probably a coincidence. A happy one for us, since we've gained the benefit of her knowledge in our efforts to hold off the pirates. If we survive our next experience with them, we'll owe Doctor Minegar a debt of gratitude, whoever or whatever she turns out to be."

Smiling, Deneuve watched him leave. Yes, she had been right: Humans did love a mystery.

19

On a hunch, Dedrick looked for Leslie Eberhart in the ship's mess. There was something he hadn't told her yet, something that he now understood she desperately needed to hear.

"He's going to be all right, Leslie."

Eberhart looked up from the java she'd been sipping and gestured to him to sit down across the table from her. She was still angry, still keeping some distance between them. With a sigh, he swung a leg over the bench and sank down onto it.

"He doesn't know a soul on Earth," she muttered, frowning.

"Actually, by now he should know quite a few. And I'm not talking about the staff at the Oncology Center."

Intrigued, Leslie put her mug down and leaned towards him. "And you know this because...?"

"My contact on Earth is an old friend of the family — Barry Novak. He owns a medium-sized company called SecuriTech. I asked him to meet Sam at the airfield and take him under his wing, so to speak, for the duration of Sam's stay onworld. The last commburst we received included a message for me from New Chicago. Barry was so impressed with Sam that he offered him a job at SecuriTech, and Sam has accepted. He won't be alone, Leslie. He'll have friends and co-workers. A whole support network to help him get through this."

Anything else Dedrick planned to say flew out of his head as Leslie sprang to her feet, grabbed his face with both her hands, and planted a warm, dry kiss on his lips.

"Don't get any ideas," she warned him, settling back down on her bench. "That was just for helping Sam. I'm still mad at you for not telling me about it."

"Understood," he replied, as solemnly as was possible for someone whose heart was swelling with happiness inside his chest. *One down, one to go.*

—— «» ——

That night, Ixbeth's dream was her own. She was back on Dimmla, one hour before dusk, putting on the traditional loin strap and chest band in preparation for the ritual of *mar'ruk*. They had been woven by her brother. He had used his own blood to dye them. Red was the color of a defender.

"You've grown into it very well." Tal suddenly stood beside her, nodding his approval. Her brother's garb was the dark blue of a midnight sky. Blue for a scholar. It even sparkled a bit, she thought. "Stars," he said, answering her unspoken question.

"Does mine contain stars as well?"

"Not yet, but it will," he assured her. "We're together, and that's the first step."

Ixbeth glanced down at herself and shivered a little, in spite of the heat. The bands of cloth showed nearly all of her golden fur.

"It's all the protection you need, my sister."

Together, victory.

Ixbeth arrived at the clearing just as the sun was completing its evening descent, smearing the sky behind it as though with blood. The clearing was actually a huge, grassy depression in the ground. It spread out before her, the scaffolded wooden platform rising from its center seeming to pin it in place. There was sufficient room in the broad shallow bowl to hold their entire community several times over. One thousand Kularians.

It looked as though they were all there. But where was Tal? Ixbeth's eyes roved anxiously over the crowd, slipping past manes that were too yellow or brown, bodies that were too short or tall or thin, costumes that still clung to hints of red or green or orange in the rapidly waning daylight.

Eventually, it grew too dark to continue looking for him. Crossing the lip of the bowl, Ixbeth positioned herself on the margin of the crowd and watched as the four Guardians, in their respective capes of office, launched themselves at the scaffold from four different directions. They climbed it with smooth, powerful movements of their arms and legs, then took their places on the high platform and stood facing outwards, arms folded over their chests. They waited, unmoving, until the clearing was completely dark and a reverent hush had fallen over the assembly.

Then a voice sprang up and split the darkness, a proud, clear voice, singing out words that soared over the heads of the gathered Kularians with breath-stealing power: *MAR'RUK DEL'LOYIT, AL'LOYIT OHE'ELU.*

The Guardian of Light was issuing a summons.

In response, fire bugs came streaming from every direction, thick swarms that looked like glowing golden ribbons undulating through the air. The arcing ribbons met directly over the platform, where they wove themselves into a luminous, living vault, filling the clearing with their light. As one person, the assembly breathed a sigh of pure awe.

Ixbeth felt a stirring deep inside her.

"It is beautiful, isn't it?"

Tal's voice beside her completed the moment. The faint, sweet taste of his affection for her was unmistakable. "Yes, it is," she murmured gratefully. "I'd almost forgotten how startling the contrast is between light and darkness here."

"Almost as startling as the contrast between understanding and ignorance. I'm glad you ran this way instead of back to Altera."

The oldest Guardian, the one identified by his yellow cape as the Guardian of Truth, stepped forward now and spread his arms in a welcoming gesture to the crowd. "When Avo'or, the Great Presence, created the Children of Kula'as, he gave us four great gifts, and enjoined us to guard them with our very existence. Wherever there are Kularians, there are four Guardians to watch over these precious gifts and keep them safe. The gift of Time allows us to remember and learn from what has gone before. The gift of Light allows us to be creators of that which we need and that which gives us pleasure. The gift of Truth allows us to know what is right and what is wrong, and to follow the path of justice. The gift of Life allows us to enjoy all the other gifts. *Eluya'at elumi'in.* The Truth lives and is spoken."

The crowd responded in unison: *"Ohe'elu!"*

Krodus stepped forward now. Ixbeth's heart constricted with pride. Her father looked so strong, so imposing up there. His voice was deep and resonant. It rolled over the crowd like a wave.

"This is a very special *mar'ruk*. It requires us to remember what for many years we have obediently striven to forget. Now, on the eve of the Reyot Quest, I restore for you this piece of our history: three hundred and forty years ago, the first of four ships landed on this very spot where we stand now. The ship contained 3,000 Kularians, adults and children, serving every domain, seeking a place of concealment, as they had been ordered to do by the Oracle."

"Eluya'at elumi'in!" shouted the Guardian of Truth, and the people roared in response, *"Ohe'elu!"*

Krodus was continuing: "Now the Oracle has spoken again, and a new Reyot Quest has begun. For the benefit of the chosen ones who will be leaving us very soon, many never to return, we must repeat the old legends one last time.

"In the beginning, Avo'or was alone in the universe. He was able to travel it from one end to the other, and could even be at both ends at the same moment, but he had no companion to share it with. He felt the need of a friend. So he took a star and shaped it into a being with eight arms and eight legs, and he named his new friend Raku'ula — the First Companion. Raku'ula was a good friend and never left his side, but soon Avo'or grew tired of this constant companionship. There were times when he wanted to be alone. So he changed Raku'ula into an air-breathing creature and set him down on a planet. This way, he could visit Raku'ula whenever he felt the need of company, but could go away and be by himself when he needed solitude."

"We have a very selfish deity," Ixbeth couldn't help commenting.

"What we have are selfish neighbors."

"But the Dimmlesi haven't been selfish," she protested.

Tal only smiled.

"...and when Avo'or saw how the male and female beings cared for each other, protected each other, shared each other's lives, his heart was gladdened. He decided to give them a very special gift. He gave them the power, when they joined together in pairs, to create life in their own image. And this gift he called *Evo'OrLemAlli*."

"*Eluya'at elumi'in*," chanted the Guardian of Truth.

"*Ohe'elu*," responded the crowd, minus Ixbeth's voice this time.

"Don't you want to hear the Truth?" Tal teased.

Ixbeth shot him a disdainful glance. "You must be joking. I didn't believe this when I was five years old."

Now the green-caped Guardian of Life stepped forward, arms raised and outstretched, and began to chant: "Great Presence, help us to cherish those who weep with fear, for they are your children and must be comforted."

"*Ohe'elu*!" groaned the crowd.

"Help us to cherish those who weep with compassion, for they are your merciful spirit among us and must be honored."

"*Ohe'elu*!"

"Above all, help us to cherish those who cannot weep, for they are the lost and must be guided home."

All at once, Ixbeth was alone, crouching in a corner of a small, dark room, and terrified. She was filled with the emotion, projecting it. Her own fear was frightening away anyone who might help her.

Silence. Then, footsteps. Heavy, deliberate, getting closer. Halting. She tried to breathe but couldn't. A key was rattling in the door. As it swung open, Ixbeth reached out instinctively and found her fingers closing around the handle of a long knife.

A gigantic, faceless figure loomed over her. It was her captor, come to torture her to death. He'd come directly from another victim. His clothing reeked with her blood. Desperately Ixbeth lunged, burying the entire blade in his chest. And as he fell backward, into the light, she saw his face for the first time and shrieked with horror.

The man she had just killed was Commander Dedrick.

Ixbeth!

Ixbeth awoke with a gasp. Teeth chattering, fingerclaws fully extended, she kicked off her bedcovers and staggered across the darkened cabin to the light switch. She spun as she tripped it and leaned against the wall for a moment, catching her breath. Then she dropped into her chair, her head throbbing with remembered terror, and willed her senses to clear.

Ixbeth! What just happened?

Tal's confusion was a sharpness at the back of her throat.

One of the Humans had a nightmare, she told him.

That was no Human dream. I shared it.

Impossible! *You shared the dream?*

It cut through my sleepshield like a toothed blade, he confirmed. *Be careful, Ixbeth. The young one—*

Of course. After all the reading she'd done, Ixbeth should have been prepared for this.

Nightmares are normal after a psychological trauma, Tal. Her father abused her for years. It will take time for her to integrate the memories of that fear and—

Not fear, Ixbeth. Guilt, strong enough to be a projection. 'Life out of death' has already killed once, and now she relives the killing in her sleep.

He could possibly be right. The voice log from the sprint ship had already confirmed Deneuve's suspicion that Abner and Rose hadn't died of the plague. Nonetheless...

Until the Human healer has had a chance to examine Abner's remains, it is wrong to assume that Lania killed him. The dream could have been a wish-enactment. And there were others on that planet, Tal, much larger and stronger than a half-grown child and with just as much reason to hate him.

All I'm saying is, be careful. The prophecy states that 'life out of death' will kill. It's important that none of her rage be directed against her own kind.

Her own kind? And just who would that be, Ixbeth couldn't help wondering. The Humans aboard this ship? or the Kularians within sensing range? The young one was trapped between two species. It was an otherness Ixbeth was quite familiar with.

Kularian blood, born of Humans. Was it even possible?

If Avo'or wishes it, Tal reminded her, *anything is possible.*

20

There were a dozen beings at the meeting in the strategy room, including Captain Takamura, and none of them were smiling. In fact, as Doctors Kuzinski and Hesl of the Field Physics laboratory began their joint report to the command staff, Lieutenant Mbuku's expression was positively grim.

Keenly aware of the urgency of their situation, Takamura had ordered the Engineering Department to begin implementing the conversion as soon as Field Physics had successfully completed a simulation test of the schematics. Mbuku's people had been working on the new systems nonstop for just over a day now, and Ixbeth had tasted his deep frustration from the moment he stalked into the room. She had heard that he was now a 'hot head' but couldn't help noticing that there had been no change in the Engineering Specialist's appearance. Perhaps the heat was felt on the inside only. With luck, they would not have to find out.

Lania was present as well, at Dr. Kuzinski's request. Like the Humans, the young one was broadcasting apprehension, her otherness giving it a slightly metallic taste. Not even the generally inscrutable Takamura was immune today. The entire crew had been hard at work making the ship battle-ready. It helped keep their minds off a fact that their captain dared not forget: that the pirates could return at any time, armed with a far superior technology that made the *Marco Polo*'s chances of surviving the encounter slim at best.

Interesting. Lania's otherness was common knowledge aboard the ship; and yet, not for one second had anyone, including Mbuku, entertained the idea of simply giving the pirates what they wanted in order to make them go away.

"Now you're saying this is some sort of organic technology?" Takamura demanded incredulously. "How is that possible with inorganic components?"

Discomfort. Dr. Hesl cleared his throat twice before replying. "What we said was that the wiring in Ms Dedrick's computer and in the control room of the sprint ship appeared to follow the same organic principles. It's really quite logical, Captain. We have levers and hydraulics and chemical signal processes in our own bodies, and because we build machines as extensions of ourselves, we tend to make them work the same way as we do. As we deepened our understanding of brain electrochemistry, for example, high-definition interactive virtual reality became possible. One day, if research continues, we may even have artificial intelligence as sophisticated as the device constructed by this young lady."

"The organic principle that drives Ms Dedrick's computer," Kuzinski chimed in, "reflects the organizational patterns of an intelligent mind. The reason it seemed so illogical to us on first inspection is that the mind in question is not Human."

An almost palpable silence descended over the group around the table. A second later Mbuku's indignation sliced through it. "So this is an alien artificial intelligence? Engineered by a Human girl using Earth-made parts? Call me a cynic, but I find that very hard to believe, Doctor."

"Precisely why she and her device are both present at our briefing, Mister Mbuku," said Kuzinski.

All eyes turned toward Lania. Seated between Commander Dedrick and Doctor Deneuve, still carefully avoiding physical contact with either one of them, the young one straightened in her chair and drew her lips into a hyphen. It was a practiced façade, mused Ixbeth, who could clearly taste the girl's rising anxiety. She reached out to Tal.

You can only project what you feel, my sister, he reminded her. *She trusts you because you trust yourself. She trusts her cousin and the Human healer because you do as well, with your life.*

And if I want her to trust in the knowledge of the Human scientists, the skill of the Human engineers?

She'll do it as long as your own confidence in them is unconditional. Is it?

Ixbeth could not answer.

The physicist continued, "We have reason to believe that this artificial intelligence is not only designed and built by Ms Dedrick, but also powered by her."

"By her mind," Hesl hastened to add. "The brain scans supplied by Med Services were extraordinary, to say the least. Unusual differentiation of cells. High synaptic density. Electrochemical activity right off the scale. We made four attempts to measure the energy generated by her neural matter, and each one succeeded only in creating a feedback stream powerful enough to burn out relays in our biogalvanometer. If her mind was capable of doing that, it might explain why her device will only operate in her presence and with her consent."

It's psi-powered! This young one is definitely Kularian.

How, Tal? By the hand of Avo'or?

Not directly. The Dr'rava Kula'as states, as a basic principle, that there is a rational explanation for everything in the universe, whether we understand it or not. Think, Ixbeth! Didn't your Human superior say that Lania's parents had escaped together from Thrygg?

Yes, she had. And while what Tal was suggesting should have been unthinkable, knowing the Thryggians it made perfect sense. Ten generations earlier, all the Kularians had 'disappeared'. How typically Thryggian it would be to try to resurrect the species through genetic manipulation of another race's nucleic matter. Not to repopulate Kula'as — that would be far too altruistic. Perhaps just to see whether it could be done. Or maybe for some more self-serving purpose.

"This just gets better and better!" sputtered Mbuku. He was halfway to his feet now, leaning across the table toward the two scientists and radiating incredulous rage. "It's not enough that the pirates have a technology our own systems can't defend against. Now you're saying that the lives of everyone aboard this ship will be in the hands of a child because the new systems we've been installing won't work for anyone else?"

Fear, assailing Ixbeth from all directions. She saw Lania stiffen and grow pale. The young one needed an infusion of trust. But Ixbeth could only project what she felt herself, and the Humans had good reason to be afraid.

Takamura sprang up, glaring at his Engineering Specialist. "That will be enough, Mister Mbuku!"

"With all due respect, sir, I must protest this intolerable situation."

"Your protest is noted. And to spare you any additional anguish regarding this *situation*, as you put it, I am also relieving you of any responsibility for the systems conversion. Until further notice, I will expect to see Mister Tsieng at these briefing meetings."

Amazement. "Then you're still determined to go ahead with this suicidal scheme?"

"Unfortunately, the Thryggians have left us no other option," Takamura pointed out patiently. "I agree, it's a huge risk, but with luck, it's one the enemy won't be expecting us to take."

His rage finally beginning to dissipate, Mbuku straightened to attention. "Understood, sir. Permission to return to Propulsion Control?"

"Very well," said Takamura. "You are dismissed, Mister Mbuku."

As the strategy room door slid closed behind the departing officer, everyone at the meeting exhaled a sigh of relief. Ixbeth realized with a start that she had been holding her breath as well, half-expecting the Engineering Specialist's 'hot head' to explode.

"Now, then," Takamura resumed, nodding an invitation to Doctor Kuzinski to address the remaining group.

Anxiety. "Mister Mbuku was essentially correct in his analysis of the situation, Captain. I'm sorry I can't be more positive. Perhaps, if we could figure out a way to stabilize the controlling AI, make its responses less 'Human' and more reliable... Back on Earth, we'd be applying for grants for such a project, setting aside three to five years for its completion. Out here?" He shrugged helplessly. "We've used the schematics to continue running tactical simulations on a conventional computer. However, once the AI is brought online to operate the converted systems, we'll have two variables, not just one, and no valid sim data to help us anticipate the outcome of real-time battle strategies."

Puzzled disbelief. "I thought that was what testing was for. And given that we're pressed for time and may not be able to field test these systems, will you tell me, please, why the AI is not already online and assisting with the conversion?" Takamura demanded.

Dr. Hesl replied apologetically, "As earlier noted, Captain, the device can only be operated by Ms Dedrick, and Med Services has informed us that the young lady's — ah — condition is still quite fragile."

"So they've denied you access to her? Clearly, there has been a misunderstanding," said Takamura, directing his stern gaze toward the group at the far end of the long table.

Large swallows small, and small corrupts large. Tasting the captain's tightly controlled anger, Ixbeth sighed inwardly.

The 'alienization' of the *Marco Polo*'s defences was only half-completed and already causing disharmony shipwide. She had been sensing it for hours. It would only get worse once the modified technology was brought online. The moment shields and weapons were activated, the ship would begin to die. Some systems would fail immediately, others more slowly, but all of them would eventually be affected. Harmonic resonance was a fact, and field testing was not an option. The Humans would have just one chance to defeat the pirates, and the victory would need to be swift and decisive, or they were lost.

"We cannot wait until the thick of battle to discover whether we are capable of defending ourselves," Takamura declared. "Doctor Deneuve, Doctor Minegar — you will make Ms Dedrick available whenever and wherever she is needed during the conversion process. The survival of all of us depends on this. Do you understand?"

Fear! Searching her heart for any conviction strong enough to be projected as a buffer, Ixbeth glanced at Lania. As if on cue, the young one's eyes rolled upward in their sockets, and a second later she was unconscious, a limp bundle in her startled cousin's arms.

—— «» ——

Lania lay in Rehab with her head tilted slightly to one side, short tendrils of her long dark hair curling at her temples. Except for the pallor of her skin, she looked as though her eyes could open at any moment.

"What's wrong with her, Doctor?" Dedrick asked tautly.

Deneuve shook her head. "She's comatose. These are the same vital readings as I recorded the other day: pulse, respiration, brain function, all steady but depressed. And no physical injury or pathology to account for it. Sometimes," she added reluctantly, "unconsciousness can be induced by massive psychological shock. The mind simply decides it is safer not to be awake."

Fear. "I don't understand," said Dedrick. "What exactly has she done? Is she willing herself to die?"

She has put herself into a healing sleep, Tal fretted. *Only she isn't healing, Ixbeth — she's hiding. And we're running out of time.*

Ixbeth couldn't help sympathizing with Commander Dedrick, a fellow defender. Lania, his last remaining relative, had been entrusted to his care. Now, standing at the foot of her bed, he was having to face the possibility of losing her, just as he was coming to know her.

"She won't die, Commander," Ixbeth assured him. "But the prospect of holding all our lives in her hands terrifies her, especially when there may be no chance of success. As an officer, you are accustomed to taking responsibility for the lives of others in potentially hopeless situations. She's just a child."

"All right, so she's scared," Dedrick insisted. "I could understand it if she ran away and hid, but this? This is not normal."

"Not normal for Humans, perhaps."

A soft gasp of recognition from Deneuve. Growing excitement. "But normal for Dimmlesi? Of course! Jump in a hole and pull it in after you! Remember how we brought them both back from the planet, Commander? Lania wasn't knocked out of that tree — she was frightened and shut down her mind, just as she did in the strategy room. Doctor Minegar, you were able to reach her before. Can you do it again, now?"

You can do it, Tal said. *Tell her you'll do it. I'll help you. Sister, we have to wake the young one up. The prophecy...!*

Ixbeth tried unsuccessfully to swallow the lump forming in her throat. The prophecy laid even more responsibility on Lania's shoulders. Without her help, the *Marco Polo* would lose the coming battle. It would mean the destruction of not only a ship but possibly a world, along with any hope for peace in the galaxy over the next ten generations.

You can help her, Tal repeated quietly.

Ixbeth shook her head. "She was already conscious when I made contact with her before. I don't know whether it will work, but I can try."

Concern. Deneuve was having second thoughts.

"Don't worry, Doctor," Ixbeth assured her. "If she doesn't respond, I'll break off the contact before she pulls me in."

Reluctantly Deneuve nodded.

All right, Tal, what do I do now?

You must identify the emotion that is paralyzing her mind and neutralize it by projecting its opposite. But remember, you can only project what you feel yourself.

Ixbeth sat down on the edge of Lania's bed. The young one had put herself into the healing sleep to escape fear — fear of exposure, fear of consequences, fear of failure — especially fear of failure. And what emotion could be considered the opposite of fear? Perhaps one that produced the opposite effect. Fear was paralyzing; anger was motivating. Anger might be the key. And Ixbeth had plenty of it right now.

You have to project pure emotion, Tal warned her. *Cleanse your mind of all other feelings. Focus your entire being, as you did before.*

Ixbeth took Lania's hand. Then she sucked in a long, steadying breath and made a conscious effort to clear her mind. At once, anger began to fill her. This was what remained when every other emotion was stilled. Anger that bubbled hotly each time she thought of the Thryggians and what they had done — and were continuing to do without feeling or remorse, even as they were on trial for it. Anger that swelled and overflowed like molten lava, becoming an irresistible torrent of purest…

Rage!

It boiled furiously inside her brain, dissolving walls, spilling thoughts, memories, imagined fears all together into a red-hot, galvanizing soup.

Fire! Surrounded, burning. Flames. Heat. Weaponless. Defender! I will protect—

Rage!

Now her lungs were filling up, melting down, their heat bursting her ribs.

Booted feet, huge fists, bones breaking, blood pouring… Charred corpses, arms raised in supplication. Helpless! I am a defender! I must—

Rage!

I must protect! I will defend!

———— «» ————

They wouldn't let her rest. Tucked away deep inside her mind, Lania had been startled and then outraged to discover that her peaceful place, since childhood her only real refuge, was under siege. Abner had sometimes been able to block her from reaching it, but even he had never tried to breach its boundaries once she was there.

How dare they!

Lania sensed it seeping thickly into her, the rage, sliding into the cracks of her mind, filling every corner of her being and then rising, like an unstoppable tide. It was scalding hot and smelled like blood. Abner's blood. She had felt nothing but relief when it had begun to flow. Blood would have to flow if she was ever to experience such relief again. And she needed — and wanted — that release.

Lania opened her eyes and saw her defender sitting on the side of her bed. Doctor Minegar's eyes opened as well and met hers, and Lania realized for the first time that the alien had been holding her hand.

"The Thryggians will be back. They're going to try to take you," she informed Lania quietly. "Are you ready to fight them?"

Yes, Lania decided. Blood would flow, perhaps the Thryggians', perhaps her own. Either way, there would be release. And as Abner had taught her so well, freedom always came at a price.

Sitting up, Lania grasped Ixbeth's hand firmly with both of her own. "I saw what they did to my mother. I felt what they did to my father. They're not going to do it to me."

Commander Dedrick's huge hands closed around their three. "You're right," he told her. "They're not. Because we're not going to let them."

21

Emergency klaxons were blaring all over the ship. Disharmony upon disharmony.

"They're back! Come on, ladies, it's show time!"

"Just don't break a leg," Deneuve called after them as Ixbeth and Lania followed Commander Dedrick out into the corridor. They raced to the nearest PTS stop. Tsieng stood waiting for them, holding the tube car door open. Once they were all aboard, the engineer keyed in their destination and hit the express button.

Looking over Tsieng's shoulder, Ixbeth wondered aloud, "Community sector?"

Frustration. "I was planning to move the AI onto the bridge," Tsieng explained. "Unfortunately, the pirates showed up early, so we're going to have to do this by remote, from the commander's quarters."

"What's our shields and weapons status?" asked Dedrick.

"Shields fully converted, weapons at ninety percent, and at the moment they both show green on my stat board. But they haven't been tested, so once the AI comes online that could change. And Doctor Hesl has warned me that with only a partial conversion, we can expect glitches in all our standard systems as well. Forewarned being forearmed, I've got techs assigned to every main access point in the grid. We'll use flypaper and chewing gum if necessary, but we'll hold things together."

Grim satisfaction. "How many Thryggian ships?"

"Half a dozen at last count, sir, all roughly the same size as the one that scanned us. We've sent out Gate maydays and distress beacons, but it's doubtful whether any other ships will be able to get here in time. We're on our own, Commander," the engineer added quietly. "I really hope this works."

Hope was all the Humans had, Ixbeth realized. Cornered and outgunned but refusing to surrender, they were quite literally betting their lives on an otherness none of them really understood: a Kularian born to Humans, and an artificial intelligence that was neither.

Ixbeth sampled Lania's aura and found it uncompromising and unafraid. Good. The young one spent the entire tube transit simmering silently in a corner of the car. Once arrived in the Dedricks' quarters, however, she went directly to the desk and said briskly, "Computer on."

GOOD MORNING, LANIA

"Good *afternoon*. Computer, you have been connected to other processors. Can you feel them?"

THERE ARE OTHER PROCESSORS

I CAN TOUCH MANY PARTS OF THE SHIP

Ixbeth heard grateful sighs behind her. The Humans had evidently been holding their breath.

"I need you to activate the shields and weapon systems."

The computer hummed for a few seconds, then,

I HAVE LOCATED THEM

THEY ARE NOT FULLY CONNECTED

I WILL COMPLETE THE INTEGRATION

As Dedrick and Ixbeth exchanged a startled look, the comm speaker blared, "Lieutenant Tsieng, this is Harding on the bridge. Half my board just went red. Techs are complaining all over the ship. What's going on down there?"

INTEGRATION COMPLETED

"The AI was just making a few adjustments, Mister Harding. What does your board look like now?"

"It's flashing like a Christmas tree, sir. Should I be worried?"

"Computer," said Lania, "bring up the shields to full power, please."

ARE YOU INSIDE THE SHIELDS?

"Yes."

A pause, then, "Shields just came up, Lieutenant," reported Harding over the comm, "but weapons are still showing red."

"Computer," said Lania, her confidence growing by the second, "can you activate the weapons systems?"

YES

They waited.

"Weapons still not activated, sir," said Harding a moment later in a tight voice.

"Computer," she repeated, a little more urgently, "I need you to activate the weapons systems so you can defend me."

YOU ARE SAFE BEHIND THE SHIELDS

WEAPONS ARE USED TO KILL

KILLING IS WRONG

"A pacifist computer. I don't believe this," muttered Dedrick.

Bemusement. Tsieng's lips quirked briefly in a smile. "Hesl did warn us about incompatibility, Commander."

Not just pacifist, Tal warned. *Remember her dream, Ixbeth. Maximize your senses and you'll taste it.*

Ixbeth reached out and placed a hand lightly on the casing of the AI. Yes, this device and Lania would be in perfect harmony.

Like twins who have bonded, Tal said. *Their minds are joined. They reflect each other's emotions. What are you tasting, Ixbeth?*

Guilt. Ixbeth's heart dropped. Tal had been right.

"The Thryggians are losing patience with us, Commander," warned Harding's taut voice. "You'd better brace yourselves. The inertial dampers just failed and it looks like we're about to field test those newfangled shields."

All at once the room rocked, nearly pitching Lania out of her chair and Ixbeth against the wall.

"Harding, report!" bawled Tsieng in the direction of the wallcomm.

"Shields still green, sir. They work!"

"Give me numbers, Mister Harding."

"You're not going to believe this, sir. All shields are at one hundred percent, except for numbers six and eleven, port side, which are at one-fourteen. Hot damn! They take a licking and we're still ticking."

A second, female voice came over the speaker. "Commander, this is Leblanc. The captain wants you to hear this. You can still use your comm unit to talk to the bridge."

"…interesting shields you've managed to acquire, Captain Takamura, but they cannot last forever. And please do not insult my intelligence with semantic hair-splitting. On our last sensing pass we detected the genetic patterns of a test subject that one of your species stole from our laboratory on Thrygg. A being with the genetic patterns of this female who is not this female could only be her offspring. Since the mother was part of a multi-generational experiment, that means the child is also contracted to us. We have legal entitlement and you must surrender the test subject to us!"

"Well, that certainly clears up a lot of questions," Dedrick commented grimly.

Fear. Lania was staring up at the wallcomm, tears glistening in her eyes. She and the computer were like twins, bonded, and fear was a paralyzer—!

Moving quickly, Ixbeth placed her hands on either side of the young one's face and forced her to meet her gaze. Then, carefully keeping her fingerclaws retracted, she summoned up all the anger she possessed and began projecting. "They want you to be afraid, Lania, because if you're scared you won't fight, and they know they can't win if you fight them. They have no feelings, no soul. They cut into your mother's body. They took away your father's Humanity. They did it because they hate and fear what they can never have. They're afraid of you, Lania, and they want you to help them destroy you. Don't give them what they want."

The *incharna* eyes were smoldering again, filled with rage. Excellent! "Help us defeat them instead," Ixbeth urged. "The part of you that's inside your computer is feeling guilty over Abner's death. I can sense it. That's why it won't activate the weapons systems. To defeat the Thryggians and save this ship and everyone on it, you need to stop your computer from feeling guilty. You need to make it as angry as you are."

Lania clamped her lips together and nodded.

Dedrick was leaning across the desktop toward her. "We need those weapons, Doctor, and we don't have time to put the computer through guilt therapy to get them."

"Commander, I'm working on it."

Without warning, the room rocked again. Ixbeth was grateful for Dedrick's hands on her shoulders, holding her steady.

"Harding, report!" Tsieng commanded.

"The shields are holding, sir. They seem to get stronger each time the Thryggians hit them. I don't understand this, but I love it. The bad news is that we still have no weapons online, and the alien circuitry is interfering with just about all of our standard systems. We've got glitches popping up everywhere. It's all minor stuff so far, nothing the techs can't handle. But Captain Takamura's taking us out of orbit in case we lose maneuvering thrusters."

Dedrick punched the button on his deskcomm. "Tell the captain we're doing our best, Harding. We'll keep you posted."

A shudder ran through the ship as another Thryggian hit registered farther along the hull.

"Computer, we are under attack," said Lania. "You must return the fire."

THE SHIELDS ARE STRONG

YOU ARE SAFE

"Safe for how long?" she demanded. "Those are Thryggians out there. They know I'm on this ship."

Another shudder, on the opposite side.

THRYGGIANS?

"Yes! They know that I'm Rose's daughter. They want me very badly. They won't give up until they own me. You have to defend me, now!"

THE THRYGGIANS MUST NOT HAVE YOU

WILL NOT TAKE YOU

SHIELDS WILL PROTECT YOU

The ship was rocked twice more. Ixbeth lurched forward, nearly toppling onto Lania's lap. Tsieng and Dedrick, grasping wildly for anything that would stop them from falling, found only each other and were thrown together onto the sofa against the far wall.

Exasperation. "Don't these Thryggians have a learning curve?" Tsieng demanded.

"They're scientists, Lieutenant, and we're their latest experiment," Ixbeth told him. "They'll hit each shield once and observe the effect before drawing any conclusions." By then, of course, disharmony would have claimed every vital system on the *Marco Polo*, leaving it a derelict in space…

…helpless. Others trapped, panicking. Defender!

Ixbeth, we're running out of time!

The lights flickered. Lania gasped and jerked upright in her chair.

"Commander," said Harding's voice on the comm, "we've got glitches in the power systems now. Captain Takamura says, whatever you're doing down there, could you please hurry?"

Sudden decisiveness. Dedrick reached out and, before she could shrink away from the contact, put his two large hands on Lania's shoulders. Immediately, Ixbeth could sense the quiet strength that underpinned this Human male, the discipline, the determination. And to her amazement, it was also flowing outward, toward her, toward Lania, steadying them both.

Stars! He's projecting, Tal!

The Thryggians had to have a genetic starting place for their experiments, Tal pointed out. *Latencies, recessives… And if Abner had them, it's reasonable to suppose that they would be found in other members of his family as well.*

Of course, Ixbeth realized. The singleton offspring of same-gender twins would be twins themselves, the light and dark halves of a single soul.

Dedrick had been speaking quietly to Lania. "That's your leverage, cousin," he concluded. "Bring it the bad news. We're depending on you."

Lania nodded and relaxed her posture. "Computer," she said, "the shields are putting a strain on the ship's power systems. They're weakening. If the power goes, the shields will shut down, and I will be unprotected. Do you really wish to save me?"

The computer hummed softly for several seconds, apparently digesting this new logic.

WE MUST SAVE YOU

"Then don't just hide me behind the shields. Defend me. Attack the Thryggians. Destroy or disable every one of their ships. But do it right now, before the power supply is interrupted and you lose your chance forever."

As the cursor flashed silently on the screen, four beings waited, motionless, forgetting even to breathe. Then, all at once—

Rage! The ship was filling with energy, shaking and spasming all over.

"What the hell—?" yelped Tsieng. "Harding, report!"

Disharmony, strong enough to make Ixbeth's muscles twitch. The ship was dying. These must be its death throes. Had they failed?

Tal!

Trust the prophecy, Ixbeth. And trust yourself. Together, victory!

"Whoo-ee!" Harding's voice burst out of the wallcomm.

In the silence that followed, Ixbeth felt the room flood with relief.

"So what do you think, Commander?" Tsieng asked after a beat. "Did that sound like we won?"

Dedrick pretended to consider for a second. "I think we won," he said, barely suppressing a smile.

Tsieng reached out and punched the button on the deskcomm. "Mister Harding, when I ask for a report—"

"The shields became weapons, sir! They all discharged at the same moment, in all directions. The Thryggians never had a chance."

"Any Human casualties reported?" Dedrick wanted to know.

"Some bumps and bruises from being shaken around, but nothing serious. Techs are still assessing our situation, Lieutenant, but I can give you a partial status report. Hull integrity is full green. Life support is yellow, and auxiliary power is being brought online to cover it. Long range communications has been knocked out. Bolivar estimates three standard days for repair. And the weapons console is down, sir. An overload — it blew most of the circuits. Shields with an attitude. Man! I don't understand it, but I—"

"—love it," Tsieng concluded for him, grinning broadly. "Yes, Harding, we know."

Something made Ixbeth turn at that moment, some muted disturbance colliding with her and Tal's shield. "Commander!" she cried.

Lania lay sprawled in the chair, her head lolling to one side. Her eyes were closed, her lids rimmed by tears.

Just then the computer emitted a short buzzing sound, drawing their attention to the final line on the screen:

KILLING IS STILL WRONG

———— «» ————

The words fell like early morning mist on her mind, gently present but not penetrating. Lania knew they must be words because she recognized the voices: Doctor Deneuve and Doctor Minegar and her guardian, Commander Dedrick. Singly and in pairs, taking turns, nonstop, they spoke to her, coaxing her, then begging her, to open her eyes, to return to them. They didn't understand.

Words. They pattered softly on the outermost margins of her being, a distant memory of meaning that was meaningless now that they couldn't reach her.

Couldn't hurt her. Nothing could hurt her here, floating safe and alone in the cocoon of her mind. Knowing without caring any longer that her heart continued to pulsate, her lungs to respire, her cells to repair themselves. Remembering with growing regret the well of sorrow she had once seen in the commander's eyes, the reassuring touch of his hand on her shoulder. He would have died to save her. The whole crew had been willing to die to keep her safe. Now she had to save them from the monster that she had become. Or perhaps she had always been that way. Rose had died to give her a chance at a normal life, not realizing that it was reserved for normal people...and none of them — not Abner, not Rose, not Lania — was normal or ever would be. Abner had known this from the beginning. However cruel he might have been, however selfish, Abner had always been a realist.

And Lania had killed him, without hesitation or remorse, and had convinced her computer to do the same to the Thryggians on those ships. Monster! She had to stay all alone inside herself now, and for their own safety, Doctor Minegar and Commander Dedrick had to remain outside. It was the only way.

PART VII

The Return

Nicknamed 'the fighting rabbi', **Leon Goldman** (b. 2331 C.E.- d. 2450 C.E.) was born on Earth and served as chaplain aboard the star cruiser *Vasco da Gama* from 2382 to 2420 C.E., a total of 38 years. Goldman distinguished himself at the Battle of Daisy Hub in 2402 C.E. and was subsequently awarded the Fleet's highest commendation for bravery. He was also the second of only two Humans ever invited to join a Nandrian shield clan, and the first and only Human known to have participated in the Nandrian planetary sport of *tekl'hananni*. Goldman spent the last thirty years of his life establishing and governing Yerushalayim, the self-declared Jewish home world in Sector 5 of Earth space.

— *Sic Transit Terra, An Unauthorized Planetary History*
(2673 C.E.)

Fleet Control Headquarters, Earth

MEMO

EARTH DATE: 20 March 2399

FROM: Vice-Admiral Kendra Nelligan

TO: Captain Sven Nordstrom, commanding the star cruiser *Vasco da Gama*

ENCRYPTION LEVEL: Highest

Effective immediately, the *Vasco da Gama* is removed from census duty and given the following assignment:

You are to rendezvous with the *Marco Polo* at MF-307, where you will take aboard one alien passenger, named Doctor Ixbeth Minegar. You will then transport her directly to the planet Kula'as, where she is to appear as a witness before the Interplanetary Tribunal. Coordinates are attached.

You are guaranteed safe passage to Kula'as by the Galactic Great Council. However, you are advised to take all precautions against the possibility of attack by Thryggian pirates.

Good luck and godspeed.

22

The excitement had been over for thirty standard hours when the two Earth ships rendezvoused. It was clear who had won the fight. The *Marco Polo* was back in orbit, intact, with the scorched wreckage of a number of smaller vessels drifting lazily around its hull. Repairs were already in progress. After an exchange of greetings, Captain Takamura gave Captain Nordstrom a status report to relay to Fleet Control, since the long-range communications systems aboard his own ship had been damaged in the battle. And Nordstrom, making no effort to conceal his embarrassment, swore Takamura to secrecy before passing along the reason for the request from the *Vasco da Gama*'s chaplain.

Takamura raised an eyebrow. "He believes that the Dedrick girl has a message for him from God?"

The other man's face crumpled with distaste. "Maybe not from God directly, but he's convinced she has something to tell him. I know it sounds crazy, but after a standard year of census duty, counting up bodies, performing mass funerals on about a dozen plague-dead worlds, we're probably all riding the edge. So, when we found this beautiful child alive in the middle of all that lifelessness, the rabbi naturally took it as a sign from above. Goldman's quirk is pretty innocuous when you think about it, Hiro. He just wants to talk to her."

Takamura nodded thoughtfully. "As it happens, Ms Dedrick was injured during the battle and is presently in a coma. However, provided there is no objection from Med Services, I am willing to give him access to her. She has so far been unresponsive to our attempts to waken her. Perhaps your chaplain can succeed where we have failed."

—— «» —— *

Ixbeth stood just inside the landing vehicle dock and watched the *Vasco da Gama*'s chaplain step down from the short-hopper. His grizzled chin-mane was full and neatly trimmed. His eyes were calm and clear. Over the shoulders of his Fleet uniform he wore a lustrous white scarf, and a small round black cap clung to the crown of his balding head.

He was a Believer. Even from a distance, Ixbeth could taste his unshakable faith, his serene acceptance of self and purpose. His aura was almost as calm as Takamura's. Rapidly filling with awe, she stepped forward to introduce herself.

"Rabbi Goldman? I'm Doctor Minegar."

He froze, staring wide-eyed at her face. If there had been anything in his hands, she was sure he would have dropped it.

"Rabbi?"

Her voice seemed to break a spell. "Forgive me, Doctor," he said, flustered. "I didn't mean to be rude. I just—"

"Never saw an alien before?" she inquired, smiling.

He sighed, emanating a strange combination of wonderment and loss. "No, it's your hair. All that fiery red hair. I once loved a woman with hair that same color. She's dead now, but for just a moment, I—" Shaking off the rest of that thought, he concluded, "It makes you look very beautiful."

Caught off guard, Ixbeth paused. Humans usually noticed her eyes first, and then her ears. But this being saw the universe in a different way. Felt it differently, too. Perhaps it was no accident that he had arrived wanting to see Lania just when no one else seemed able to reach her. Perhaps the Great Presence and whatever god this Human believed in had even worked together to make it happen.

"The young one is in Medical Services," she offered, leading the way to the PTS. "If there is anything you can do for her, we would be most grateful."

"As will I be for whatever message she brings me," he replied.

Ixbeth had begun keying in their destination. She halted briefly and glanced up in confusion. "You're expecting a message, Rabbi?"

"From my God."

He looked far too relaxed to be anticipating that sort of contact, she thought. Gods didn't whisper politely, and neither did their messengers, if the Oracle on Reyi'it was any indication.

"Has your god spoken to you before?"

Sadness. He let out a long breath. "*Adonai* hasn't spoken directly to any of us in a very long time. He sends us signs and places us where we can see them. Sometimes He tests us with difficult choices."

"Like a docent. Or a parent. He helps you to learn."

"Just so," he said with a nod. "And how does your Creator communicate with you, Doctor Minegar?"

He was entitled to a response. Ixbeth picked her words carefully. "Our Creator calls out to the chosen among us every ten generations. To give us a task."

Goldman reflected for a moment. "Like a boss. Or a brother-in-law. He gets in touch with you when he wants something."

The humor in his voice reminded Ixbeth of Docent Ribara. Involuntarily she grinned. "I am looking forward to traveling with you to Kula'as, Rabbi."

He returned the smile. "And I would be honored if you would join me in my cabin for a cup of tea once you've settled into your quarters on the *Vasco da Gama*, Doctor Minegar."

By the time the tube car door slid open again in Med Services, Ixbeth found herself wondering whether Avo'or and Adonai were, if not sibs, then at least related to each other.

——— «» ———

Docent Ribara had been Ixbeth's favorite teacher. At the Archives on Altera, he had spent many midday meal breaks in the principal atrium, holding forth on a variety of philosophical topics. One he kept returning to was the definition of intelligence. An intelligent race, he maintained, was one that could contribute something to the universe. The Corvou were master engineers; the Mitrades had their perfect sense of direction; Kularians were dedicated to the Quest which ensured the peace of the galaxy; even the

Thryggians could contribute greatly if they chose to share their scientific genius. But the Humans? What could such a selfish and primitive species possibly give to others?

One day Evin Lurrlo had suggested, jokingly, that the Humans might be Avo'or's 'bad example', put in place to teach other races how *not* to do things. At the time, Ixbeth recalled, she had laughed as heartily as everyone else present. None of them had ever actually met a Human, of course, but there was plenty of information available on the database, none of it flattering — and very little of it accurate, as Ixbeth now knew.

Rabbi Goldman was a holy man, a Believer. From a distance Ixbeth watched as he stood quietly beside Lania's bed, gazing softly down on her, stroking her cheek, and vocalizing words in a language Ixbeth did not understand. She didn't have to understand them, she suddenly realized — she had begun to taste them. They were delicately sweet, almost fragrant, with the slightest tang of sadness. Then, in an instant, they were riding the crest of a powerful surge of emotion, one that flooded the room; and Ixbeth found herself greedily absorbing that emotion, rejoicing in it, and hungering for more.

She had never experienced such a rapturous sharing. His voice wept from his throat, and there was such love and loss and redemption and ecstasy in his song that Ixbeth felt as though the Great Presence himself had reached down and touched her soul.

The holy man paused when the child opened her eyes and gazed up at him. "Don't stop," she begged. And his joy at hearing her speak broke over Ixbeth like a mighty wave, draining her of every other feeling. Cleansing her. Renewing her. It was such a powerful projection of Human emotions that even if she had wanted to she could not have shielded herself against it.

In the past year, Ixbeth had listened to hundreds of pieces of music composed and performed by Humans on a variety of manufactured instruments; but these were pitiful shadows of the music that had issued from the holy man's mouth. Lania was part Human and had found a way to create a bridge between technologies. Rabbi Goldman was completely Human and had used his voice to create a bridge between souls. So had Commander Dedrick, during the battle. Humans were bridge-builders. And this, Ixbeth realized, could be their gift. Docent Ribara was wrong. Humans weren't selfish or primitive — they were young. And they were learning. Given time to mature, she felt certain, they would one day make a mighty contribution to the universe.

——— «» ———

In her sleeping module, Lania lay very still, keeping her eyes closed and her senses open, and listened to the music. It resided in every voice now. Each had its own tones and timbre, its own melody. Rabbi Goldman's had been the first. Now she was eager to experience them all. Some voices were already familiar to her — Ixbeth's, Doctor Deneuve's, Commander Dedrick's — but now that the missing dimension had been added, it was as though she were hearing them for the first time. As they conversed in the commander's sitting room, Lania could hear a symphony. And then her focus shifted to the words they were speaking, and she realized that they were talking about *her.*

"She isn't going to be happy about this," sighed Deneuve. "You were the first person she trusted on this ship, Ixbeth, and she doesn't form attachments easily."

"It is very important that I present this evidence against the Thryggians at the Tribunal," Ixbeth pointed out. "It's what I was meant to do. And Lania won't be alone. She'll have you and Commander Dedrick. Her strongest bond should be with him, since they are related."

"Ixbeth is right," said the commander. "The DNA doesn't prove it, but anyone with eyes can see that she's a Dedrick. It will be good for us to spend some quiet time alone, getting to know each other. I can only imagine the kind of life she had with Abner."

"She has scars from that experience that may never heal, Commander," Deneuve warned. "She'll need therapy for a very long time."

"Doctor, Abner left his marks on every member of the Dedrick clan, and I confess, I fantasized about killing him myself on more than one occasion. Lania and I are the only Dedricks left. That makes two things that we have in common. Maybe we can use them to build something resembling a normal family relationship."

Normal family life...

The music had faded now, but Lania didn't mind. Her heart was filling with anticipation. The commander wanted what Rose had wished for her — what her mother had died to give her — what Lania had given up hope of ever having. And he didn't see her as a monster. None of them did.

"Lania also has some abilities that will set her apart from other Humans," added Ixbeth.

"So I've noticed," Dedrick replied drily. "And to answer your next question, no, I don't believe those differences will present any major problems for us. She's family. She'll stay with me, wherever Fleet Control assigns me."

Deneuve cleared her throat. "I'm afraid her future is not that clear-cut, Commander. Her DNA is not Human. I can override that determination and certify her as Human based on heritage, but then once she's on Earth's database as your cousin, she'll be classified Eligible or Ineligible. And you know what happens after that."

"So, I'm going to end up taking on either Fleet Control, or the Relocation Authority, or both." It was a statement, not a question. "Well, if that's what I have to do, then that's what I'll do, Doctor. I repeat, Lania is family, and I *will* protect her from the stupidity of Earth's bureaucracy."

...and a new defender. In a family, the older members protected the younger ones, just as Rose had described in those stories so furtively whispered by the flickering light of Abner's hearth. Lania's heart was too full to let her remain hidden any longer. She swung herself out of bed and headed for the door.

"You won't be fighting this battle alone, Commander," Deneuve was saying. "I can put off transmitting my report on Lania for as long as you need. And I can think of at least one other officer who will gladly join your cause. Leslie has never stopped caring about you, you know. You do plan to ask her?"

Dedrick nodded thoughtfully.

Ixbeth was the first to notice her, standing in the doorway. "Lania!"

"I wish you didn't have to go," Lania blurted. "Will we ever see you again?"

Ixbeth walked over to her and gently took her hand. Once again Lania knew an enveloping sensation of utter security. This being would always be her friend, if no longer her defender.

"I will contact you as soon as the Tribunal is over," Ixbeth promised. "In the meanwhile, be patient. Each of us has a purpose, and this is mine. Yours may not be clear yet, but one day, in a moment that belongs to you alone, you will understand what a great gift you bring to the universe."

The alien's voice was a song.

PART VIII

Trial And Judgement

Available records contain little information about the Interplanetary Tribunal empaneled in 2346 C.E. to try the Thryggians for scientific atrocities against other races, other than to confirm that testimony was completed and judgement rendered in 2399 C.E., on the Kularian home world of Kula'as. There was no Human involvement in any of the proceedings.

— *Sic Transit Terra, An Unauthorized Planetary History*
(2673 C.E.)

23

Yorell Enne carefully smoothed her robes across her lap before clasping her hands to rest them there. She was being watched by two clerks who had become extremely nervous when told who she was. Their anxiety amused her It also confirmed that despite her advanced years and exalted position with the Reyot High Council, she was still considered by many to be subversive, even dangerous. A rebel in her one hundred and twentieth year. An icon and an iconoclast at the same time. What a delicious paradox!

Yorell let her gaze wander over the rows of seats in the old Kularian meeting hall and across the floor, to the raised dais where the tribunes would sit once the session was formally convened. The clerks were probably afraid that she might try to disrupt the proceedings — she'd done it often enough in the High Council chambers back on Reyi'it — but they needn't have worried. After declining the honor of sitting on the Tribunal herself, Yorell had fought like one possessed to convince the tribunes to hold this session on the abandoned planet of Kula'as.

The hall was huge. A circular room beneath a lofty golden dome, it held gallery seating for more than a thousand spectators. Historically, the Kularians had always been an extremely pragmatic race. That explained the lack of furniture in the center of the hall, where the stone floor had been worn shiny by the feet of hundreds of generations of decision-makers as they stood debating and deliberating. Government tended to run much more efficiently in the absence of chairs.

Yorell leaned forward intently as several more witnesses entered the hall and took their places in the roped-off area to the left of the dais. They had been arriving sporadically by twos and threes for intervals now; and for intervals Yorell had sat in the spectators' gallery, counting. She had been very specific about the number of seats the witnesses would require. The tribunes had indulged her, probably out of deference to her age, but she had known exactly what she was doing.

Two hundred on a world, wandering together.

The truth was returning to Kula'as. Soon, the prophecy — and the Great Presence's purpose in sending it — would be fulfilled. Yorell had been preparing for this day for the last thirty years.

She realized with a start that the last seat had been taken. By another Reyot? Cautiously, she reached out with her mind and queried the other female. No answer. Was she blocked, or simply unheard? Communication over a distance was a talent that tended to weaken with age, Yorell knew; nonetheless, even if the message were unclear, any Reyot of average mental ability should have at least felt and acknowledged the attempt at contact. She tried again, and a third time, before it struck her what the female must be. Of course! Now she knew she was getting old. The verification request from the Earth ship almost a year earlier had slipped her mind.

Yorell felt the vibration begin deep in her chest. After watching the witnesses' dock fill up with hybrids of every size and shape, she had all but abandoned any hope of seeing the face of the pure-blooded Kularian female again. She had suspected when the request first arrived that it was a sign from Avo'or. Now, watching Ixbeth Minegar take her appointed place, she was certain. The child had arrived, and the machine was ready for her.

Kula'as would rise again.

——— «» ———

Yorell hadn't questioned it initially, hadn't stopped to wonder why, after so many years of indifference toward Kula'as, she suddenly felt a compulsion to visit the place. She was ninety years old and a fully-accredited Prime Docent at the Central Archives. Her data input had been crucial to the winning of a sizable royalty for her city from a corporation developing telepathic translation devices for the Galactic Great Council. Her reward from her people had been an invitation to serve the entire planet as a member of the Reyot High Council. To the dismay of the Council, her first official action once installed had been to take a leave of absence to investigate the foothills near the Kularian capital city.

Her students had attempted to dissuade her. It was a dangerous undertaking, and they did not want to lose their highly esteemed teacher. Her peers had attempted to talk her out of it, too. What could she be thinking, starting over at her age as a novice in the study of artifacts? Weren't there already enough trained specialists infesting that treacherous rock in the neighboring orbit? Yorell had simply smiled and departed, leaving a great deal of horrified indignation in her wake.

Kula'as, she discovered, was hardly a rock. Rather, it was a huge forest, punctuated by mountains and cool, transparent lakes, all bursting with life. Its flora and fauna had been growing wild for more than three hundred years, attracting scientists from almost every member planet in the Council. Yorell spent the first moontide of her stay watching and talking with these visitors, observing their techniques, learning as much as she could about the native Kularian ecosystem. The more she learned about the planet, the more convinced she became of her purpose there.

About 310 years earlier, the Kularians had evacuated their home, taking only what they could carry. Not one being had remained behind. From that day, Kula'as could have been annexed and colonized by any of the other races, including and especially the Reyota — but it hadn't been. Cities, parks, mines, factoria, cleared farmland, all had been abandoned furnished and intact. For nearly three centuries, the galaxy had waited expectantly for the Kularians to return, as though from an extended vacation, to reclaim their world. Only in the last twenty years had curiosity overcome courtesy, bringing scientists to investigate. And they had found a planet that also waited, like a fanged pet for an absent master, not only expectantly but watchfully, protectively. Kula'as had become a dangerous place for uninvited guests, as many scientific teams had discovered firsthand. There were poisonous plants that mimicked the appearance of harmless shrubs and flowers, insects with painful, even lethal stings, nocturnal predators both small and large that stalked silently and attacked without warning. Yorell had no reason to expect that the danger to her would be any less because she was Reyot. And yet, somehow, she felt safe here. She felt invited.

At the end of her self-imposed indoctrination period, Yorell traded for the necessary gear and supplies for a moontide-long trek to the foothills. She purposely led the outfitter to believe that she would be traveling with several strong, well-armed male comrades. She didn't want any well-meaning aliens insisting she accompany them, or they her. Yorell knew that something was waiting for her out there, and that she was meant to find it alone.

The city was walled. It dated back millennia to a time before the Great War, when the Reyot and Kularian races had explored space together, and the Kularians had worked their planet using alien materials and legendary tools. They had fashioned the walls of their living spaces from a stone-like substance that could be made transparent literally at will. The city wall, made of that same material, showed a seamless surface that somehow absorbed and then redirected the energy of any weapon fired against it. This remarkable place, called simply Capital City, had continued to stand long after the technology that created it had been lost, repelling every enemy but one — the surrounding forest. During a period of more than three centuries, its roots and vines had crept over and under and around, clogging streets and dwellings, weaving a near-insurmountable wall of its own. It had taken more than a year to reclaim enough of the city to provide a base of operations for all the scientists staying on Kula'as. After that, approximately five kilopaces of road to the northeast had been cleared before the effort had been abandoned. This was the road Yorell could sense calling to her.

As she walked, shouldering one heavy pack and dragging a second behind her on a sledge, she could feel primitive minds all around her, watching from concealment in the bushes. Animals were observing her progress, perhaps sizing her up as a potential meal. Yorell deliberately straightened her spine, standing as tall as possible. Her fingerclaws were trying to extend. She pulled her clearing-blade from its sheath and held it in plain sight as she walked, and gradually the feral presence faded from her awareness. Soon enough, she needed the long sharp blade to hack her way through the brush that had overgrown her path. It was tiring work. For the first time since embarking on this adventure, Yorell could feel the weight of her years on her shoulders and arms. Still, she persevered, determined to finish what she had begun.

She already knew how quickly night fell on this planet. The moment she sensed a change in the quality of the daylight, Yorell began looking for a place to make camp. Something flashed yellow-white off to her left, beyond a stand of trees. She paused and saw it flash again. Perhaps another traveler had chosen this path before her and built a fire, she thought, as curiosity drew her away from the road to investigate.

In a small clearing stood an even smaller cabin crafted of wood. Its front door was ajar and swung gently back and forth in a breeze Yorell could scarcely detect. Attached to the door was a shiny metal ornament. This decoration, catching the light of the setting sun each time the angle of the door changed, was the source of the flashing she had seen from the road. Yorell knew better than to question her luck. She spent the night in the cabin with the door bolted.

It took her a full five days to reach the foothills. Each night, as though summoned by magic, a shelter or structure appeared precisely where she needed it, allowing her to sleep safe from the cold and the forest animals. Each night, her certainty grew that she was intended to be here, doing exactly what she was doing, despite her age and her inexperience, and despite the fact that she was not Kularian.

On the sixth day, she stood at the base of a gentle rise carpeted with wildgrasses and gazed northward at a serration of tall, craggy peaks caped in clouds. Yorell shivered with anticipation. It was here, whatever it was, and it would be the most important discovery of her life.

—— «» ——

It had taken all of Yorell's powers of persuasion to convince the Galactic Tribunal to convene on Kula'as. An abandoned world? they scoffed. Who would there be to testify? What evidence could possibly remain after artifactitians had picked over all the cities and burial sites? But Yorell had persisted, had coaxed, had reasoned, had used every iota of influence that an Elder Councilor could command, and one by one the tribunes had acceded. And, as though in response to a summons, Kularians had begun to appear. As foretold by the prophecy, two hundred of them now sat in the witnesses' dock, each bearing a piece of the truth.

A gong sounded and a hush fell over the hall. Moving with solemn dignity, the seven tribunes entered and made their way in single file past the spectators to the high dais. After them came a pair of advocates, walking side by side, their shiny black robes identical to the tribunes' garb, only shorter. A Reyot had been chosen to represent the interests of the host world. The other advocate, speaking for the Thryggians, was a Proat, Yorell noticed. How fitting. The Proats were great orators, often called upon to mediate disputes and rescue lost causes. And whether or not the Thryggians realized it, this time they were lost.

For the past thirty-five standard years the Tribunal had been traveling from planet to planet, collecting evidence and depositions against the Thryggians. So far, because of the rule that testimony could only come from citizens of the host planet, the complaints had all been minor. The tribunes had been examining small local details, when what they needed to do was step back and take in the much larger picture. Only then would they comprehend the true, horrific extent of the Thryggians' crimes. Here on Kula'as that was finally about to happen. After hearing testimony brought from all parts of the galaxy by Kularians coming out of their concealment, the Tribunal would finally have to stop deliberating and reach a verdict.

If it didn't, Yorell had decided, she was going to demand to know why. And she wouldn't be discreet about it, either. Enough was enough.

Yorell was too old and too disenchanted to be impressed by all the pomp and ceremony that surrounded these sessions. She had been pressured herself to join the panel, not because she was better or wiser than the other beings on her home planet, but simply to get her out of the way. It was the same with all the tribunes. Each of the seven represented one of the major worlds on the Great Council. Yorell scanned the bored and weary faces floating above the lustrous dark ocean on the dais and could put a name to every one. Thorns in the sides of their respective governments, all of them. They ought to welcome the chance to bring this sorry spectacle to an end and return home.

A second gong sounded and resounded inside the hall, triggering a brief flurry of activity as the clerks and record-keepers took their places for the start of the official proceedings.

"The record will show that the Interplanetary Tribunal convened on this date on the planet of Kula'as, to hear testimony sworn against the Thryggians by the citizens of Kula'as. Let the first witness come forward," sang out the Prime Tribune.

A being with dark skin and bright yellow hair stepped forward. This creature, a male, wore a tunic and tight-fitting trousers made of soft leather with rainbow markings . They were disturbingly similar to those on the skin of the Proat advocate. Yorell heard him hiss softly as the witness took his place in the center of the stone floor, facing the tribunes, and bowed.

"I am named Orrin Phail. I am a Kularian born on the planet Murrala 5, and I come before you so that all may hear the truth."

The Prime Tribune leaned forward impatiently. "Truth is a strange word in the mouth of an impostor," he challenged. "You bear no resemblance to a Kularian, Orrin Phail."

Yorell had been waiting for this moment. "Nonetheless, Arfan D'Ull, he is a citizen of this planet by direct descent, by the tacit consent of the member worlds of the Great Council," she called out from the gallery.

"Councilor Enne, if you wish to speak to a member of this panel, you will address him by title," D'Ull reproved her. Yorell couldn't help noticing that he was suppressing a smile. "Now, what's this about the tacit consent of the Council?"

"Great Tribune D'Ull of Reyi'it, since the beginnings of interstellar travel it has been accepted as a given that citizenship is a portable attribute, passed down from parent to child. A Reyot parent produces Reyot offspring, regardless of where the children are born. Ten generations ago, the Kularians left their home world without renouncing their citizenship. Since then, all Kularians have been born offplanet, and many of them have mixed blood; however, by unwritten galactic law, they are still citizens of Kula'as, eligible to testify before this tribunal. If you require further proof, ask Orrin Phail what made him leave his home world one standard year ago."

D'Ull sat back thoughtfully. "Are you referring to the Reyot Quest? But that's just a—"

"It isn't a legend, Arfan. Ask and you'll discover that every witness here today received the call of the Oracle. And everyone knows that only a Kularian can be summoned to the Quest."

There was a great murmuring and emphatic nodding of heads in the witnesses' dock. After a moment's consideration, the Prime Tribune announced, "It will be recorded that the citizenship and entitlement of the witnesses has herewith been confirmed."

There was no opportunity for anyone to object to his arbitrary decision. As one body, the 199 beings in the witnesses' dock leaped to their feet and exclaimed, "*Ohe'elu!*" Their outcry startled the tribunes so badly that three of them almost slipped off their seats.

"They're Kularian, all right," one of them grumbled.

"Let's just get on with the proceedings," D'Ull declared, cutting off any further comment from the panel.

Prompted by a clerk, the first witness resumed speaking. "Great and glorious Tribunes from the planets—"

"You see what you've started, Yorell?" D'Ull shook his head in disgust. "I apologize for interrupting you, Orrin Phail. Please, just tell us what evidence you have brought and give us your testimony."

Phail reached into a leather pouch hanging from a thong around his neck and withdrew a datacube and a cylindrical metal object. "In this specimen container is a sample of plague virus taken from the body of my friend, Dravin Jule. Before ending his own life, he recorded a confession on this datacube, which I also offer in evidence. Twelve standard years ago, he traveled to Thrygg to receive an unapproved medical treatment which he was told would greatly extend his lifespan. Instead, the Thryggians implanted a strain of Angel of Death into his body. When he returned home to Murrala 5, the toxins released by this virus into our environment destroyed every unborn child in its mother's womb. Since then, no female has been able to deliver a living infant on our world. This was the doing of the Thryggians, who developed the plague virus and sent him home without warning him that he was carrying it. Our scientists have made a detailed analysis. They have isolated and measured the toxins. Every fact is documented right here," he declaimed, brandishing the cube as he turned, resonating with passion, toward the witnesses' dock. "Hear the truth!"

Every Kularian in the hall shouted again in response, "*Ohe'elu!*"

Yorell smiled as the tribunes began to fidget uncomfortably in their soft chairs and shiny robes. The truth would be delivered — and heard — 199 more times. Truth was often unpleasant to contemplate, but its results could be satisfying. Here on Kula'as the trial would end. At last the Thryggians would get what they deserved. And Yorell knew exactly how it would be accomplished.

——— «» ———

The artifact's size was impossible to measure at first. Sheer happenstance had brought her to that side of the ridge, had caused her to stand for a moment, admiring the majesty of the mountainside that lay beyond it. Had placed the sun in the sky at precisely the angle necessary for its light to reflect off the small, curved piece of metal that sat exposed at Yorell's eye level. It shone as though polished. As she probed around it with her fingers, she felt the metal curve under slightly on the right-hand side. It wasn't a seam — it was the edge of an opening of some sort.

Excitement swelling in her chest, Yorell opened her pack and selected a digging tool. There were hours of daylight left, sufficient time to uncover the side of the artifact and begin estimating its dimensions.

Yorell got no sleep that night, or the next. The curved metal turned out to be part of a door, and she simply could not rest until she had exposed all of it and found a way to get through it. Something important was waiting for her on the other side of that door, she was certain. It had been waiting a long time to be found. It was the reason she was here. She knew she mustn't delay any longer.

Yorell set out light sources and worked nonstop, never pausing to question whether she would be safe. She had sensed all along that whatever had brought her to this place had also been watching over her. It would not let her be harmed this close to the goal of her journey.

Two days later, exhausted, Yorell stood staring at the gentle silver curve of the object's flank — the several paces' length that she had managed to unearth, and the featureless ovoid slab of door that blocked her way inside. This was no simple artifact. Artifacts were bits of evidence that a race had existed: food containers, small tools, reading materials. What Yorell had found was huge, and the entrance was airtight. It could be an ecopod, a laboratory, perhaps even a ground-to-space ship. If she could just make it let her in, she would be able to identify it. So far, however, the door had defied all the tools in her kit.

Open, curse you! she thought, frustration draining her of all strength and patience.

In that moment she heard a muted click, and the door swung slowly inward in response to her telepathic command.

Psi-powered, she realized with a shock. According to legend, the ancient Kularians had developed and operated such machines, but nobody had ever found one intact. Until now. Until this, whatever it was, that she had found buried in the foothills. No, she amended, not buried *in* the foothills — it *was* a foothill. If she hadn't chanced to notice the sun glinting off that tiny piece of its hull, she could have climbed right on top of it for a better view, never suspecting what lay just beneath her feet.

Retracting her fingerclaws, Yorell swallowed the growl at the back of her throat and stepped gingerly through the open doorway. She found herself in a long, narrow space with a sealed door at each end. Turning right, she issued another telepathic command and watched the door slide noiselessly away, admitting her into a large control room of some kind. A circle of reclining seats surrounded a single upright chair in the center of the room. All were equipped with headsets. It looked innocent enough, and yet, something told her she was trespassing. Only Kularians were meant to be here. Yorell backed out slowly and turned around.

At the other end of the hallway, the door led to a different kind of control room, a kind Yorell recognized from her youthful exploration days. This was a pilot's cabin, with additional seats for a secondary and navigator. The panel indicators were labeled in one of the ancient languages, but Yorell had flown into space often enough to guess what they displayed. Her 'artifact' was clearly an interstellar craft, equipped for Gate maneuvers. As she watched, enthralled, a small yellow light began to flash in the middle of the navigator's console. Knowing instinctively that this was a message intended for her, Yorell sat down in the chair and put on the attached headset. A voice began to speak.

It resonated inside her head, like a huge gong. It wrapped her entire being in its words. It spoke Reyot. And it knew her name.

YORELL, YOU ARE THE CHOSEN ONE. KNOW THE TRUTH AND GIVE IT LIFE.

Without warning, she was enveloped in a huge ball of white-hot thought. She burned inside it for an endless moment, her mouth framing a scream. Then she winked out.

Yorell awakened on the ground outside, in the cool air of dusk. She had no memory of leaving the Kularian ship-machine. Perhaps the owner of the voice, after giving her her instructions, had caused her to be transported here. Yorell knew without trying it that the door wouldn't open again, not for her nor for anyone else, until she had completed her task. But she now also knew what the device was and how it was meant to be used, and the knowledge made her glad to be locked out.

She should probably have been afraid, but she wasn't. For Yorell was a researcher of history, living every historian's dream. She had made personal contact with the ancient past; and, if she was successful in her mission, she would be using this deadly machine to make living history.

—— «» ——

The final witness was the full-blooded Kularian female.

"I am named Ixbeth Minegar. I am a Kularian born on the planet Dimmla, and I have come here so that all may hear the truth."

By now a sense of inevitability permeated the hall. The parade of witnesses had taken almost a moontide to cross the stone floor. All told variations of the same story, supported by physical evidence from every corner of the galaxy: a journal entry, a voice log, a visual record, a laboratory specimen, all thoroughly documented. The Tribunal's verdict was a foregone conclusion. So why, Yorell wondered, was the Proat advocate looking so unconcerned?

"...I was also present aboard the Human ship when it was attacked by Thryggian pirates. On this datawafer are the Human captain's records of the attack, including a voice communication in which the pirates identified themselves as Thryggians..."

She made an impressive witness, Yorell observed. In her size and her manner, this Child of Kula'as conveyed an authority far beyond her years. She descended from a long line of defenders, most likely, in a community that had safeguarded the undiluted genome of a very special race. Yorell hoped fervently that there were other such communities out there. It would be a shame, after hearing the truth, to have to witness the death by assimilation of the species that had been entrusted for so many cycles with bringing it to light.

The Proat had remained seated and relaxed throughout the proceedings, not even bothering to make notes for his final appeal to the Tribunal. It was not like the Proat to default a judgment. They kept fighting to the end, even when the cause was already lost. This advocate must have a secret weapon. Eaten alive by curiosity, Yorell had to restrain herself from probing his mind. A procedural impropriety now would taint the entire session, and the last thing she wanted to do was hand the Proat a reason to demand that it be expunged.

"Ohe'elu!"

Yorell started and felt her fingerclaws try to extend. Even when it was expected, that lusty shout still took her by surprise.

Now the testifying was done. It was time for the concluding formalities.

"Does the advocate for the Thryggians have anything to say?" asked the Prime Tribune.

Slowly, with an air of infuriating confidence, the Proat rose to his feet. "Tribunes," he began, "there can be no defence against the testimony we have witnessed here, and so I will offer none. However, I must remind the panel that any system of justice must be predicated upon the ability of a governing body to administer fair and appropriate punishment. Yes, the Thryggians have committed many criminal acts, and they must be made to pay the penalty. But what should that penalty be? What would be fair and reasonable?

"Tribunes, it is not your mandate to avenge the Thryggians' victims or their families. A life taken in vengeance does not restore the life that was lost. Although many tragic deaths resulted indirectly from their actions, the fact remains that the Thryggians themselves took no lives. Consequently, to take their lives in punishment would be nothing less than government-sanctioned genocide.

"Similarly, Tribunes, it would be excessive and ultimately fatal to the Thryggian race to strip their home planet of its resources. Yes, you must find them guilty of the crimes with which they are charged. The evidence is incontrovertible. But in the interests of justice, I ask you to impose not a vengeful punishment, but rather a fair and feasible punishment. Governments everywhere have learned the futility of levying harsh reparations against an impoverished race, or of sentencing a criminal to imprisonment where there is no cell to contain him. The Thryggians have already spent thirty-five standard years in planetary confinement — *in planetary confinement*," he repeated, raising his voice to be heard over the angry muttering now emanating from the gallery and the witnesses' dock.

"Please, don't suggest that we simply extend that pretence a while longer," warned the Prime Tribune, scowling.

"I was merely going to point out that while imprisonment would seem to be the only fair punishment, the past thirty-five years have shown that it cannot be effectively carried out. Fair, but not feasible," the Proat concluded smugly.

Very clever, thought Yorell, getting to her feet. But the Great Presence was several steps ahead of him.

"Tribunes!" she exclaimed. "There is a way to imprison the Thryggians effectively."

"I'm not done yet—"

"Yes, you are, Advocate," D'Ull declared, shooting him a look that instantly silenced the objection. "Continue, Councilor Enne."

"Using a machine built by the ancient Kularians, we can seal the Thryggian system up in a pocket of space. I found this relic out in the foothills while on an artifact-gathering expedition years ago. It can be made to work again, using the psi-power of the Kularians gathered here."

As the witnesses' dock erupted in excited murmuring, the full-blooded female stepped forward, her head cocked as though she were listening to a whispered message. "There has to be a focusing lens to direct the energy," she pointed out tautly.

"That would be you, Ixbeth Minegar," Yorell replied. "A pure-blooded Child of Kula'as."

There was a soft gasp of recognition from the witnesses' dock, and Ixbeth Minegar began to smile. "A machine with the heart of a Child!" She whirled to face the other witnesses, her expression fierce. "A machine with the heart of a Child of Kula'as! Together, victory!"

With one proud voice the 199 responded, "And Kula'as rises again! *Ohe'elu!*"

"A what?" demanded the Proat, flustered. "What child? What victory? What's going on here? I insist on being heard!"

Yorell almost felt sorry for him.

—— «◊» ——

The machine was magnificent. Twice as large as a sprint ship, it sat as though on a pedestal, five days' journey from Capital City. Yorell Enne had spent years excavating the device. Its smooth gray skin glowed faintly in the sunlight. It looked ready to lift off at any moment. And Ixbeth could sense it calling out to her.

"It's alive," whispered Ixbeth.

Beside her, Yorell replied softly, "It contains the spirit of Avo'or. I have already received my instructions from the Great Presence. Now it is your turn."

In a moment that belongs to you alone. As she recalled Tal's words — it seemed a lifetime ago that they had had that discussion — Ixbeth shivered. He had been right, about everything.

Tal?

We are one. I'll never leave you, my sister.

A featureless sweep of metal, the door swung inward as she walked toward it, inviting her inside. It closed behind her and sealed with a faint hiss. An instant later, the air was filled with energy. It seemed to radiate from the bulkheads. It made her nerves itch.

Disharmony, all around her.

Tal!

It's a test, Ixbeth. A first step. You'll be receiving mental projections from twelve others. You'll have to harmonize all their resonances with your own before you can activate the machine.

Remembering what had happened the last time her body had been flooded with incompatible energy, Ixbeth struggled to breathe.

No! In the SPA room, I — I can't do this—!

Ixbeth, listen to me. You have more mental power than you realize. When a community becomes inbred, recessive traits are strengthened. The brotherhood keeps records. When my docent found out you and I were bonded, he showed them to me. For the past five generations, psi power on Dimmla has been steadily increasing. And by joining, we've more than doubled your strength. You can do this, my sister. You must. There's no one else.

He was right. And he was projecting. By sheer force of will, Ixbeth relaxed her body and opened her mind to receive his trust in her.

Tell me what to do, she said at last.

The shields on the ship absorbed the energy of the Thryggian weapons fire and made it part of themselves. You have to do the same. Feel the resonance pattern that surrounds you. It's not completely different from your own. Embrace the similarities. Then adapt your pattern to match the differences. Let your mind become a bridge between the two....

Ixbeth tried. For hours that felt like eternities she strove, first to create harmony out of disharmony, then simply to gain control over her own resonance pattern. Finally, exhausted, she was forced to stop.

I'm sorry, Tal.

It was your first attempt, he consoled her. *I would have been surprised if you'd equaled the skills of an ancient Kularian on your first try. Don't worry, my sister. Avo'or is patient. You've made progress today. He'll see to it that you have sufficient time to practice.*

On the third day, Ixbeth managed to harmonize herself with the resonance pattern of the machine.

On the fourth, with Tal's assistance, she was able to sustain the harmony for several hours.

On the fifth, she felt herself drawn to the control room at the end of the corridor, where a yellow light was blinking on the navigator's panel.

I have already received my instructions from the Great Presence. Now it is your turn.

Without hesitation, Ixbeth sat down in the navigator's seat and put on the headset.

In a moment that belongs to you alone.... Ixbeth knew everything now. She knew who she was and what she must do. She knew that everything in her life had been leading to this moment: every choice, every trial, every failure. And she knew that Tal was right, and Avo'or was real.

The first stage in her training was complete.

Ixbeth blinked, opening her eyes in a room she didn't recognize at first. Several times during the preceding days, she had stood at the threshold of this chamber, staring at the seat in the middle of the circle but knowing in her soul that it would be premature, even dangerous, to try sitting in it. Now Avo'or had placed her there.

She wasn't alone. She turned her head and met the steady gaze of Orrin Phail, already occupying one of the twelve seats in the circle.

"Have you been instructed?" she asked.

He nodded. "I'll begin projecting on your mark."

Once she had successfully integrated Phail's pattern into her own, another sender would be added, and then another, until all twelve seats were occupied. With Tal's help, she knew she wouldn't fail.

With Avo'or's help, he corrected her patiently, *we will not fail.*

24

One moontide after the Interplanetary Tribunal had delivered its judgement, the Kularian ship-machine lifted off, its course plotted for Thryggian space. Agents of the Great Council had found and evacuated all non-Thryggians from the planet's surface, and had removed all experiments involving non-Thryggian organic substances from the Thryggian laboratories. Meanwhile, the combined fleets of the Great Council's member worlds had located Thryggians on well over forty spacecraft scattered across the galaxy. The ships had been destroyed and the beings returned to custody on Thrygg.

The sentencing had been, in everyone's estimation, both fair and feasible — life imprisonment for the entire Thryggian system. After all, the Thryggians were a highly intelligent race living on one of five resource-rich planets. As long as their sun continued to burn, and if only half their population turned from pure science to other pursuits, Thrygg could survive indefinitely in complete isolation. Not even the Proat could complain.

The seven tribunes, the two advocates, and Yorell Enne were designated as official witnesses to the execution of the sentence. Standing in the observation chamber of a Reyot ship, they watched the Kularian vessel rotate in place, directing its energy emitters at the Thryggian planetary system.

The ship was smooth and graceful, and it hung in space like a curved, shimmering blade poised to strike. Yorell shivered as it began to glow with a pale blue light. The tempered weapon, aware that it was about to exact a well-earned retribution. No, she corrected herself, it wasn't the ship that radiated that attitude, but rather the Kularians inside it.

She could visualize them now, the dozen strongest senders in the circle of reclining chairs, transmitting the energy of their minds to the occupant of the central upright seat, the proud Child of Kula'as, owner of the purest talent. She was the filtering lens that focused and directed the energy stream, powering the ancient device.

Yorell had selected the executioners, had taught them how to fly the machine, had overseen their practice with it, exactly as the voice had commanded her to do. She hadn't really wanted to know more. Like their ancestors, the legendary Gate-builders, these Kularians were preparing to harness the stellar power of other universes in order to shape the fabric of space itself. They were doing this with their minds, for no mechanical device could possibly contain or direct such magnitudes of energy. In the Great War, the Kularians had used their heavy ships to destroy entire fleets, even worlds. Today, they would be using this one craft to create a brand new universe, with just a single star and five planets in it.

Distractedly Yorell wondered what the Thryggians were doing at that moment. Would they see any difference in the space detectable by their scanners? Would they try to contact anyone to beg for more time? It was unlike the Thryggians to simply accept their fate in silence, unless they, like Yorell herself, had some sort of contingency plan in place. Was it possible?

Before she could speculate any further, her attention was drawn to the Kularian machine. The glow it emitted was intensifying. Soon it was pulsing white, rivaling the Thryggian sun in brightness. The pilot of the observation ship was forced to back his vessel away from the powerful radiation. It was difficult to believe that thirteen beings sat safely inside that fierce ball of light, channeling all that energy.

Planet-killing energy. For a single treacherous moment, Yorell's resolve faltered. These were Kularians. Could it possibly be right to let them, to let any beings possess such strength? Then she heard an echo of the voice inside her head, and it came to her that no matter how much power mere mortals held, it could only ever be a shadow of that owned by the Great Presence. The thought was strangely comforting.

A moment later it seemed to Yorell as though the Thryggian system itself was moving away from them, slowly at first, then more quickly. Enthralled, she watched it shrink in size to a pinpoint and finally wink out.

"Is that it?" Standing beside her, D'Ull sounded disappointed.

Yorell couldn't help smiling at the utter youthfulness of his question. "What were you expecting? Lightning bolts?"

"I'm not sure. Something more dramatic, I guess. Space opening up, a glimpse of another universe..."

"Trust me, Arfan. This was preferable," she advised him.

Gradually the energy glow from the Kularian ship was subsiding again, and the other eight beings could resume breathing. The tribunes shared a feeling not of satisfaction, but of closure. The Thryggians were gone. At last the Great Council's member worlds could put the Tribunal behind them and get on with the business of day-to-day life.

The Prime Tribune clapped his hands three times and announced, "Let the official record show that the sentence was carried out against the Thryggian race at this time on this date." The clerk at his side bowed and scurried off to close the file.

That left just one thing more to do, Yorell thought grimly. She turned and met Arfan D'Ull's steady gaze. "Are you ready?" he asked.

"No. Does it make a difference?"

He smiled wearily. "Has it ever made a difference in the past? We do what we must do, Yorell. This relic of yours has served us well, but the Great Council was quite specific in its order and—"

"Prime Tribune!" squealed the Proat. "Look!"

All eyes turned to the Kularian machine, which had rotated to face the observation ship. The energy glow, far from fading away, was almost as bright as it had been before.

And its diameter was shrinking. The entire Kularian ship was growing smaller as they watched.

"Open fire!" D'Ull commanded. "Do it now!"

"On what, Prime Tribune?" called the secondary from the control room.

Yorell stared at the empty space where the Kularian ship had been. "Too late, Arfan," she sighed. "They made themselves a Gate and went through it."

"And probably locked it behind them," he fretted. "They must have found out about the Council's decision. But how? Yorell, you didn't—"

"Don't be ridiculous, Arfan. I may not agree with all the Great Council's orders but I'm a loyal Reyot, and if the Kularians ever decided to use their device as a weapon, Reyi'it would be a natural first target. I want that threat eliminated as much as anyone does."

He nodded solemnly. "I know you, Yorell Enne, and I believe you."

"And I know you, Arfan D'Ull, and I believe that you would not have destroyed the device without first removing to safety the beings who were aboard it. So I ask you to consider this: the prophecy promised an end to the Kularian exile once the criminals were punished. Is it not possible that the Kularians aboard the ship-machine were simply anxious to return to their ancestral home world as quickly as they could?"

A thoughtful pause, then, "You think they might be en route to Kula'as?"

Yorell gave him her most charming smile. "I would wager a large amount on it, Prime Tribune."

"And what odds would you give on their turning over the device to the Great Council for disposal once they've arrived, Councilor Enne?"

"Not as favorable as the odds of their already having disposed of it themselves," she replied. "The Kularians were once great explorers. For at least the next cycle, however, their descendants will be kept far too busy on Kula'as to think of looking elsewhere."

"What makes you so sure of that?"

"The prophecy. 'And Kula'as rises again.' They'll all be coming back now, you know. All those hybrids, representing many different cultures, returning to reclaim their ancestral world. Your official recognition of their citizenship made it possible."

"So we shall have neighbors again," D'Ull remarked with a grin. "It should be interesting to see how they get along with one another."

"And with us," she added. "It occurs to me that the Reyot High Council could be called to account very shortly for all those scientific and artifact-gathering parties that have visited Kula'as: all the permits and licenses the Council sold them, the royalties payable on any relics removed from the system, not to mention the various supplies available onplanet at a price...? Those fees were exorbitant thirty years ago. Now they're even higher. I would say that an inquiry is definitely in order."

"How fortunate then that my duties as Prime Tribune are concluded and I am once more available to take a hand in Reyot planetary affairs," he mused, the grin widening. "Life is such an adventure around you, Yorell."

"We are all docents and we are all students. You were one of my best. That is why for you life will always be an *education*, Arfan," she corrected him.

"Like mother, like son?"

He always had to have the last word. This time Yorell smiled and permitted him to keep it.

—— «» ——

They were thirteen in number, the 'doubly chosen ones', as one of them had jokingly said moments before the linkage. Afterwards, they stood near the hillock they had made between the forest and the mountains, staring mutely at the sky, fearing even to make eye contact with one another in case the connection hadn't completely broken.

They had all grown up with the old legends. They had heard descriptions of the ancient power that could split the heavens, but none of them had believed — *truly* believed — until now. The air thickened with their collective horror.

"We should have buried that psi monster in pieces," declared Orrin Phail. "It was evil. I could feel it. If Ixbeth's concentration had slipped, or if the energy stream had lost constancy, even for a split-second…!" Sensing sympathetic anxiety from the others, he became even more agitated. "People, we all could have died out there!"

Rage. Dread. He was right, but he was wrong as well. Ixbeth raised her voice above the chorus of discontented muttering to reply, "Councilor Enne's instructions — and mine — came from the Great Presence himself. That is how she was able to teach us how to use this machine. That is how I know with such certainty that it will be needed again someday. But you're right about the danger it poses, Orrin. Soon this hillock will be covered with vegetation and only we will know what lies beneath. We must all swear to protect the secret for as long as we live, or until the Great Presence commands that we reveal it. If we love our people, if we love Kula'as, we dare not allow this much power to fall into anyone else's hands. Will you swear?"

"I will, Ixbeth," called out a female voice, and then another, and then a male voice. A moment later the group of thirteen was of a single mind once more, and Ixbeth reached a further decision.

"We need to have a *mar'ruk*," she said, "for the two hundred. It's been at least a year since the prophecy. And we need *ohe'elu* as well. There are so many differences now, to divide us. The rituals will be a reminder of what has brought us back together."

——— «» ———

Ixbeth stood on the floor of the meeting hall with Nance Preta, Olf Rugh, and Effre Janno. It was minutes before dawn. Once the sun had cleared the horizon, its light would begin filtering through the dome overhead, bathing the hall in a soft golden glow. The first time she had seen the effect, Ixbeth had sighed with recognition, remembering the fire bugs. This couldn't be a coincidence, she realized. Her ancestors had to have come from Capital City. The glowing roof was probably one of the small, significant details they had taken with them to Dimmla to keep them connected to their home and heritage during the cycle of concealment.

Gradually the gloom in the meeting hall lightened, revealing 196 Kularians seated in a block in the gallery. Not one of them had moved restlessly or made a sound from the time the four Guardians had taken their places. Now, as they became able to see one another, Ixbeth sensed a collective aura of wonder and excitement.

Effre Janno stepped forward and sang out the ancient summons to light in a proud, clear voice: *MAR'RUK DEL'LOYIT, AL'LOYIT OHE'ELU.*

As though in answer to the call, the room grew brighter still, warming as the air suffused with gold. Then it was the turn to speak of Nance Preta, their acting Guardian of Truth: "This is a very special moment in the history of our people. The cycle of concealment has ended and a new cycle — a new era — is about to begin. When the remaining Children of Kula'as have returned home, they will join us in the enormous task that lies ahead. In order to be successful, we will have to do two things. We must first respect and celebrate our differences; and then we must look beyond those differences and remember what we all share. One of the things we share is the ritual of *mar'ruk*. In celebration of our differences, we have combined the traditions of several worlds in today's ceremony, the first of what we hope will be many innovations marking this new beginning for our peoples. *Eluya'at elumi'in.* The truth lives and is spoken."

As one, the assembled Kularians replied, *"Ohe'elu!"*

Smiling, Ixbeth fingered the softly draped brown sash that curved from shoulder to waist across her chest. At last, a ceremonial garb she felt comfortable wearing!

It was her turn to speak. Suddenly aware of 199 pairs of eyes directed expectantly toward her, Ixbeth felt her fingerclaws try to extend. Stars! How did Krodus do this year after year?

Tal was repressing laughter. *Just say it the way we practiced*, he told her.

Ixbeth inhaled a steadying breath and began, in a voice that grew stronger with each word: "This has been a year of greatest triumph for our people, but also for some of us a year of great loss and sorrow. We are the forerunners. We have come here from many different planets and cultures, by 200 different routes. It would be arrogant of any one of us to presume to speak for the experiences of all of us; and so I wear this sash and the clasp that holds it in a ceremonial capacity only, until the rest of our peoples have arrived, each community with its own Guardian of Time."

Pausing, she cued Nance with a nod.

"*Eluya'at elumi'in!*" cried the Guardian of Truth.

"*Ohe'elu!*"

Ixbeth resumed speaking. She and Tal had discussed the significance of this *mar'ruk* at great length, what it meant and what it must do. More important than either of these was what the ritual must *not* do.

As she had expected, Ixbeth's journey to Kula'as aboard the *Vasco da Gama* had been extremely enlightening. Rabbi Goldman had told her many stories about the diversity of religious beliefs among the Humans, and about the grief and poisonous hatred that inevitably resulted whenever any one group decided that it was right and the rest were wrong. Rejection of otherness had always been part of the Kularian culture. Now the tradition posed a real threat, for Kularian culture had become a mosaic of othernesses. If even one community claimed to hold the only real Kularians on the planet and rejected all the others, there would almost certainly be a war. The ancestral home world to which they had fought to return would die.

"Ten generations ago, the Great Presence realized that in order to defeat the evil that he could see spreading across the galaxy, the Children of Kula'as needed to operate covertly. And so, instead of sending one generation out on a quest, he sent our entire race on a mission. We were instructed to abandon Kula'as, to submerge ourselves in other cultures and other genomes and await further orders. But the Great Presence also realized that only a full-blooded Child of Kula'as could provide the focus necessary to control the ancient machine; and so he ensured that at least one community of Kularians was not able to interbreed with its host race.

"When the time was right and the Children of Kula'as had so disguised themselves that we were concealed even from one another, the Oracle called out once more. And we responded. Because we had been scattered and hidden, we were successful. We have fulfilled the prophecy. We have defeated the Thryggians and ensured the peace of the galaxy for the next three hundred and forty years. And now we must send word to every Kularian community on every planet that the cycle of concealment is over, and that the Children of Kula'as can finally come out of hiding and return home — if they wish, and if they are able."

Into the silence that followed her final words, Nance threw a rather unsteady *"Eluya'at elumi'in,"* receiving back a subdued *"Ohe'elu."*

Clearly, in the excitement of the Tribunal and the shock that attended the sheer power and finality of the Thryggians' punishment, none of the chosen ones had taken time to think about a future beyond the Quest. Gingerly Ixbeth sampled their auras.

They're afraid, Tal.

Understandable. For them, what the ancient legends call 'home' is an alien planet.

And I've just reminded them that they're aliens everywhere else, she thought bitterly.

No, my sister. You've just put a name to something they've always wanted but have never been allowed to ask for — their birthright.

Olf Rugh was singing something. The lyrics reminded Ixbeth of the closing coda used on Dimmla, but the lilting melody made the words even more poignant.

For they are the lost, and must be guided home.

Ohe'elu, Tal whispered softly.

Ixbeth felt a tear slide slowly down her cheek.

25

Ixbeth heard the muted roar of a ship punching through atmosphere and looked up from her work table. Another community was arriving from another distant place of concealment. Another hybrid race to swell the growing population of Kula'as.

The Children of Kula'as who had left the home world three and a half centuries earlier had been a single race. So far almost twenty hybrid varieties had claimed the right to return, and the number was still growing. Settlements were springing up all over the planet, populated by beings of various shapes, sizes, and skin colors, with and without fur. They seemed to have taken to heart the message of that first *ohe'elu*. Each new community had chosen one of the empty places on the planet and settled peacefully into it. Capital City had had two market days already, and the communal ovens had been extricated from their thick shroud of foliage and made operational once more. It was too soon yet for anyone to be baking bread, of course. That was an after-harvest activity. But a growing season had already begun, and from the window of her office at the Archives, Ixbeth could see a patchwork of cultivated fields greening up.

Involuntarily she sighed. It was a safe bet none of those plants would be producing *elibans* or *lalava* beans.

Ixbeth had walked the streets of Capital City on that first market day. The air had been thick with curiosity, mingled with apprehension as members of each race surveyed their new neighbors. Despite the optimism of the prophecy, she realized, time alone would tell whether Kula'as would rise again.

Ixbeth?

Tal!

Regret. *Father called another ohe'elu, and the community has decided. Ixbeth, they won't be coming home. Not because they don't want to. They felt it would be better for Kula'as if there weren't any pure-blooded Children there.*

But, Tal, the inbreeding! You warned me—

They're not staying on Dimmla, or on Altera. They're going to build or buy a ship and negotiate their own piloting contract with the Mitrades. They've decided to search for the others.

The others?

The other pure-bloods. They're certain there must be other communities like ours in the galaxy somewhere. And now that the cycle of concealment is ended, they have a new quest. A Kularian quest this time.

And will you be going on this quest?

Ixbeth tasted a mixture of feelings. Sadness. Excitement. *The brotherhood are close to a breakthrough. They've asked that as many scholars as possible remain here and help them unravel the secrets of the ancient writings. Ten of us have agreed, including Father. So, Mother is staying as well.*

Ixbeth sighed. She had been hoping to see her parents again, on Kula'as.

They miss you too, her brother whispered.

I can't go back to Dimmla, Tal.

Sad resignation. *I know. You must look ahead, not over your shoulder—*

That's not the reason. I have work to do on the home world. I've accepted a post at the Archives: Docent of Human Studies. And I've contacted the Marco Polo and requested that Doctor Deneuve spend a term here as a guest docent, and that she bring Lania with her. The young one needs to be trained in the use of her talents, and I believe it would be beneficial for her as well to spend time with others like herself.

Kularians who no longer resemble Kularians?

She's a hybrid, Tal, and she needs to feel that she fits in somewhere. What better place than Kula'as, at a time when hybrids from all over the galaxy are coming together?

And what about you, my sister? Don't you feel the need to fit in anymore?

Ixbeth smiled. *Let's just say that I've discovered other needs.*

You've found a mate?

I've found a mission, she corrected him primly.

Fortunately he had chosen to make contact with her during daylight, she later reflected. For there were many stars in the night sky, and Ixbeth could sense them calling out to her. By the time the *Marco Polo* arrived, she hoped to have convinced the Council of Docents to make Doctor Deneuve an irresistible offer — to take Ixbeth's place as Docent of Human Studies.

And then she would look ahead, as Avo'or had always intended, and find her future.

———— «» ————

Appendix:

A Kularian Lexicology

The words *KULA'AS* (home world) and *KULARIANS* are derived from the ancient term *KU'ULA*, meaning 'companion'. According to the Kularian mythology, the race is descended from a being called *RAKU'ULA* (the Very First Companion), created by *AVO'OR*, the Great Presence, to be his friend.

KULARIAN IS A LANGUAGE OF ROOT WORDS, PREFIXES AND SUFFIXES.
For example:

VAN is the root word denoting an emotional connection while physically apart

SIMM is the root word denoting physical proximity, with no emotional connection

U is the suffix which creates the adjectival form in the present tense

OI is the suffix creating the adjectival form in the past tense (used to be, but not any more)

OR is the suffix creating the adjectival form in the future (not currently, but expect to be)

<u>When these are put together with various prefixes, we get:</u>

lemvanu – emotionally connected to one's family (*lem* = family)

lemvanoi – emotionally withdrawn from one's family

lemsimmoi – no longer in the vicinity of one's family (moved to another town, for example)

lemsimmor – planning to pay a visit to one's family

disvan – sexual attraction felt by a female to a male or a male to a female (*dis* = blood)

disvanu – in a period of sexual receptivity

disvanoi – no longer receptive (coming out of heat)

dissimmu – just friends for now…

disvanor – …but that could change.

errivan – the connection specific to childbirth, when twins who were physically connected in the womb by the *abital* (soul cord) are born separately — the cord dissolves in the last stages of gestation — but retain their emotional connection with each other (*erri* = once physically connected, now apart)

drovan – an emotional connection to someone outside one's family; friendship (*dro* = outsider)

drosimmu – part of a group but not emotionally bonded to any of them

allovan – the special emotional bond between mates (*allo* = second; a mate is one's second self)

allovanoi – emotionally withdrawn from one's mate

allosimmoi – physically distant from one's mate

natvan – an emotional attachment to an object or a non-sentient creature; fondness for something that can't form the same attachment in return (*nat* = a thing, empty, without a soul)

natsimmu – not letting something out of one's sight

norivan – an unhealthy emotional connection (usually refers to twins whose 'soul cord' does not dissolve to allow them to be born, but can mean an emotional connection that interferes with the bonding between mates, or that threatens the community in some way) (*nori* = danger)

norisimmu – in physical danger

pritvanu – like newborn kits, unable to control one's emotions and therefore spewing them all over the place (*prit* = without shape)

pritsimmu – present but hidden or disguised

pritsimmoi – unmasked, discovered

pellavan – a connection strong enough to be made from far away (*pella* = a great distance)

pellasimmu – daydreaming, distracted (near and far at the same
   time)

IN THE KULARIAN MYTHOLOGY

Avo'or is the Great Presence, the intelligence that guides the
   universe and who created all the life contained in it.
   Whenever *Or* appears as a prefix, it means "by the hand of
   Avo'or done/created".

OrRaKu'ula – by the hand of Avo'or, the Very First Companion is
   created

(*Ra* = original; *Ku'ula* = Companion)

OrErriKu'ula – by the hand of Avo'or, the Companion, once
   together, is now physically divided

OrPellaKu'ula – by the hand of Avo'or, the Companions are
   separated by a great distance

OrErriKu'ulallo – by the hand of Avo'or, the Companions are
   divided a second time

Evo'OrLemAlli – the gift of reproduction

(*Evo* = life; *Or* = given by Avo'or; *Lem* = family; *Alli* = of/belonging
   to the two)

elu – truth

eluya'at elumi'in – the truth lives and is spoken

(the subject of the verb becomes a prefix which must be repeated
   each time, since the Kularian language does not have a
   separate word meaning 'and')

ohe'elu – hear the truth

(in the imperative mode, the object becomes a suffix. Please
   note that the apostrophe has no grammatical function in
   Kularian. It is a diacritical mark directing pronunciation.)

mar'ruk – a tally, an accounting.

Mar'ruk del'loyit al'loyit ohe'elu – First we will have a great
   accounting; second, we will have a hearing of the truth.
   These words are sung, with great power, to summon light
   to the ceremony.

(*Dello* and *allo* are ordinal numbers. *Yit* is the suffix that makes
   them adverbial.)

THE PROPHECY

The language of the Oracle tends to be more cryptic, because the ancient Kularians did not speak only in words – some of their communication was empathic and some telepathic. The words may not have been entirely clear, but their meaning always was, provided the receiver had Kularian blood:

Jann grosta'an virtod simmsal hr'ruv

Hark! World 200 (tod=belong to) gathering (return to proximity) wide movement

Tal's version: 200 on a world, wandering together

grent fan m'mhjordor gefsal m'mhjordor

emerge shake off death to give again (sal=back, return) death

Tal's version: life out of death, dealing out death

nurr krechtod l'ljev do'ovani

final heart (tod=belong to) machine of child (suffix 'i' is possessive)

Tal's version: and a machine with the heart of a child

nurrsal straffmr'rand Kula'as angs'slim

at end again battle glory Kula'as back in place

Tal's version: Together, victory, and Kula'as rises again.

If you enjoyed this read

Please leave a review on Amazon, Facebook, Good Reads or Instagram.

It takes less than five minutes and it really does make a difference.

If you're not sure how to leave a review on Amazon:

1. *Go to amazon.com.*

2. *Type in The Otherness Factor by Arlene F. Marks and when you see it, click on it.*

3. *Scroll down to Customer Reviews. Nearby you'll see a box labeled Write a Review. Click it.*

4. *Now, if you've never written a review before on Amazon, they might ask you to create a name for yourself.*

5. *Reviews can be as simple as, "Loved the book! Can't wait for the Next!" (Please don't give the story away.)*

And that's it!

Brian Hades, publisher

About the Author:

Born and raised in Toronto, Arlene F. Marks found her muse at the age of 6 and has been writing and sharing her stories ever since. Her work has appeared in *H.P. Lovecraft's Magazine of Horror* and has been published by *Daily Science Fiction*. Her first science fantasy novel, *The Accidental God*, was nominated for the 2015 Stephen Leacock Medal for Humour. Arlene lives with her husband on Nottawasaga Bay but spends an inordinate amount of time in the Sic Transit Terra universe. She welcomes visitors to her website:

www.thewritersnest.ca

Need something new to read?

If you liked The Otherness Factor, you should also consider these other EDGE-Lite titles:

———— «» ————

The Rosetta Man

by Claire McCague

Wanted:
Translator for first contact.
Immediate opening.
Danger pay allowance.

Estlin Hume lives in Twin Butte, Alberta surrounded by a horde of affectionate squirrels. His involuntary squirrel-attracting talent leaves him evicted, expelled, fired and near penniless until two aliens arrive and adopt him as their translator. Yanked around the world at the center of the first contact crisis, Estlin finds his new employers incomprehensible. As he faces the ultimate language barrier, unsympathetic military forces converging in the South Pacific keep threatening to kill the messenger. The question on everyone's mind is: Why are the aliens here? But Estlin's starting to think we'll happily blow ourselves up in the process of finding that out.

Praise for The Rosetta Man:

"The cover and synopsis had me expecting a light-hearted comedy. I didn't realize I was getting a geopolitical first contact thriller that somehow still managed to be a light-hearted comedy. I really enjoyed this book! The characters are rich and diverse. Estlin and Harry are great, Beth and Bomani made me cry. The story is fast paced and engaging and again, completely unexpected. Great book for fans of first contact scifi, but also fans of thrillers and mysteries. And so well-executed that I give it a solid 5 stars."
— Scott Burtness, author of Wisconsin Vamp (Monsters in the Midwest)

"This book ranks up there with many of the classic sci-fi "first contact" stories and Claire McCague's scientific background comes through in waves."
— Cameron Arsenault, Amazon Reviewer

"A completely enjoyable read. Good action, lots of humor, and a global setting. Strongly recommended."
— Diane Lacey, Amazon Reviewer

For more on The Rosetta Man visit:
tinyurl.com/edge6004

——— «» ———

The Salarian Desert Game
(Book 2 in The Unintentional Adventures
of Kia and Agatha)

by J. A. McLachlan

What if someone you love gambled on her life?

Games are serious business on Salaria, and the stakes are high. When Kia's older sister, in a desperate bid to erase their family debt, loses the game and forfeits her freedom, Kia is determined to rescue her.

Disguised as a Salarian, Kia becomes Idaro in order to move freely in this dangerous new culture. When she arrives on Salaria, she learns it's a world where a few key players control the board, and the pawns are ready to revolt. Kia joins the conflict, risking everything to save her sister. As if she doesn't already have enough to handle, Agatha, the maddeningly calm and unpredictable Select who lives life both by-the-book and off-the-cuff shows up to help, along with handsome Norio, a strong-willed desert girl with her own agenda, and a group of Salarian teens earning their rite of passage in the treacherous desert game.

What can an interpreter and former thief possibly do in the midst of all this to keep the people she loves alive?

Praise for The Salarian Desert Game

I couldn't put it down! This exciting story had me reaching for my kindle in every spare minute I could drum up. Kia and Agatha are constantly in danger in this, their second space adventure.

Kia only cares about saving her sister. That's the only reason she agrees to alter her appearance and accompany Agatha to the planet Salaria. Little does she know, she'll be forced into participating in a barbaric coming of age custom, the Salarian desert game.

Will she lose herself in the game? Or will she be able to keep her wits about her, and stay focused on her goal?

Read The Salarian Desert Game, by JA McLachlan, and find out for yourself. It shouldn't take more than a single sitting, as long as you have five or six uninterrupted hours...

— Bridget Keller

Readers of The Occasional Diamond Thief will be delighted by the further maturation of the heroine Kia. The prickly, prideful and interesting protagonist journeys to a new planet and a bigger challenge in The Salarian Desert Game.

This is the sequel to the excellent first book, in what I sincerely hope becomes a series of adventures detailing the increasing complexity and maturation of this engaging heroine. Mindless bravery is not nearly as admirable as the true courage exhibited by a real character who is terrified - and does the morally right thing anyways. Will resonate with fans of Robin McKinley and Tamora Pierce

— Linda Stortz

For more on The Salarian Desert Game visit:
tinyurl.com/edge2087

———— «» ————

Dreamers

by Donna Glee Williams

Driven by duty towards a sleepless death…

By the time she's sixteen, the town's Dreamer has long ago given up her own life. She only dreams for others now, every morning delivering up to them the divine guidance that comes to her in the night. In exchange, they treat the Dreamer like their queen. All her bodily needs are provided, but love and relationships are forbidden to her. Now something unexpected is happening. Something entirely new. A foreign man has come to the village, wearing a scarlet vest and a gold finger-ring that is far, far too good for a mere Water-Bearer. His strange amber eyes have found the Dreamer's and she longs to be free. But maybe freedom isn't the only cost of being the Dreamer: When her dreams begin to question the authority of the self-serving Chief Interpreter, will she survive his fury? Or will he quietly entomb her in the Dreamer's Chamber, clearing her away like so much litter to make room for a hapless new young girl to take her place? Her fate will be kept as silent as the sacred Garden that is her prison. Unless she can find a way to give voice to her own dreams.

Praise for Dreamers

Dreamers transports the reader to a distant land where you can feel the yarn beneath your fingers and taste the sweet

water left by a secret friend. Williams spins a moving and eloquent tale of love and dreaming, rich with well-observed details of how people live, work, scheme and hope. She writes with the resonant voice of the story-teller, drawing you in to share this beautiful dream.
— Elaine Isaak

After twining a world in her first novel, The Braided Path, that is different from any other yet totally believable, even to the extent that everyone in it is kind, Donna Glee has woven another with Dreamers in which the strands of evil are revealed as gradually as rebellion is awakened. I love the way she lets us get to know the characters by building the story from many different points of view, from threads of conversation that build gradually into an ending that is right - but oh, so shocking.
— Anne Lane

For more on Dreamers visit:
tinyurl.com/edge6009

——— «» ———

For more Science Fiction, Fantasy, and Speculative Fiction titles from EDGE and EDGE-Lite visit us at:

www.edgewebsite.com

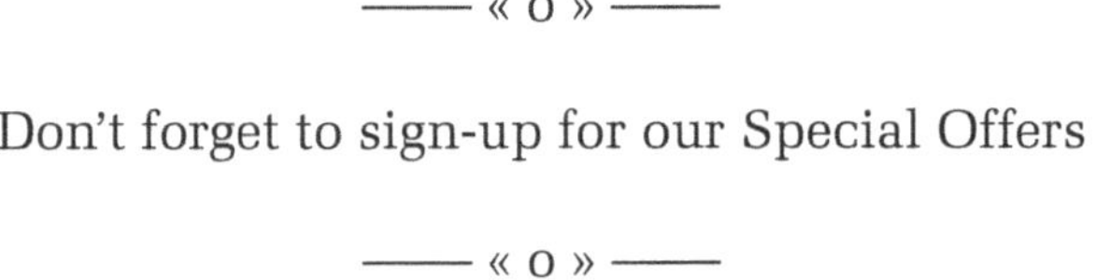

Don't forget to sign-up for our Special Offers

* 9 7 8 1 7 7 0 5 3 1 4 0 6 *